the
spellkey

the Spellkey

ann downer

atheneum   1987   new york

Atheneum
Macmillan Publishing Company
866 Third Avenue, New York, NY 10022
Collier Macmillan Canada, Inc.

Composition by ComCom, Div. of Haddon Craftsmen, Allentown, PA
Printed and bound by Fairfield Graphics, Fairfield, Pennsylvania
Designed by Marjorie Zaum
First Edition

10 9 8 7 6 5 4 3 2 1

Library of Congress Cataloging-in-Publication Data

Downer, Ann,
The spellkey.

Summary: During a dangerous journey through the
thirteen kingdoms, a witch girl and an outcast
stableboy find their fortunes intertwined with nefarious
agents seeking a powerful Spellkey.
[1. Fantasy] I. Title.
PZ7.D7575Sp 1987 [Fic] 86-28709
ISBN-0-689-31329-2

A Lucas/Evans Book

To my mother, and to my father

contents

1

the cat is belled

hat morning the old witch Abagtha had set out to gather mushrooms, the silvery, fragile kind that spring up in the night and are gone by the time the sun is very high. She went out, her meager shawl clutched about her against the damp, to gather what she needed before they could vanish. Her quick, curranty eyes soon spied a white shape among the dried leaves and pine needles, and she stooped with a grunt to pick it. But Abagtha snatched back her fingers and sucked in her breath and peered more closely. It was not a mushroom but a toe. At that moment the toe wiggled, and Abagtha swept the leaves and twigs away to uncover a sleeping baby. The child opened its eyes and smiled at the old woman bending over it. Abagtha saw the child had one blue eye and one green, as true black cats do. Considering this no trifling omen, the sibyl placed the baby in the bundle on her back, with the mushrooms and herbs, and brought it away to her home in an oak, with a red door, in the heart of the forest. The tree was as ancient as she was herself, and among its roots she nursed the child on wild honey and goat's milk.

Abagtha had always lived in the Weirdwood—or as long as her memory served her. She knew a little of the grey arts, if not the black ones, and could make up a spell or two if the sack of copper was heavy enough, but she didn't have a license to practice the weightier magics, for the Necromancer alone held the franchise for magic in that kingdom.

So, with the foundling on her knee, the old woman sold paltry spells to those brave enough to venture into the wood, taking cockles and eels in return for spells to raise the wind, and barley and oats in return for spells to bring rain.

The child grew at a wicked rate. When she had cut her teeth, Abagtha taught her bird lore: how to tell their eggs and calls apart, and then all their names, the man-given ones such as nightjar and nuthatch, and then the names in the language of the birds. Abagtha taught her how unlucky it was to kill a wren, how owls' eyes could be eaten to cure night blindness. And when the child was late learning to speak, the old woman made her eat the tongues of birds. The girl cried, swallowed, pushed the plate away, and spoke.

"No."

This gave Abagtha satisfaction, and she ate the rest of the tongues herself.

When the child had been with her seven years, Abagtha summoned her and told her to make cakes of millet and honey: "Make them round, mind." Then, putting on her many shawls, Abagtha instructed the girl to put the cakes in a napkin and bring them along.

They went out. The child trotted obediently at the old woman's heels. It was growing cold—the bears had already taken to their dens —and she was barefoot. But never having had shoes, or a name, she did not miss them. Hugging the napkin of cakes to her, the girl breathed in the smell of fresh baking. They walked a long time, long enough for the light in the wood to change, the birds to stop singing and the crickets take it up. The trees came farther and farther apart until, just as the sun was beginning to disappear, they came to the edge of the wood.

The girl had never seen the sun set; indeed, she had never seen the sun except as long streaks of light that fell from the treetops and dappled the forest floor. She stood and squinted at the fiery egg in its nest of purple clouds and said not a word.

Abagtha inspected the cakes, found them to her liking, and pinched the child for being inattentive.

"Roll one down the hill."

"But aren't they for our supper?"

She got another pinch. Abagtha took one of the cakes and set it bouncing down the hill. "There! Ha! So—roll it so."

The girl-child's cake rolled down the slope, flew over a pebbled ford in the stream, and disappeared. Abagtha chewed her fingers thoughtfully.

"Yes, yes, yes," she muttered. "As I thought. Come," she said to the girl-child, settling her old body under a tree and spreading the cakes out in her apron. "We'll eat the rest."

"Why did we roll the cakes, Batha?" the girl-child asked, her mouth full of sweet millet cake.

"You can tell a fortune by the way the cake rolls."

"And what was my fortune?"

But Abagtha ate another cake, and would not say.

After the day they rolled the cakes down the hill, Abagtha began to change. She had taught the girl all she dared, not having a license to do more, and her pupil's aptness began to sit ill with her. Abagtha became unreasonable, querulous, forgetful. She started to speak to the girl in foreign tongues, scolding her without cause, howling at her in tempests of hilarity and tears. She stopped working her magic: The farmers came less and less often, so that there was less and less to eat. The old cat, Mambo, became melancholy.

Still, the child soon forgot these episodes, until the unlucky day the old woman discovered her scrawling runes of great power on the scullery wall. A palsy shook Abagtha as she menaced the girl, who shrank, terrified, into the corner.

"Have you been looking at my book of incantations, you meddlesome little toad?" Abagtha hissed. "Didn't I forbid you ever to put your dirty paws upon it?"

The book of incantations never left its wooden stand by the hearth. Three ribbons marked its pages—one silver, one blue, and one green— and its pigskin binding was stamped with the shapes of herbs and animals: mandrake and hyssop, crocodiles and hedgehogs. Wary of its iron clasps, the child had never looked inside, except to catch a glimpse while Abagtha was reading from it. All she had seen was a dog curled up asleep in a capital *P*, monkeys swinging in the margins, and thick, scowling letters that meant nothing to her.

"I didn't touch it! It's locked, and you wear the key."

"Where else did you learn to make runes like that, you nasty little liar?"

"I dreamed them, Abagtha, truly!"

Often she dreamed things. She would dream of a farmer with a toothache, riding a spotted horse, and the next day such a farmer would arrive at the oak with the red door. Other nights the girl-child dreamed things less simple: men in black on horseback, battling; fire in the air; a garden under glass, full of birds; two people kissing by a hedge. One of Abagtha's other books had pictures of knights, and people kissing, but the she liked the one with colored pictures of beetles better.

Abagtha was in no mood to hear about dreams. "Lies!" she spat. "Even *I* don't know the workings of those runes, and you scrawl them with no more care than if they were a game of crosses and oughts! Now, get a pail and rag and scrub this wall, and the floor, too, while you're about it! Ha—mark this wall again, and you'll rue it!"

When she had gone the girl-child cried silently for a while, out of fright and relief. After a while she fetched a pail and wrung out a cloth. Kneeling before the wall, she paused with the rag in her hand, knitting her brow at the runes. Abagtha had never taught the girl-child her letters, so that the runes meant less than nothing to her. But some urge moved her tongue for her, made her hand trace the elbows and tails of the letters as she said softly:

"Spellkey. . . ."

After the incident of the runes the girl kept her dreams to herself, playing quietly with the dried lizards she took from Abagtha's jars.

Years passed, and the girl grew tall and slender, a seedling seeking light among the taller branches. Her skin was smooth and white as almond meats, for it never saw the sun, and her dark hair fell past her waist, heavy as wet silk and tangled with burrs and cobwebs. In winter she wove it about her into a cloak to ward off the cold. Abagtha, now fearful of her charge's powers, kept her in the thinnest muslin well into the winter, and fed her on sour beer alone, to keep her submissive. But the girl sought out berries and roots and groundnuts to sustain her, and suffered not too much from Abagtha's abuse. This is what Abagtha had dreaded most dearly of all. She knew the girl's eyes to be seer's eyes, the eyes of an otherworld daughter. For this reason she hesitated at outright cuffs, resorting instead to sly pinches. The girl met this malice with wit and quickness, doing the endless chores set for her without complaint. Where kindness is not known it is not missed. This even temper maddened Abagtha beyond endurance, and she witheld even the sour beer, even a blanket.

It was because she had no bed that the girl found the catstone. The bottommost room under the oak tree was a nut-cellar deep among the roots. From her youngest days the girl hid there, for though it was dark the cellar was warm, and Abagtha had forgotten its existence, so that the girl crawled there to escape both the cold and Abagtha's rages. This time, as she bit into a nut, the girl chipped a tooth. She lit the lamp, a dish of fat with a bit of rag for a wick, and held the nut to the glimmer curiously.

It wasn't a nut, but a pebble, shaped oddly like a cat, carved by some hand to enhance the chance resemblance. The girl made a cord out of strands of her hair, and put the catstone around her neck, hiding it well under her rags.

After she found the catstone, the girl began to dream in daytime. She would see faces in the basin as she did the dishes. The songs of the birds were as clear to her as human speech. And the ancient cat,

Mambo, who had always resented the girl, suddenly took to her with a fierce affection, rubbing against her legs and making a curious, croaking purring.

As the cat had a history of scratching and spitting, the girl continued for some time to kick it away. But the cat's affection began to wear away her resistance, and one day at last she picked up the cat and stroked it clumsily.

"There, old Mambo," she said to it softly.

The cat burrowed its head under the girl's chin, purring. Then an extraordinary thing happened: The cat, tapping the catstone with a paw, suddenly let out a great yammering that brought Abagtha at a trot. Her gaze fixed on the catstone, and she stood before the girl, shaking with emotion, eyes bright. The girl waited for the slap, but it did not come. Instead Abagtha stretched out a greedy finger to touch the stone.

She was rewarded with a shock for her pains, blue sparks limning her arm with pale light. Abagtha gave a short shriek and stuck her fingers in her gums, nursing the burn with noisy suckings.

Then her countenance changed, and she smiled a toothless smile.

"Give it me!" she crooned. "Sweet childling, give it to your old nurse, your tender granny, who has cared for you this many a long year. Can you grudge her it? It is a cheap bauble, a nothing. Give it me!"

But this speech, so opposite Abagtha's nature, terrified the girl more than would have an unreasoning rage. She fled.

Driven home by cold and hunger, she crept back at evening. Her keeper extended a civil greeting, and plied her with hot mutton broth and barleycakes—unimagined delicacies. The girl ate, too starved to be wary, the firelight picking out the stone where it lay nestled in the hollow of her neck. A white cinder appeared in each of Abagtha's eyes as she chortled to herself and cracked her toes with quiet glee.

The girl's spoon fell to the tiles with a clatter, and the room rippled and swam. Flushed and numb, the girl slid senseless to the floor.

"The pepper! The pepper!" giggled Abagtha. "A subtler herb, that." The old woman knelt by the girl and unknotted the cord of hair, depositing the charm tenderly in a box of carved horn. She then wrapped the box in a bit of cambric, and hid the whole in her breast.

The girl woke a great while later, the arm twisted under her all pins and needles. Her hand went to her throat and found it bare, and she sat up with a cry. She went into Abagtha's chamber, where she found the old woman abed, the blankets clutched under her chin. Her eyes were staring, their malice replaced by bright fear. The box of horn lay open on the covers, the catstone resting on Abagtha's open palm. The old woman ran her thumb over it feebly, and didn't resist when the girl gently pried it from her grasp.

After she had put the catstone back around her neck, the girl brought steeped herbs and poultices and nursed the tiny form in the bed. But Abagtha hadn't the will to live; she seemed preoccupied by some distant vision, and the girl could not interest her in food, not even cakes of millet and honey, perfectly round.

Inside of a week the sibyl was dead. The girl without a name tucked the covers well about the body, and left a candle burning nearby. Then she put on a clean blouse and smock belonging to Abagtha, and went away from the oak tree with the red door, locking up carefully and hiding the key under a stone.

The Blue Toad in Moorsedge was crowded. The stranger stood on the threshold of the tavern looking for an empty seat. At last he spied a stool near the fender and struck out through the noisy throng toward it. He was weary, and wanted to sit awhile and nurse a cup of mulled wine. He managed to flag down one of the alewife's daughters and request his refreshment. The serving girl looked askance at him, informing him that he could have beer or ale, neither mulled. Supper was eight coppers: rabbit stew or hen pie. The stranger ordered his meal and gave instructions for a room to be made up for him at the adjoining inn.

The stew, when it came, tasted more like squirrel than rabbit. He chased it well with ale, then pushed the empty pannekin aside and drew his seat well into the shadows.

At the next table a cluster of men conversed in low tones. Seven strained to catch the eighth's whispered words.

". . . thought he saw a light in the wood and went and found the old witch locked in her lodgings, deader than a doorknocker."

"One attic too many, if you get my meaning."

"It's not a sound mind that shuns its own kind to live alone in the Weirdwood."

"They say madmen lurk there, and deserters."

"And the Direwolves."

There was a universal shudder, then a lull for drinking. One of their number wiped his mouth and spoke.

"You'll think me drunk or mad, but hear me out. In winter I've a scanty income, and hire myself out to the charcoal burners to pad my wage. We were working on the edge of the Weirdwood one day when all of the sudden, I, get gooseflesh all down the back of my neck. I turned around and saw a girl run off through the trees. And she were no village miss, men! No, she were as wild and dark a creature as *I* ever seen. Mark me: She had seer's eyes.

"Well, she threw me such a look it made my heart go cold, and the next day I went out to my stock and found my best milk cow writhing with colic. There now, what do you think of that?"

"I say the old witch has only shed her skin."

"What does she find to live on in the winter, d'you think?"

"Whatever's unlucky enough to cross her path, I reckon."

"I lost a ewe a week or so ago—"

"The miller over Stillwine way told me his last lot of grain was full of rats, and he had to burn it."

The traveler, in his sooty corner, lit a pipe and smoked quietly. The smoke curled toward the timbers in pale ribbons, obscuring the traveler's face with a silver cloud. His hair glinted copper bright in the firelight, and his grey eyes never turned from their thoughtful contemplation of the speakers. He spoke, and suddenly the whole room was still.

"It's not safe to go abroad anymore, if you ask me."

Every head in the tavern turned and took in his profile, gaunt and made gaunter still by the shadows. The traveler didn't blink.

"She sounds a regular menace." He said this very softly, but even the cellarer asleep among the vats woke and was afraid, so piercing was his tone.

"He's right," said the farmer who had spoken first. "We'll lose our livelihood at first, but when she's done with that sport, what's to stop her from plying her spells our children?"

There arose an ugly mutter.

"It's an unpleasant task," said another, "but it must needs be done. John, fetch a stout rope, and Ian! torches."

They spilled out into the street. The stranger remained, smiled at the serving girl, and called for another ale.

The girl without a name was raiding the squirrels' caches of nuts for her supper, her keen eyes spotting the signs of hiding places, her roughened hands digging through the snow and earth to find a nut or two the squirrels had forgotten, the worms had missed. Her hand kept returning to the catstone, no larger than any of the nuts piled in her lap, which hung around her neck on its cord of hair. Suddenly she stopped sorting the nuts, her hand lingering on the catstone. The girl leaped up and around, the nuts scattering on the snow.

Behind her two dozen men brandishing spades and torches advanced through the trees, shouting and calling to their dogs. The girl swore under her breath and began to run through the snow. She splashed through an icy stream and, clambering up its bank, remembered the foul-smelling musk she carried to keep the Direwolves at bay. She took the vial from her pocket and uncorked it, but before she had a chance to smear herself with the oil she tripped on a tree root and sprawled headlong on the snow.

The dogs were on her in a minute. The men bound her hand and foot and slung her from a pole like a carcass of venison. They cut her tresses from her with wool-shears, and pared her fingernails to char and make into an antidote for her magic. The blood rushed to her head, and before they were out of the wood the girl had fainted.

Someone prodded the girl with a broom handle until she woke. At the sight of her eyes, one blue, one green, an exclamation escaped the throats of the spectators gathered in the village square.

"A potent witch, no doubt about it," said one man. He was the wealthiest shopkeeper in the town and was expected to know such things. "We're lucky she hasn't done greater wickedness."

"Well, what are we going to do with her?" They had never caught a witch before in Moorsedge and were wondering how to proceed.

"We can't drown her—it would taint the wells."

"Burn her, then," someone said uncertainly.

"What, and have unholy ashes over every farm in the county? Are you mad?"

"We could—hang her."

"No, we can't *kill* her at all. A witch's blood revenges itself. Any fool knows that."

"Then just what are we to do, answer me that!"

The man with red hair and grey eyes unfolded his arms and lit his pipe. "Are you men, or mice? Are you men not even mice enough to bell your own cat? You needn't kill her, only render her harmless."

"And how are we to do that?"

"Weren't you listening? I just told you."

2

the tanner's daughter's son

t the bottom of the garden it was so still that it seemed the very wind had been lulled to sleep. Drugged by the drone of bee and hummingbird, the Badger lay between the roots that burrowed beneath the garden wall.

He was not a badger, but a boy, a youth really, for he was grown—not very tall—but with the lean and supple frame that comes from work with horses. It was a season of religious feasts, and there had been a steady stream of pilgrims to the Abbey of Thirdmoon See. There had been a steady stream of horses as well, so the Badger had spent the morning mucking out the stables, watering the horses by the well, and putting them to graze in the pasture above the belltower.

It was tiring work, but he hadn't been too tired afterward to raid the spice orchard. The grass around him was littered with orange rinds, and the acid juice still stung when the Badger ran his tongue over his upper lip. He was wondering whether he should go see if any of the pears were ripe when a voice hailed him. He opened his eyes reluctantly.

"How then, Badger!" A monk came up, removing a beekeeper's

veiled hat from his head, and sat down beside the Badger in the shade of the tree.

"How then yourself, Asaph."

"Hold your tongue, you insolent wretch. Been poaching again, I see. Put the peels in the hedge and come along. If you're late for prayers again you'll forfeit your ration of meat and butter."

"It's not time for lauds already? I must have fallen asleep. Damn." The Badger took his shirt from a tree branch and put it on. "What's for supper?"

"Suet pudding."

The Badger pulled a face. "The cat'll eat well, at any rate."

They started for the courtyard.

They slipped into their places at table barely in time to recite the creed and blessing. The words rattled off seventy-seven tongues and bounded off the ceiling like moths in a lampshade, words worn shabby with long use, slurred by anxious appetites. Seventy-seven index fingers hastily traced pentacles in the air, hands falling from the gesture of piety to seize cup and knife and trencher.

The suet pudding had few qualities to redeem it, its flavor and texture defying description, but it managed to take the keenest edge off the Badger's hunger. He slipped his hunk of bread into his shirt unnoticed. During vespers, while his head was supposed to be bowed in devotion, he would secretly gnaw at the crust.

After the requisite prayer—at the close of the meal—had been mumbled through, the Badger fled to his loft quarters over the stable to savor a rare hour free of horses, and prayers, and the growlings of a demanding stomach. Yesterday he had caught a bat in the chimney; the Badger took a pencil and notebook out from under his cot mattress and began to draw the face of the bat as it slept hanging from the top of a birdcage. He whistled as he worked, a lively ballad, secular bordering on bawdy. Certainly, if the abbot had heard him, and had he further divined the tune's indiscreet origins, it would have so unsettled his troubled bowels as to put him on a regimen of boiled milk gruel for a month.

The Badger had finished the bat's head and was starting on the wings when Asaph's familiar face appeared in the entrance to the loft. The short, rough fleece of his beard was wet, a sure sign he had been summoned from his medicinal gargle of brandy in order to run an errand for the abbot.

"Where did you learn a song like that?" Asaph asked, hoisting himself up into the room.

"From the knifegrinder," said the Badger. The bat began to stir. "Look, you woke him. How do you know what kind of song it is, anyway? I was humming."

"I can certainly tell a bawdy house ballad from a hymn! Just be careful you're not overheard by someone with less than my abundant charity."

"You didn't come to tell me that."

"No, the abbot wants to see you."

The Badger digested this news solemnly. "Ho!" he said softly, "so he's going to try and get me into a cowl and tunic, is he?"

"Yes, and he'll need nine strong men and a shoehorn to do it, too, by the looks of it! Come, come. You'd best resign yourself to it, my friend. He's ninety-seven, and he isn't going to die until he sees you shave your head and take the oath of the Pentacle."

The Badger threw down the pencil and slammed the notebook shut. "Then he'll live to be one hundred and ninety-seven! Why does he want *me*, anyway? Why not the butcher boy or a beggar off the street?"

Asaph's glance slid discreetly over the other's wild hair, stable-mucked boots, and sorry clothes. "Perhaps he can't resist a challenge."

"I see." The boy's laugh was easy, but his eyes had clouded. "If he can save the tanner's daughter's bastard, he can make the very devil tell his beads like a regular pilgrim."

"Don't take that tone with me. You know very well what I meant."

The Badger colored, abashed. "Yes. You're right. I do."

When they had come to the courtyard, Asaph turned and straightened the Badger's collar. "Be careful how you choose your words. His
Grace is in a holy temper tonight."

The Badger grinned and sounded a tattoo on the door to the
abbot's apartments.

"Enter."

The abbot was standing on a stool in the center of the room while
a tailor pinned the hem of a new habit. Assorted monks and tailor's
apprentices hovered nearby, clutching prayerbooks and pincushions.
The noise was fantastic.

". . . Grace! Your Grace! The butcher says we can no longer have
credit until we reconcile our delinquent accounts—"

"Your Grace, about the blessing. Was it cretins at four, and lepers
at six, or lepers at . . ."

"Could you hold your arm so, while I pin the sleeve? Oh! I am
terribly sorry. . . ."

The abbot quitted his perch and calmly withdrew the pin. He sent
a look in the direction of a rabbity monk, who hastily cleared the room
and scuttled off himself in search of sticking plaster. The abbot's gaze
fell on the Badger, who was standing just inside the doorway, twisting
his cap in his hands. The abbot frowned, squinted at his watch, and
addressed the youth before him.

"Martin, is it?"

"Matthew, your Grace."

"Quite." The abbot waved him to a chair, arranging his own
well-upholstered form in the chair opposite. He looked at the Badger,
who looked at his feet. The abbot tugged at the hair in his ear for a
moment before he spoke.

"I will be blunt. Your presence at the abbey has become a trial to
me, and I am at an age when I must economize my trials. When I
contracted with your grandfather to undertake your bringing-up, I as-
sumed you would take the vows and vestments of our order when you

came of age. It is now clear to me that I made that assumption ill-advisedly."

Here the abbot paused and meshed his fingers over the accumulation of puddings at his waist, as if anticipating a reply. But the Badger's eye held its fascination for his bootlace, and the abbot went on.

"Furthermore, it has been brought to my attention that you have taught yourself to read and work mathematical problems. In doing so you have not only reached above your station in pursuit of a gentle education, you have doubled your offense by reading poetry and other reactionary works. You knew such behavior went against all the tenets of the Pentacle and yet you persisted."

The Badger scowled. When the abbot saw no answer was forthcoming, he continued.

"I am therefore persuaded to let you go. I have made inquiries in the nearer counties; it is possible that I may secure you a place with the apothecary at Moorsedge. You will go tomorrow."

At this the Badger leaped from his chair with a great, gleeful crow. "The apothecary? Really?"

The abbot went to the cupboard and rooted among the woolen stockings and bundles of parchment. "Yes, I think it will answer." He produced writing paper and sealing wax, swiftly wrote and dusted a letter, folded and sealed it.

"There, your letter of introduction." Then the abbot pressed a small felt purse into the Badger's hand, "For expenses, mind you."

"If I am going to go tomorrow . . ."

"Yes, go and make your preparations. And Matthew"—

The Badger paused, his hand on the doorlatch.

"You will get receipts for everything."

The next morning the Badger saddled the horse the abbot had given him and rode out the gate before the dew had burned off the grass. The abbot's letter was pinned in his shirt, the purse of coins struck his hip in time to the horse's gait, and he was wearing a grin as rakish as his cap. As soon as he was out of sight of the gatehouse, the Badger nudged the old piebald's ribs with his heels and sped down the road with a quickening heart.

He made Moorsedge by early afternoon and turned the horse's head toward the marketplace. The shops lining the square were crowded, the people close and agitated as bees in a hive, with the same murmur and hum among the stalls of plucked chickens and new shoes. The horse, Motley, picked his way neatly between merchants, servants buying their masters' dinners, and dirty urchins begging for sweetmeats. The Badger spied a fortune-teller setting out a carpet and some tiles, which she was marking with colored chalk; he noticed the woman had one blue eye and one green, only the green eye was glass. She looked up and glared at the Badger.

"Rein him in, will you?"

Motley had begun to mouth the fringe of the carpet. The Badger felt in his pockets for some coins. "Here," he said, swinging down from the saddle, "how much do you charge?"

"Twelvecent." Her good eye roamed him up and down.

He extended his hand. The fortune-teller removed, polished, and replaced her glass eye before peering at the Badger's hand.

"You will make a perilous journey, lose something you prize highly, and come into a great inheritance."

"What, a fortune with no talk of love?"

"Love is three pence more."

"Well, then, another day." He placed the copper coins on the tile, spoiling a little the drawings there, and rode off. How shrewd she was! he thought. She told someone dressed for hard riding that he would make a difficult journey. And everyone loses something of value, if they love their life.

A knot of young men was unloading a cart of cabbages. The Badger recognized one as the smithy's son, who came with his father when there was more shoeing than the abbey could handle alone. Once he had tried to hold the Badger's head under the water used to cool metal from the forge, and another time he had put the Badger's hand on a hot iron.

Seeing the Badger, he elbowed his neighbor. A great sniggering and exchange of whispers followed, and one of the louts called out in a loud voice.

"Bless us, boys! If it isn't Matthew, the glover's son." He smiled; it was an unpleasant smile.

"No, Tim, you're quite mistaken. That's the son of Giles, the clock-case maker."

"Not at all," said a third, laughing through pursed lips. "His father's Lucas, you know, the cooper."

This was followed by laughter like the noise from a rookery.

The Badger had heard these taunts too often to risk a brawl and certain humiliation. He merely tipped his cap and grinned like an idiot, which sent them into fresh seizures of amusement. The Badger made his escape.

Suddenly he remembered, and the memory picked him up and bore him along like a leaf tumbling before the wind. He was six again, and his grandfather had brought him to the market on some errand. Walking through the marketplace, his bright hair blown about his face by the wind, the word followed him. Whispered among the glistening heaps of fish with their awful eyes, among the piles of oranges and bread stacked in pyramids, he heard it. It was meant for him.

Bastard!

But in his young ear the word was warped. He spent his days not with a copybook but watching the creatures that lived in the hedgerow. "Bastard" meant nothing to him. When a merchant handed him his parcel and counted out the pennies, he smiled at the boy, for he was a handsome child.

"And what is your name, little man?" he asked, pushing the coins at him across the counter.

"Badger," replied the boy.

The Badger blinked and the memory faded. The horse had stopped by a well and was having a noisy drink of water from the trough. Seeing

Motley was not about to budge, the Badger dismounted and drank from the gourd that hung from the pail.

"Make yourself comfortable, old friend," he said, knotting the bridle around a post. "I'm going to get my supper."

He let his nose lead him to a stall that sold penny loaves and stood in line flirting with the girls kneading bread at the back of the shop, up to their elbows in dough and giggles. When his turn came, the Badger bought ten penny loaves and ate three on the spot while the baker, a fat, red-faced woman, wrapped the rest in greasepaper. Suddenly the laughter wilted in the throats of the girls, and the Badger saw the ruddiness drain from the baker's face. Everyone waiting to buy bread had fallen silent as well, and in the eerie quiet the Badger heard a shop bell peal. The open-air stall had no bell, just an awning, and the Badger turned, puzzled.

The crowd had parted, and in the rift stood a woman, tall and dark and dressed in what must once have been some garment, but was now pieced together with animal skins. Her extraordinary hair tumbled, blue-black, past her waist, all but hiding her face, but the Badger could just see that her eyes were a strange, pale blue. At that moment she put up a hand to push back her hair, and the Badger saw the hidden eye was green. He was less astonished by this, however, than by the collar —also hidden and now exposed—that was fastened about her neck.

It was made of leather and iron and was hung with sleigh bells. Her hands, too, were manacled and belled, so that her every movement caused the bells to sound. The Badger had heard of bellings. It was a punishment usually reserved for very severe crimes—blasphemy, and adultery.

Now the woman stepped to the counter, drew something from a pocket, and threw it into the balance. It tipped the scales noisily. The object was crusted with mud but here and there the Badger thought he saw the gleam of a gem. The baker filled a napkin with loaves, trembling in her haste, and handed the bundle across the counter. Without a word, the belled woman took up her bread and left.

Once she was out of earshot, the power of speech returned to the onlookers.

"Wanton!"

"Devil's woman!"

"Light some incense, someone."

"Call a priest."

"Hold, now; I've a little holy water with me." The vial was passed like a jug among thieves. Everyone was anointed, and there was a smell like celery. Soon the girls were back to kneading bread, and the baker scowled impatiently at the Badger.

"Yes, yes, what else?"

"That's all, thanks."

"Then on with you, nuisance! You're holding up the rest."

On his way out the Badger paused by the girls wrestling with the bread dough. Their mother's reproach of him had put a polish on the Badger, and they answered his questions eagerly.

"Oh, yes," said the shorter and plumper of the two, "she comes in very regular. Nasty thing."

"Always pays with bits and pieces of swords and things, all stuck with rubies the size of chestnuts."

"One of the pearls, once, was the size of a goose egg," said her sister.

"Oh, Hannah! Tell me another tale," said the other, and they started to bicker. The Badger took up his bundle and left.

He had to drag Motley from the shade so he could get a foot in the stirrup. They were headed toward the district where the apothecary had his shop when the Badger saw the belled woman surrounded by the same pack of louts who had insulted him earlier. The woman was trying to ignore them, but they had circled around her and were slowly advancing.

"Here, kitty, kitty—"

"Ho, darling, isn't our cream good enough for you?"

"She's been to see the queen—the faerie queen—and won't talk to the likes of you and me."

"Did you sit under the queen's chair at court, kitty?" One of them seized her around the waist, wrapping her hair around his hand and pulling her head back. Her teeth were bared, but she neither struggled nor cried out. The Badger had seen animals like that, tensed for the dog's spring.

"If she doesn't like cream, maybe she'll like fishes' heads. What do you say, pet? Would you like that?" The one holding her suddenly caught sight of the horse and rider out of the corner of his eye. He grinned.

"Look who's joined us. Good afternoon, bastard."

"Let her go."

"Ask me nicely, bastard, and maybe I will."

"I wasn't asking."

The one holding her let the woman go and ambled slowly over to the Badger. He took hold of Motley's bridle.

"Let's continue this conversation some other time, bastard," he said, squinting up at the Badger. "I'm fascinated."

At a gesture from him the rest followed out of the square.

"Not hurt, I trust?"

The woman didn't reply, bending silently to retrieve the bread, which had been trampled in the dirt. She found all the loaves, cleaned them as well as she was able, and wrapped them up again. As the Badger approached, she straightened and hugged the bread to her.

"Stay away."

"Here, why don't you let me see that collar," he said gently, putting out a hand.

She bit it. There was a quick exchange of blows as the belled woman swore: "Dog! Dead dog! Worm in a dead dog!"

"Worse and worse!" the Badger said, parrying her attempts to land a blow. He managed to grab both her wrists and was getting a good look at the collar when she gave a howl of fury and brought her knee up sharply. He gave a yelp and dropped to the ground, cursing.

She was suddenly perfectly still, though her ears were bright red and she hiccoughed lightly.

"Get up," she said after a bit.

"No—get away from me." The Badger rocked on the ground, hooing softly.

"Here, get up," she said, hauling him to his feet.

He shook her off. "You're a madwoman," he informed her. "What exactly were you trying to do, geld me?"

"You'll mend." She began to walk away, loosing dust and a faint music of bells as she made her way across the square.

"Mad," said the Badger.

The abbot's directions led the Badger to a disreputable district of the town. He stopped a man carrying a wicker cage of cats and a large sack.

"Can you tell me where the apothecary is? I'm a stranger here."

"Well, you needn't bother to advertise it," replied the man. The cats paced in the cage with a swift restlessness, crying loudly. "If you're wise," he added, "you'll carry your money under your tongue instead of in your pocket."

"But the apothecary . . ."

"My, aren't we in a hurry? Straight on, past the bawdy house and the baths. Can't miss it."

"I'm grateful, I'm sure. Your cats are certainly full of quick."

"They smell the rats," replied the rat-catcher, hefting the sack.

Suspended above the door of the apothecary's shop was a stuffed crocodile, patched here and there with bits of green oilcloth. It revolved slowly on its cord, grinning none too endearingly. There was no answer when the Badger knocked, so he gave the bell a good hard pull. The second-story shutters banged open, and a head, bald and snaggle-toothed, popped out like a cork.

"What do you want?" the head screamed.

"I was sent by the abbot of Thirdmoon See to take a place with the apothecary."

"Take a place? Take a place? At table, do you mean? In a witness box, in the jailor's house, on the gallows?"

The Badger wondered whether every single inhabitant of Moorsedge was insane. "No, man, an apprenticeship," he said, seized by misgivings.

"The apothecary is in prison, I tell you. Jail. Ha, ha! They'll hang 'im. A fine holiday, though, a hanging. They close the banks, and there's free rum punch."

"Hang him? What has he done?"

"He's a debtor, a loathsome debtor, a poisonous, villainous debtor. Oh, sir, a scurrilous sinner, wallowing in debt. Debtor's prison. Ha!"

"Now what do I do?" the Badger asked, of no one in particular.

"Do? Do? Stay out of debt! Ha! ha! Stay out of debt!" The shutters were slammed shut, but the Badger could hear distant whooping somewhere within.

"Well," the Badger said to Motley, "I don't know what I expected, but it wasn't this." His thoughts turned to the lodgings he had outfitted in his mind, the suppers with new-made friends, the amusements in town.

"Do? What to do? Back to the abbey, I suppose, my friend. It makes debtor's prison sound as good a holiday as hanging."

If any had happened to be in the apothecary's shop just then, they would have witnessed an extraordinary transformation. Into the fire fell some bits of black wax, and lo! the snaggleteeth were gone. The wax was followed by some putty, and the warts and ragged ear disappeared as well. Some serious business with a stiff brush and some soap restored the unshaven face to a flawless pink. The red-haired man with grey eyes stirred the fire to make sure all of the disguise was consumed. He went out the back door just as the apothecary was coming in the front.

Old Caraway returned in a bad temper. A note had called him to the potter who sold him his jars; the potter knew nothing of the note. Furthermore, there was no sign of the boy he had been told to expect. At least he would be able to sup in peace.

The apothecary—thought the stranger as he donned an unremark-
able costume in the alley—would have been very surprised to learn that
he was in prison for debt.

The penny loaves were long gone, and the horse's pace had slowed
when the Badger stopped that evening at an inn halfway to Thirdmoon.
He was no sooner down from the saddle when the tavern doors flew open
and a number of lewd drunks spilled into the street—and into the
Badger.

"Can I believe my eyes?"

"He's following us. Go home, bastard."

"What's that smell, the horse or the rider?"

"Do you *sleep* with your horse, or just bathe with it?"

The Badger had escaped a brawl twice already that day and knew
it was fruitless to hope for such good fortune a third time, especially
since a match would have set the breath of any one of them alight.

A great number of the blows were poorly aimed, but he was prettily
thrashed just the same. As he was lying in the gutter, the rest of the
rioters in the inn came to see what the din was about. They hooted at
the Badger's cowardice, drenching him with beer and pelting him with
insults. Aching and wet, the Badger sat on the paving stones and
thought that by now he couldn't argue with the insult about the smell.
Someone brought a bottle down on the back of his head and the Badger
saw a burst of brilliance, and then darkness.

3

the BARROW downs

he Badger came to his senses in total darkness and had to blink several times to know whether his eyes were open or shut. The close air of the place filled his nostrils with an awful stench, and his veins with a cringing fear. He did not know this place, but he knew it.

His hands searched around him for something that would tell him where he was. They found only earthen walls, and then something else. He snatched back his hand, the hair rising on the back of his neck. His hand had closed on a bone.

He was in a grave. They had buried him alive!

Alive—the Badger felt cold air move against his cheek, and his pounding heart calmed a little. There was air, at least. Perhaps they had only bundled him into a cellar, after all. His eyes had begun to sort out faint shapes in the darkness, and he saw the bone was a mutton leg. Now he could make out niches in the earthen walls. He scrambled up to examine them. They held porcelain jars and bottles; by peering hard the Badger could just make sense of the labels: Confect of Canthar, Oil of

Mastic, Solutive Honey of Roses, Pilular Extract of Cassia. Nets hung from the ceiling—full of onions, by the smell of them; the Badger brushed, shuddering, against a ham like a hanged man. No, this was no grave, he thought, but no ordinary cellar, either, for all the hams and onions it might contain. His head ached, and he still heard bells.

As he struggled to remember why bells were important, he saw an approaching light cast a glow on the earthen walls.

Someone rounded the corner with a lit dish of tallow. Before the light showed her face, the Badger heard the bells and remembered.

The village witch silently placed a bundle on the ground beside the Badger and lit a lamp from the dish in her hand, not spilling any of the tallow despite the manacles on her hands. The Badger found he had been lying on a bed of dry heather and that his head had been skillfully bound. He touched the bandage gingerly and winced, remembering the bottle splintering in his ears.

"Where am I?"

"In my barrow."

That made him sit up again. "You mean . . ."

"On the moor, yes." She untied the bundle, which contained the heel of a loaf of bread and two eggs.

She handed the latter to him. "They're boiled. Would you rather they were raw?"

"No! Thanks," he said quickly. "They're fine this way." His hunger won out over his curiosity, and he barely looked at her as he peeled and ate the eggs. She watched him eat without comment, handing him the loaf when the eggs were gone. The Badger paused, chewing, and looked at her bashfully, wiping the crumbs from his mouth with the back of his hand.

"Why did you help me?" he asked, and swallowed.

"You didn't seem to be very good at defending yourself. And as long as I was taking your horse—"

"Motley? What did they—"

She firmly pushed him back down on the mat and began to undo the dressing on his head.

"He's fine. He seemed distressed at the thought of leaving you, but he's eaten a dinner of moor heather and finds it quite to his liking. The village idiots didn't touch him, but if they had thought of it they might have made him into a mock-venison dinner, for spite." She held a rag to the mouth of a jug and tipped it twice. A smell of vinegar assailed the Badger's nose.

"What of the Direwolves? They might have made a meal of him," the Badger said.

"They won't touch a creature shod with iron. Or belled with it. This is going to sting," she warned him. He gritted his teeth as she began to clean the wound. "You see, there's dirt in it, and I have to clean it or it will fester." The woman looked at him closely. "How did you manage to get into the good graces of that lot, anyway?"

"We're childhood friends, they and I. I'm a bastard, you see, and that's reason enough for a drubbing."

"My eyes are the wrong color for their liking—though the rest of me seems to suit them. There, I've done with you. Your shirt is in the other room, drying by the fire." She gave him a sidelong look. "There are more eggs, if you're still hungry."

The other room of the barrow was dominated by the bronze bier of a long-dead warrior. The stone likeness had been detached and now stood in a corner; in its place were a lot of blankets and cushions. Several chickens nested in the rafters. The woman ransacked one of the nests and popped three newly laid eggs into a kettle boiling on the hearth. One corner of the room was taken up by war chests overflowing with armor, much of it broken up by grave robbers themselves long dust.

"Your shirt is on the chair by the fire. Mind the bees."

Near the hearth an old suit of armor was serving as a beehive; one of the bees exited through the visor and flew by the Badger's ear.

The Badger gingerly removed his shirt from the chair and dressed himself. As he did up the buttons, he thought of the woman with her manacled hands putting him across Motley's back, lowering him into the barrow, dressing his wound, undressing him. . . . A high color rose in the Badger's cheeks, which did not come from the fire. He turned to face her.

"You're no witch, whatever they say. What are you?"

She turned on him a cool, blue-green gaze. "But I am a witch. Make no mistake about that. I am full of all sorts of volatile magics, my friend. I might slit your throat from behind while your back is turned and have you for supper." She laughed, yawned, stretched, and addressed him again. "I know something of magic. Call me what you like. I was never named. At least, I was never given a name I cared to keep."

"What do you mean? Don't you have a name?"

"The woman who raised me called me lots of things—Lizardling, Underfoot—none of them names, really." She seemed to have a thought. "Call me Catling."

He was having trouble with her accent. "Caitlin?"

She laughed. "Yes. Call me that. Caitlin." Her hand went to a small stone that hung around her neck. "Do you like waffles with honey? But of course you do."

The waffles were baked in the fire on a piece of chain mail, but tasted very good for all that. After they had eaten, the Badger hoisted himself out the trapdoor onto the moor. Motley neighed a greeting and the Badger passed his hands swiftly over the horse's legs with no little relief.

"Hey, ugly old thing. Don't get any ideas about this being a holiday for you, just because you get to dine with a view." The Badger beat the dust and sweat from the horse's coat as best he could, and saw the tether ropes were secure. Then he stepped down onto the rafter and swung onto the floor of the barrow, cheerfully rubbing his aching head.

"I believe the moor agrees with him."

"It will have to. You will both have to stay until morning. The moor isn't safe at night."

"Then why do you stay?"

"They think the moor is haunted; it keeps them away. It's the grave robbers and wolves that keep *me* in."

"How . . . how did you come to be . . . belled?"

She paused so long he thought she would not answer. "There was a sickness among the children," she said at last, "and some cows went dry. Nothing very remarkable in that, except it happened all at once. I grew up in the Weirdwood, alone with my guardian. That would have been enough, even if she hadn't dabbled in spells. So they blamed her, and when she died her blame was my inheritance. They would have killed me, only they were cowards. So they belled me instead, to know when I was coming."

"How did you lift me?"

"I have learned to live with these," she said, shaking the manacles so the bells rang. "Even to use them. How I hate them."

"I could take them off for you."

She looked at him. "Why should you?"

"Well, why should you have helped me?"

"Because I hate the ones that beat you—not because I bear *you* any love."

"And I bear no love for those who belled you."

A riot of emotions fought to fix themselves on her features.

"You're not doing this out of kindness?"

The Badger hesitated, not sure which answer she wanted.

"Kindness is a lie," said Caitlin, the fire making her face fearsome. Then her face softened, and she asked, tantalized: "Could you really get them off?"

"I'll try—to spite them."

"Yes," she said, "to spite them." But when the tools were fetched from the saddlebag, and the manacles and collar fell noisily to the barrow floor, Caitlin clutched her ears, tears starting up in her eyes.

"It's so quiet," she said, her voice full of surprise. "I had forgotten."

She then instructed the Badger how to make a salve for her neck and wrists. Bandaged, Caitlin settled on the bier among the cushions and chickens.

"Tell me a story. Tell me where you came from, Badger, and then tell me a story with dragons in it. Then we will sleep, and in the morning I will show you off the moor. But a story first."

The rat-catcher was in his rooms, placating his cats with scraps of mackerel after a day spent deratting a brewery and a judge's chambers. The cats swarmed over the rat-catcher's legs, joggling for the fish. The rat-catcher chortled and helped himself to a few mackerel, teasing the cats on his lap by dangling the fish near his lips.

"Oh, yes, delicious, my pretties, yes! There, go on; have it. I bought liver sausage for *my* dinner." He stood, scattering the cats, which yowled and fled to the corners of the room with greasy bits of mackerel.

"Do I have mustard?" mused the rat-catcher aloud, going to the cupboard with a heavy tread. One foot was shorter than the other where a rat had gnawed the heel. He found only old traps and some cheese suitable for rat bait but not human consumption. A loud knocking interrupted his search, and the rat-catcher limped to the door. Through the little shutter the rat-catcher could see a clean-shaven cheek and a grey eye.

"Yes, what do you want?"

"I want some rats caught."

"Off hours. Come tomorrow." The rat-catcher started to close the shutter, but quick as a wink the visitor slid a coin in before it had closed all the way. It was a gold coin, newly minted, and the rat-catcher felt his palms begin to itch, and his mouth water.

"There are many more like it to be had," said the stranger, "if only I could remember where I put them."

The rat-catcher opened the door, motioning for the man to enter. The cats came clambering around, and the man with the grey eyes picked up a particularly noisy one, holding it to his chest and languidly stroking its fur.

"How ratty are you?" asked the rat-catcher as he put the liver sausage in the pan and looked for a knife with which to pare some potatoes.

"Not very. There are only two, but they are very *large* rats."

The rat-catcher looked up sharply and spat with elaborate disdain into a corner. "I don't do that kind of rat-catching. I have no ambition to put my head into a noose, thank you very much. If you want your wife and her fancy man sent to hell by the quick road, you needn't've come to me. There are cutthroats a plenty in the street, and you wouldn't have interrupted my dinner." This was a very long speech for the rat-catcher; he had to sit down at the end of it.

"You mistake me. I have no wish to kill my rats, I merely want them displaced. You aren't going to eat that sausage without mustard, are you?"

"Haven't got any," said the rat-catcher ruefully.

A small felt sack appeared on the table, its contents settling pleasantly, coin against coin.

"That will buy a considerable amount of mustard, my friend. Watch for me in an hour by the tavern and I will direct you. Enjoy your supper."

Above on the moor Motley paused in his grazing and whinnied nervously. A man, his hair glinting like tarnished copper in the dark, stepped up to the horse and stretched out a palm full of lump sugar. Motley's wariness deserted him, and he nosed eagerly at the confection offered by the black glove. The man stroked the nap of the horse's broad nose, speaking in a lulling tone.

"Nothing to be anxious about, my fine fellow. We're going to be famous friends, very famous friends, indeed. The burglar must throw a bone to the faithful dog if he doesn't want the household roused."

In the barrow Caitlin woke and lay crouched on the bier, listening intently with her ears, with her very skin. She heard nothing but the light snore of the Badger asleep in front of the fire. Some coals settled into ash, and the horse on the peat overhead shifted his weight. Slowly Caitlin relaxed, her cheek reluctantly coming to rest against the cold of the ancient stone. At length she closed her eyes, and at greater length perhaps she slept.

She did so fitfully, and dreamed. They were uneasy dreams, dreams of being punished by Abagtha, being locked in the smokehouse where Abagtha dried her herbs, being put to bed in a cellar full of rats.

Caitlin stirred in her sleep uneasily, then woke with a shudder and start. The barrow was full of hundreds of rats, rats panicked by the thick tar smoke that choked the rooms. Gagging on the foul, stinging smoke, Caitlin felt along the wall, stepping on rats all the way, and found the Badger. He hadn't woken, though the rats had crawled onto him where he slept and had begun to chew his boots. The smoke! thought Caitlin, and she hauled him to his feet.

The trapdoor was shut and the tunnel was full of smouldering rags soaked in tar and lamp-oil. Everywhere the rats scurried in panic, making an awful noise. Caitlin's clothes began to smoke, and there was barely room in the space of the tunnel to put out the flames. At last, their eyes streaming and throats raw with smoke, the two stumbled out into the black, cool, blessed night.

When the fits of coughing had subsided, they saw Motley standing a little apart, a large red handkerchief tied over his eyes.

"Our friends," said the Badger.

"No—they would have stolen the horse, or killed him."

The Badger knelt to pick something from the moor at the horse's feet, turning it in his hands in a puzzled manner.

"What did you find?"

"Footprints. And—it's odd—a sugar-lump."

Caitlin's hands went to the amulet around her neck.

"Badger. You must leave at once. Now, not in the morning."

He heartily agreed. "But you're coming with me."

She didn't argue.

The bed in which the abbot of Thirdmoon See slept was an unyielding one unlikely to encourage dreams or even luxurious sleep.

The abbot rose at his usual hour, said his morning prayers, ate his coddled egg, and awaited the arrival of his secretary.

When a monk with a harelip arrived bearing a tray with a razor and a bowl of lather, the abbot settled in a chair for his morning shave. The monk lathered the abbot's sunken cheeks and began to sharpen the razor. That instrument poised, the monk cleared his throat.

"Your Grace."

"Yes?" mumbled the abbot, trying not to get soap in his mouth.

"Young Matthew, the tanner's daughter's son, is returned from Moorsedge."

"What happened?"

"We have not put any questions to him, your Grace. We thought it best to leave any interview to you. But as far as we can ascertain from his remarks to the cook who fed him on his return, the apothecary was unavailable." The monk began to shave the abbot's chin and neck. After a considerable silence he spoke again.

"Your Grace."

"Hmmm-hmm?"

"He has brought a young woman with him."

"Dear me. What sort of young woman?"

"A witch, your Grace."

The abbot took a great mouthful of lather and was forced to spit in a most unseemly manner. "A *what?*"

"A young woman who works magic, scorning the creed of the Pentacle. As I said, your Grace: a witch." The monk rinsed the razor and wiped the traces of lather from around the abbot's ears and throat.

"Send them to me. Send them to me, and make sure the woman is free of vermin first."

"As you wish, your Grace."

The woman from the dairy and her niece were recruited to wash Caitlin. They came with brushes in many sizes, meant for cattle and carpets, and with strong lye soap and specially blessed pentacles to ward off evil eyes and other spell-spinning. Caitlin was led away, and from the dye-house where they had readied her bath there could be heard at first shouts and short screams and splashing. Later, voices singing in rounds issued out over the abbey courtyard, followed by laughter and then again screams.

While Caitlin was being readied for her audience with the abbot, the Badger went in search of Asaph. Knocking on the door to the monk's cell, he got no answer; when he knocked harder, the door swung open under his hand. The room had been stripped: the beekeeper's hat was not on its peg. A young monk not much older than the Badger was sitting on a bare cot by the window, reading a missal.

"Sorry . . . I . . . I must have taken a wrong turn. I was looking for Asaph's cell."

The young monk looked at him strangely. "This was his cell. Did you know him?"

"I used to be the stableboy here. Why, where is he?"

"They took him to the asylum yesterday."

The Badger left Asaph's cell and went to his own old room above the stables. At first he thought they had given his rooms over, too, but the figure sitting on his cot turned, and he saw it was Caitlin. She was very pink, and someone had braided her hair and dressed her in a robe of bluegreen stuff that couldn't decide whether it wanted to be the color of her right eye or her left. She was holding his recorder in her hands.

"Do you make music on this?"

"Sometimes—to amuse myself."

Her eyes widened a little, then narrowed. Caitlin had never heard of music for amusement, only for charming things. She saw the Badger was troubled.

"What's the matter?"

"Nothing for you to worry about." He had rescued some of Asaph's belongings from the forge coalbox: a small gilded missal, a small treatise on bees, the barnyard animals carved from honeycomb Asaph made for village children. The Badger ranged them now on the foot of the cot.

Caitlin picked up a wax hen and rooster; she thought of Abagtha, and an old spell to make hens lay. If you said the spell backward as you roasted a brown egg in the fire, the same spell would make hens stop laying. Most spells were like that, Caitlin mused. They could be turned inside-out as easily as a cap.

"You're worried about someone," she said. "It's all right; it doesn't take a seer to read it in your face."

"Perhaps I'll tell you about it later. Right now we have to go to the abbot and convince him you're not the devil incarnate."

"Ah. Perhaps they should have dressed me in virginal white?"

The abbot's light dun eyes flicked over the curiosity before them. They noted the unsettling eyes, the blistered skin on the neck and wrists, the secular amulet. At last, after rolling his words around on his tongue like a mouthful of wine, the abbot spoke.

"Are you a believer, my daughter?"

"I don't believe you are my father."

"Don't be impudent. You have had no religious instruction, then?"

"Oh, I know of you and your Pentacle. When the Necromancer succeeds in turning lead into gold, all faithful souls will be made pure and incorruptible. Yes—I know your Pentacle." Caitlin had spoken in low tones, but the Badger thought that if her hair had not been bound it would have thrown off sparks.

"Hush," said the abbot, stretching out a hand to touch the cat amulet. "You flirt with blasphemy, and I am too old for such nonsense. This is an amulet of the black arts. Are you a witch?"

"I am an herbwoman, and an interpreter of birds. I have been known to converse with cats. I am an otherworld daughter. Would you have me dye an eye to match the other, and take in laundry, and a husband?"

The abbot bit his lip and pulled at his ear-hair. Then his consternation lifted.

"There are two courses of action open to me. You see, I have the duty of saving your soul from damnation while setting the populace at ease. The easiest way in which I might accomplish this is to have you burned at the stake." The abbot coughed; Caitlin didn't flinch. "But I am willing instead to offer you this choice: confinement for the rest of your natural life in either a convent or an asylum. I leave the choice to you. Come to me before lauds tonight and I will hear your answer.

"Now, Matthew. Kneel, and explain yourself. What is this about you trying to apprentice yourself to a witch?"

The Badger knelt. Caitlin arched an eyebrow.

"The apothecary was in debtor's prison, your Grace."

"Does that excuse or even explain your subsequent behavior? You disappoint me. You will remain here for a time longer until I decide what to do with you. I shall make inquiries of the muleskinner and the renderer." The abbot extended his hand, and the Badger touched his lips to the large ring of holy office, rose, and jammed his cap over his red ears.

"You may go."

In the courtyard, it seemed to him Caitlin looked at him with mocking eyes. "Are you a badger, Badger, or a mouse?" she murmured.

He turned on her like a dog that has had its tail pulled one too many times. "MOUSE!" he shouted, and the word rang and hung in the courtyard. Monks poked their heads out of casements to look quizzically at them as they passed.

"I wear a collar, too, invisible perhaps, but no less hard than yours! Only there is no getting mine off. Muleskinner! Boiler of lard! God help me!" He strode off toward the garden without waiting for Caitlin.

She caught up with him easily; he tripped on a jutting tree root and sprawled headlong on the path. Caitlin caught his sleeve and reached unabashedly into his shirt, pulling out the brass pentacle that hung there by a lace.

"Then why kiss his ring, if you feel that way about it? Or do you really believe third-rate alchemy is going to save your soul?"

"How can I not believe it—I was raised here, wasn't I?"

She let the pendant fall back upon his chest. "You didn't tell me you were a monk," she said reproachfully. "I thought you were going to be an apothecary."

"It seems I'm to be neither." The Badger sat on the ground and lifted his eyes to Caitlin's. "I'm nothing but a self-deceived kisser of rings. I haven't believed for a long time. But if truth is not in this, where is it? I thought it lay outside these walls, but I was wrong. I was a fool."

"Yes, you were, but no more a fool than anyone else."

The Badger got up and brushed the shreds of moss and bark from his trousers. "Come on."

They went to the kitchen gate, where the Badger spoke to the knifegrinder.

"Yes, I saw them take him away, in the back of a cart. He was raving so it took three men to hold him down."

"You're sure it was Asaph?"

"Yes—the fat one, the drunkard who kept the bees, right?"

The Badger walked away without answering, though he wanted very much to sharpen his knuckles on the knifegrinder's back teeth. Caitlin followed, but not until she had cast a small spell dulling the knifegrinder's whetstone.

4

the journey begins

rossing the yard, Caitlin and the Badger were approached by the harelipped monk.

"The abbot would have you prepare for your journey before you come to him," he said to Caitlin. "You are to be ready to depart at once." The monk hurried away, scattering the goats and geese.

The Badger took Caitlin back to the stables to outfit her for a journey; in her haste she had taken nothing from the barrow, if there had been anything fit to snatch from the smoke and rats. While the Badger searched for a pair of boots to fit her, Caitlin picked up Asaph's missal.

"Badger—Asaph's missal. It's pigskin."

He looked up; half the time she seemed to read his thoughts, the other half she acted like a simpleton. "That it is."

"Pigskin with gilt edges? You don't gild pigskin. Vellum, yes, but not pigskin."

"You're right; I hadn't thought of it that way. It would be like making a velvet coat for a pig." He took the missal from her hands. "How odd. He must have added the gilt himself for some reason. It's not like him. . . ."

"Careful. I think it's safe to say he didn't add the gilt himself, it's poison."

The Badger hastily dropped the prayerbook. "What!"

"I think that gilt has poison in it. Some belladonna, foxglove, and maybe a little mistletoe. I picked it up earlier, and I haven't felt right since. In any case, the bookworms knew enough to leave it alone."

"But poison? He's supposed to be mad, not dead."

"If he wet his thumb to turn the pages, or cut it. Over a time it would begin to tell. He would be feverish, raving—the picture of a madman."

"Surely, he would have noticed it. . . ."

"Not necessarily. How often do you suppose Asaph really *read* his missal? No, far more likely it was in his pocket, where he ran his hand along the spine when he was thinking. Just a little of the poison through the skin and his brain would begin to get foggy. He might never notice."

The Badger let the missal fall open, and gazed hard at the page before suddenly slamming the book shut.

"What am I to believe, that Asaph went mad? Or did someone plot to drive him mad by poisoning a book? I feel a little strange, myself."

"Here, put it down for now. The abbot awaits."

The abbot was ready for bed—he always took a nap at midday— and the harelipped monk had tied on his nightcap for him and fetched his gruel. The abbot sucked his teeth a little and looked balefully at the pair before him.

"Well, which shall it be? The convent or the asylum?"

"The convent."

"Very well. You shall start today for the convent at Ninthstile." The abbot held a spoonful of gruel halfway to his mouth, spilling a little on his shirt. "It is a great distance, some months' journey, and I would not have you travel it alone. Matthew here will go with you."

The Badger was dumbstruck. "I thought . . . the muleskinner . . ."

"This suits my purposes. Do you question me?"

"Of course not, your Grace."

"You ought to have a chaperone, but I can spare no one to go with you."

"If the nuns doubt that I am spotless I shall tell them my escort is a eunuch," Caitlin said coolly. The Badger went very red.

"Confound you, go as you please, so long as you go," said the abbot. "But mark me: I will not tolerate witches. I shall send word to the sisters at Ninthstile to look for you by the new year. If you have not arrived by then, I shall have the sergeant set a price for both your heads. If either of you fails to arrive in Ninthstile by the appointed time, the other shall die. You will be sent to the muleskinner, and not to be apprenticed. Now go."

While Caitlin chose a horse from the stable, the Badger repacked his belongings: his tools, the recorder, his notebook, a box of dominoes, some marbles that had been in his pocket the first day he came to Thirdmoon. Hesitating, he added Asaph's missal to the bundle, then took the brass pentacle from around his neck and hung it from a rafter.

Caitlin had chosen a grey mare, Maud. They saddled the horses and the Badger left the Abbey of Thirdmoon See for the second, and, as it turned out, the last time.

The messenger ran his hands through his hair and squinted through the eyepiece. The spyglass was trained on a dimple in the wood where Caitlin and the Badger had stopped for the night.

"Elric," he said, without turning to the red-haired man beside him, "are you sure she is the one?"

"I should hope to heaven she is, after these twenty years! Look at those eyes, man. Look at those cockatrice, those seer's, those otherworld eyes! Of course she is the one."

The messenger shut the spyglass and joined Elric by the fire. "Do you find her beautiful?"

"No. But something about her would make a man forswear beauty."

"Just don't fall in love with her."

"In love with her? My dear fellow." Elric knelt and used a stick to roll a blackened potato out of the fire. "I haven't forgotten what I was sent to do." He split the potato, reached into his pocket, drew out a peppermill, and peppered the potato.

"Are you sure you can take care of them?" asked the other.

"Don't worry; I'm sworn to. Now, did you bring me what I asked?"

"Oh, I'd nearly forgotten." The messenger threw Elric the saddlebag.

"Yes, I thought you had. Ah! Bootlaces, a razor, and . . . butter." He looked up, grey eyes darting. "Have a potato. No? Good, I'm famished." Chewing his potato, Elric walked to the rim of the hollow and gazed down on the pair below.

No sooner had they crossed into the woods than the Badger was seized with powerful misgivings: A few days ago he had been eating stolen oranges and arguing with Asaph. Suddenly all that, the whole loathed but familiar world of Thirdmoon, had vanished, and there stretched in front of him only this dark wood. What in the name of sweet heaven was he doing, anyway, with this half-witch on his way to Ninthstile? Ninthstile, a convent so remote that it would take them half the winter to reach it. It was madness. If they lost time, if they were delayed reaching the straits at Little Rim, they would be forced to wait until spring to cross, and then every bounty hunter in thirteen kingdoms would be looking for them. And Asaph, poisoned, and vanished? It was too much.

And then there was Caitlin. The first night in the wood the Badger had bolted upright to a bloodcurdling scream and found himself across the fire at Caitlin's side, shaking her awake.

"You were having a nightmare," he said to her calmly, but the hairs on the back of his neck were standing up straight.

Caitlin's face was white as death, her dark hair damp with sweat against her brow.

She pushed him away and drew the blanket to her chin. "Go back to sleep."

He hesitated. "What did you dream?"

But Caitlin wouldn't answer him.

This was not the Weirdwood, so there was no need to fear the Direwolves, but there might very well be deserters, or robbers, so they rode as swiftly as they could without leaving the path. The Badger looked over his shoulder. He could have sworn he saw something move behind them, off to the right. They came to a stream and paused to fill the waterskins.

"I don't mean to alarm you," he said, "but we're being followed."

"Yes, I know. He's been back there since early yesterday." Kneeling in the middle of the stream Caitlin was washing with neat, catlike movements.

"I don't suppose you thought to tell me," the Badger said angrily.

Her eyes widened. "Why, what could you have done?"

"You should have told me in any case," he said lamely.

They rode on in silence.

In the shadows, Elric was having a rest, leaning on the hunter's bow that came up to his shoulder. He was wishing for some ointment; his last assignment had involved masquerading as a jester at court, and the stint had made him soft. It was going to be hell keeping the two of them in sight. He was on foot now.

Elric was annoyed, and a little worried. There was no doubt in the case of the girl, but he had a bad feeling about the boy. He wasn't at all sure he was the one. It was a nuisance and no little danger, but there was nothing for it. When the time came, he would have to act. If someone got hurt who wasn't mean to, well, there was no helping it.

Elric wished he didn't feel so uneasy. I should have listened to my father, he thought sullenly, and become a lawyer.

It happened the woods in question belonged to Milo, known to his subjects as the Boy King, though he was a strapping man of thirty-three. Milo was riding through his woods with a small hunting party of two hundred, consisting of his astronomer, fifty courtiers, several dozen servants assigned to lunch detail, some sixty hunters and bodyguards, Milo's old nurse, and a yammering pack of dogs that led the way through the dense thicket.

They were going to kill the first creature they saw, whether furred or feathered, great or small. It didn't matter what kind of animal, Milo insisted.

"You see, it says: 'Kill ye the first beast ye shall find, and cook it with the heart of a fox, and ye shall understand the voices of the birds and beasts.'"

"Nonsense," said Nurse, riding at the king's side.

"Oh, no," said the astronomer, "this has very recently been proven to be so."

Milo was reading aloud in the saddle from a small, illuminated book of wonders, so that two grooms had to ride at either side of their king, poised to seize the reins if his horse should suddenly try to unseat his rider and bolt for freedom through the trees.

"It's nonsense, nevertheless," Nurse proclaimed in her rich baritone. The astronomer protested that he himself had witnessed such a case in his own lifetime. Nurse only belched gently in reply.

They had the fox already. Milo had the largest menagerie in thirteen kingdoms, and all the roads in his realm were in disrepair, the money for mending them having been spent on expeditions to capture an ibex or iguana. Milo yawned. He hoped they would find something soon. Once he had gained the speech of the animals he wanted to test it on the tame carp in the palace fountain.

The king's First Huntsman swore as he rode ahead with the hounds. He could hear old King Max turning in his grave. It was a good thing the old monarch had died when he did, that was all he could say. And they had all thought the prince would outgrow this monstrous foolishness! It was going to be dark in an hour or two, and they hadn't seen a thing.

Apart from the king's party, and from the pair traveling to Ninth-stile, the woods held a small party of the king's guards, looking for poachers. These were bad times in Milo's kingdom, and no game was safe. It happened that there was only one poacher in the woods just then, an old rascal named Purley, and he had concealed himself for the afternoon inside a hollow tree. The woods were crawling today; he hadn't seen it this bad since Prince Milo, aged six, had run off to hunt dragons' nests and had gotten lost. Well, the only thing for it was to stay put, have a smoke to confuse the dogs, and take a nap. When all these busybodies had gone home he would come out and tend to his lines and traps.

The patrol consisted of five guards, each of whom had been hoping to be assigned to hunt duty. That was easy work and a good day's outing, with better meat and drink than they got at home on feast days. As it was, they had only been given brown bread, red and white cheese, and beer for their meal—"not even a little hot wine!" they grumbled—and they were all in a nasty temper. Heaven help any poacher they caught.

Old King Max had loved to hunt. These woods had once been his deer park, before his son's indifference had condemned them to rack and ruin. They were thick with deer, but the king and his party were making such a racket that every living thing for miles gave them a wide berth.

The Badger and Caitlin were making far less noise, and now and then as they rode they would spy a hind drinking with her young. Even had they the skill to kill one, neither Caitlin nor the Badger had the heart for the butchering, or any appetite for new-killed venison. When the stores they had brought from Thirdmoon were gone, they dined on eggs from birds' nests, and climbing winter figs that ripened early in the wood.

"We're coming to the edge of the forest," Caitlin said. They had just eaten their dinner in the saddle, for they were still being followed.

The Badger reined in Motley beside her. "If we do a little hard riding, we might reach a town before dark."

Just then a huge stag crashed through the thicket, hurtling across the path. In midair it gave a shudder and groan awful to hear, and fell thundering to the ground, making Motley rear in terror.

"Sweet heaven!" cried the Badger, trying to calm the horse. Motley was skipping and snorting at the smell of fresh blood in his nostrils. The shaft of an arrow emerged from the hart's side.

Elric stepped from the brush, fitting another arrow to his bow. He had tied a kerchief about his face but (was it his imagination, or just her eyes?) he thought Caitlin put a hand to her amulet.

"Oblige me, madam, and climb that tree. Yes, that one there. Come, come, you can do better than that, I've seen you."

"What in sweet heaven—" began the Badger.

But the hunter stepped up, pressing a finger to his lips for silence. "Hush!" he said, pressing the bow into the startled Badger's hands. "You oughtn't to be hunting here, my friend. These are the king's woods." With that, he flung the quiver at the Badger's feet and vanished.

As if on cue, the patrol galloped through the gap in the trees. A sword pressed lightly into the base of the Badger's throat.

"You're under arrest in the name of the king."

In the tree Caitlin crouched very still, watching the Badger being trussed like a piece of game—the way they had trussed her, once. She was helpless. If she revealed herself, they would both be lost. Caitlin saw the Badger's face strained with the effort of not looking in her direction. Her breath seemed very loud to her.

And they led him away, with the horses in tow.

"Quick," said their leader, "I saw the other go this way."

Elric escaped. One minute the guards had him in sight, the next he had vanished. Elric smiled, vain over his marksmanship. He chuckled as he reached the edge of the forest and saw the town road stretching out before him. Carelessly, he took a step forward. A poacher's snare closed tight around his foot, the sprung trap hauling him up by one leg to dangle in the treetops.

The dogs had found Caitlin. They sat beneath the tree, panting and howling by turns. Coming up to them the First Huntsman gazed into the branches and began to laugh.

"Well, sweetheart," he called up to her, "I hope you fancy fox for dinner!" And he sat down and laughed some more.

Caitlin was too weary to answer. Let them climb up and get me, she thought.

The rest of the hunting party rode up and reined in their mounts. Necks were craned, eyes shaded as everyone looked up into the treetops.

"My word," said the astronomer.

"Huh," said Nurse.

"A princess!" crowed Milo in delight.

And a princess Caitlin became, despite the best arguments put forth by Nurse, the astronomer, and the First Huntsman. Milo ordered Caitlin retrieved from her perch and placed before him on his horse. "Or is it behind?" he thought aloud. One of his picture books had a colored plate of such a scene, if only he could remember it. "She is a mute princess," he explained to Nurse. "All her brothers have been changed to ravens by a wicked stepqueen, and she must keep a vow of silence for seven years to free them. Let's see; we will have to devise a system of hand signals." Milo hummed and fidgeted in the saddle. He loved this sort of puzzle.

"She needs a bath," said Nurse.

Caitlin held her tongue. The First Huntsman helped her into the saddle, muttering under his breath, "Ah, you can talk as well as I!"

And so the three of them—Caitlin, the Badger, and Elric—arrived in Milo's kingdom in three very different manners.

The Badger entered slung across the back of a horse and was promptly thrown into Milo's dungeons.

Caitlin entered like royalty and was immediately submerged in a hot bath, on strict orders from Nurse.

And Elric was cut down past midnight by old Purley the poacher, who revived him with rum and helped him into town on foot.

5

the magpie king

he richest men in Milo's kingdom were the money-lender, the hangman, and the rat-catcher. The capital was sooty, full of dark, sour smells, and the streets rang with an unholy, unceasing din. It was hard to tell the houses from the taverns; they alike stank of beer, with arguments spilling out into the streets. In Milo's kingdom, the man next to you would as soon slit your throat for a piece of bread as a piece of gold. On every street corner there were fistfights, and people took their children to see the public trials and hangings, since there were no puppet shows.

Caitlin saw none of this. Certain peasants were paid an allowance out of the king's treasury to keep up a rustic touch along the king's road: Children hurried home from their shifts at the glue works; their mothers smeared their faces with rouge to give them a healthy pink. Then the whole family would drag father out of bed so that he could be leading the cow on a rope and smoking a pipe when the king rode by. It was this picture Caitlin saw as she rode with Milo's arms around her waist.

She lay now, floating in the second proper bath of her life. The water had issued from an unseen source, steaming hot and bubbling with fragrant oils. Caitlin lay back in the water and thought.

She wondered where they had taken the Badger, and whether they hanged poachers in this kingdom. She seemed to remember they did that sort of thing to thieves.

She wondered, too, about the man who had killed the deer. She had an uneasy feeling that she had seen him before. In the Weirdwood? Moorsedge? She stared through the vapor at the bathwater, willing the scene to take shape out of the colored swirls of oil.

Nurse entered, hefting a huge pile of towels. A string of handmaidens followed behind, bearing clothing, a large assortment of shoes, and caskets of jewels.

"Wash your neck, and then out of the water with you! Such idleness! So you can't speak, is that your story? We'll see about that. Well, you, dry her off; you, put that gown on her, and these shoes. We'll see how she looks in blue."

After she was dressed, Caitlin was led to a banqueting hall. It was an indoor garden, a hundred evergreens lit with uncountable tapers. Cages of songbirds were suspended from the ceiling, which was painted with clouds and stars; on fair evenings the dome opened an oval eye to the real sky. Tame deer wandered here and there begging for tobacco from spent pipes, and bears in large lace ruffs capered clumsily to the piping of a musician, wagging their snouts to the music and catching in their great jaws meat tossed them by the members of the court.

If the courtiers seated at the lavish banqueting table noticed Caitlin's seer's eyes, they hid the fact well. Everyone was intent on Milo, who was cocking an ear to a nightingale in a cage. On Milo's plate was what Caitlin supposed was the unfortunate fox's heart, and a poached egg. The first animal they had seen had been a hen, but the owner had refused to part with it, finally taking a sovereign for one of the bird's eggs.

Milo shook his head, and let his napkin fall to the cloth. "Nothing

—nothing—it's really very disappointing. Perhaps it has to settle in the stomach, and brew. I will try again in the morning."

Caitlin stepped up to the king. If there had been no need to keep mute, she could have told him what the bird was singing. It was one of the first songs Abagtha had taught her: *My love has flown to the moon, the moon, and there is no consoling me.*

Milo spied Caitlin and stood, beaming.

"Princess!" Although a place had already been set for her farther down the table, Milo made a new place for her between himself and the astronomer, crowding the rest at the table down toward one end. Caitlin sat beside the king, thinking, Playact for your supper. You are a mute princess whose brothers have been turned to ravens. Behave accordingly.

Kissing his hand seemed a good beginning, and she surprised herself by even summoning up a few tears. The whole court was touched, no one more than the young king himself. He could hardly eat his soup. Between courses they played Twenty Questions until he had pieced together the whole of her tragic history.

Her name, Caitlin pantomimed, was Emeralda (here she pointed to Milo's ring). For his benefit she relived her arduous journey over the terrain of her plate, through forests of asparagus, treacherous custard seas, baked plains of beef. Pity welled up in Milo's heart.

Nurse kicked the astronomer under the table.

"Do you think . . ." she whispered.

"Yes, I'm afraid he's smitten."

Nurse peppered her meat viciously. "Not again!"

"Shh! He'll hear you." The astronomer glanced at Milo nervously under cover of his napkin.

"Rot. He's so busy playing Charades he wouldn't hear an army marching on his eardrum in hobnailed boots."

It was true. The astronomer didn't like the look of it, at all.

The guards threw the Badger down a flight of stone steps, and the last thing he remembered was hitting his head. Awake again, he slowly breathed in the smell of filthy straw and tasted the foul mattress beneath him. He closed his mouth and swallowed. His throat was dry, he ached, and his eyes burned. The place was stinking and small, and he was not alone in it.

The Badger sat up, clutching his pounding head. He blinked, trying to train his eyes on the uncertain figures across the room.

As far as he could make out, there were three of them. The first face he sorted from the darkness was pale, topped with a shock of white hair, although the face was not particularly old. The eyes were pale, too, made even less substantial by thick lenses secured with wire and string. The second face the Badger could make out was young, but its handsome features were fixed in a scowl. It was unpleasant to hold the gaze of the dark eyes beneath their thunderclap brows. The Badger released the second man's gaze to look at the last face. This one was very old, a mass of wrinkles that all but hid the eyes. It was a hairless face, and toothless; a set of false teeth hung around the old man's neck by a cord. The Badger looked from one to the other to the third again. His head was killing him.

"Hello," said the first.

The second nodded grudgingly.

The third put in his teeth, as if that would help him see better.

"I'm Fowk," said the first, handing the Badger a pitcher of water. It was warm and unpleasantly fusty, but it was water. The Badger drank, washed his face, and thanked him.

"You can call me Badger."

"This is Ulick—don't kick me! Why shouldn't I tell him?—and this here is Old Dice. How did you manage to get thrown into our good company?"

The Badger felt the back of his head, wincing. "Poaching." To his surprise the Badger saw Ulick's face light up into a pleasant smile.

"Good for you! We'll get on, you and I."

"Ulick here helped himself to one of the king's peacocks and was fool enough to put the feathers in his cap," said Fowk. He himself, he explained, was a lockpick. "I'd have us out in the blink of an eye, too, if it wasn't for those bolts." The iron bolts barring the door and window were thick as a man's arm.

Old Dice took out his teeth again. "Pleased to meet you. Pleased indeed. I myself am a purveyor of antiquities. Relics. A victim of circumstances, I assure you—I lacked a license—most unfortunate oversight. I expect to be released shortly."

But when the Badger asked how long he had been there, Old Dice fell silent. Fowk took the Badger aside.

"Best not to take that tack with him. He's been here fourteen years."

It was a fine morning and Milo took the princess Emeralda on a tour of his menagerie, the best in the thirteen kingdoms. Indeed, there were creatures Caitlin had only seen in Abagtha's books: lizards the size of a large dog, goats with great twisted horns, horses banded black and white, a creature part duck, part mole. There was a golden bear that could fit in a teacup, and a white bear that was twice as tall as the tallest man. There was a bull with heavy armor and a horn on the end of its nose. Rabbits the size of a grown man leaped across the enclosure in a single bound. They seemed to Caitlin to have a pocket of fur on their bellies, and once she thought she saw a small head protrude. They passed a pool of great tusked sea-boars and came to a golden pavilion. Milo took a key from his ring.

"These are the rarest animals of all," he said. "Even the wisest men thought they were creatures of fancy. But I have a mermaid," he whispered, "and a unicorn."

And, after a fashion, he did. Caitlin had to admit they were marvelous fakes. The unicorn was some sort of exotic deer. You could see where the other antler had been sawn off, the fur bleached and horn gilded. Now the dark roots were growing in and the gilt was chipping off.

But to the young king's eyes it was a creature of legend. The mermaid, too, was no mermaid, nor was it any creature Caitlin had ever seen. It was whiskered like a pig with the fins of a turtle and the tail of a fish. It had no golden scales, no gossamer hair to comb, and its song, if it had one, would never have lured sailors onto the rocks. It seemed sickly, pining for its own kind. Caitlin was glad when the pavilion was locked again behind them.

"My menagerie is famed throughout Pentacledom," Milo said proudly, linking his arm in hers. "I send expeditions to the ends of the earth, even in the waste of winter, to find every shape of beast, and dig them out of their dens when they are at their meekest. I spare no expense. And charlatans try to sell me fakes. Can you believe it? A man came to court only last week, with what he claimed was a griffin. He said it had died on the long journey from the mountain eyrie, but you could tell it was only half a housecat, sewn to a crow. Such fakery—"

They came to a summerhouse, with spacious porches and a grove of fruit trees scenting the air. Milo proudly showed her to her own suite of rooms.

"I regret they weren't ready for you last night. I hope you were comfortable—? Here—"

Milo showed her how to fill a silver cup with clear, cool water by turning a handle in the wall. He sat on the wide bed to show her how soft it was, and opened the cupboards to display the rich clothes that hung there. He even seized a little bell from a table and rang it. Three women appeared silently in the doorway. He waved them away again.

"Just ring that, and they will bring you whatever you want. I know you must be eager to begin your task, and free your brothers all the sooner." A boy appeared with a large basket of flowers, which he emptied on the floor. A second boy did the same. Milo handed Caitlin a little box.

"I thought twelve reels of silk thread to start. If you need more, you must tell me. And there are steel needles, as well as silver. I didn't know which kind you would need."

Caitlin looked at the flowers, overwhelmed.

Milo had taken off his crown and was turning it in his hands. "Well! I'll leave you now. I know you have a lot to do."

Caitlin sat still for a long moment after he left her. Then she threaded a needle and began to string blossoms into a chain. She hadn't reached the sixth flower when she fell back onto the bed laughing. This would have surprised Milo enormously, for everyone knows that to free a prince from an enchantment, a princess may not speak or laugh for seven years, all the while sewing a shirt of aster flowers. But then, Abagtha had never kept books of fairy tales around, so Caitlin could not really be faulted.

"Every piece of money in this blasted kingdom goes to buy freaks and monsters for the king's amusement. Let children starve, women go in rags! Let men die of nosebleed for want of a surgeon! There isn't a decent paved road from one end of the kingdom to the other. I can hear old King Max turning in his grave." Ulick paused long enough to tear a great mouthful of bread from the common loaf and wash it down with more of the water. It was that day's ration, and as a result was a little cooler, less musty than the day before. The Badger watched Ulick drink; he hoped there would be some left.

Fowk was digging a tunnel. All he had for a shovel was a bent spoon, which he was using to scrape the unyielding earth away little by little from underneath the wall. The dirt then had to be hidden: pushed out the grate, stuffed in the mattress, or, if the guard was coming, swallowed. Fowk had been in Milo's prison for a year, and now the tunnel was nearly finished. This put Fowk in high spirits, and he whistled softly as he worked. This habit had contributed to his arrest in the first place.

Old Dice was arranging his relics in their tray; each time the guards confiscated the petrified tears in an ivory vial and all Dice's other curiosities, the urchins outside the prison grate would retrieve them from the gutter and pass them through the bars. It was a good collection, and there had been a time, not so very long ago, when the Badger would have exhibited keen interest in it. But he was uneasy. He had been wondering, since his head had cleared, what had happened to Caitlin. Those eyes were going to get her in trouble wherever she went.

"This," said Old Dice, "is the head of a talking turtle that once belonged to one of the oracles of Chameol."

"Shut up, you pathetic old man," said Ulick. "Chameol doesn't even exist!"

Dice bristled. "The king sends an expedition there annually, sir. Six ships every year."

"And none of them has ever come back. There isn't a soul in the whole kingdom who hasn't lost a father or brother or been taxed to starvation to outfit the ships. It's criminal."

"You two," said Fowk. "Stop it, or you'll bring the guard, and we'll never get out."

"This," Dice went on, "is a beetle in amber that used to belong to a sorceress in the spice mountains."

Ulick started to say something, but caught Fowk's eye, and thought better of it. He moved to the grate and stared out, muttering.

"And this—this is the most precious of all," the old man said. "A lock of hair from the last woman of full elvin blood. I think you'll agree it's in a state of remarkable preservation."

The Badger handed it back, trying to mask his disgust: If it was elvin hair, then elves smelled very much like goats.

"It's very remarkable, but I haven't any money on me at the moment."

This pacified the relic-seller a little, and the Badger was at last able to drink from the jug, passing it to Fowk.

The lockpick only paused long enough to take a swallow or two. "Can't stop now," he muttered. The earth was as hard as stone and yielded slowly, slowly under the bowl of the spoon.

"Why don't you get Nix to bring you a pick?" the Badger asked. Nix was a tiny boy, one of the countless urchins who swarmed the streets of the city. He made daily visits to the grate, which opened on a dingy alley.

"No place to hide it, and the guards would beat him if they saw him pass anything like that between the bars. Besides," Fowk added, "I'm none too sure Nix would understand. He's a little touched."

The Badger had to agree. Nix was exceedingly small, a wisp of a thing, paler in every respect even than Fowk, with hair light as milkweed down and the barest flush to his skin to show he was alive. He came to the cell every day, pressing his little face to the grate, chanting singsong nonsense, and passing little gifts through the cracks, treasures culled from tavern-sweepings: snuff, apple peelings, corks soaked in wine.

Ulick launched into another speech on the rule of old King Max's only son. The Badger took out the missal and opened it.

He was surprised that the guards hadn't taken it from him. Perhaps it had gone unnoticed; Asaph's missal fit easily into the palm of the Badger's hand. They probably had taken his money and been satisfied with that. The Badger, in his boredom, had read the prayerbook through twice, a feat he had never accomplished in all his years at the Abbey of Thirdmoon See. He opened the missal again, quailing at the prospect of a third reading, and only riffled the pages idly. And that careless action revealed to his eye something that a thousand more careful readings would never have uncovered. On the fore-edge of the pages, where the gilt was, there was something written, something only revealed when the pages were spread slightly beneath the thumb. The Badger carefully held the missal up to the light at the grate, fanning the gilt edges out carefully. The ghostly writing appeared.

> *It unlocks no doors,*
> *Empties all prisons,*
> *Unbolts no shutters,*
> *Yet clears all visions,*
> *It turns no lock,*
> *But topples all towers,*
> *The SPELLKEY unlocks the lock of Hours.*

"I'll give you my necklace, if you'll trade with me."

"I wouldn't have your job for a mountain of rubies and the best-looking husband in all the world."

"Today she broke everything in her room and wouldn't eat until we brought her raw meat. She ate it like an animal, then cracked the bones with her teeth and sucked the marrow out. I'm afraid to go in the room—"

Caitlin was by now wide awake, but the handmaidens had moved out of earshot. Apparently she was not the only princess in Milo's summerhouse.

The next morning Caitlin saw the meat-eater. Breakfast had brought poached eggs, Milo, and Nurse.

"Nurse has come to help you with your sewing," Milo announced with great cheer. Since the failure of the fox heart the king himself was distrustful of eggs and demanded popovers.

One of the handmaidens hurried up and whispered anxiously in Nurse's ear. Nurse frowned, folded her napkin, and heaved her great bulk out of her chair. She padded away after the servant, and Milo and Caitlin shortly heard a distant crash, followed by a shriek. Nurse reappeared, looking grim. All she said was "Milo."

He was about to get up when a creature dashed out onto the porch from the corridor.

It was a young girl of twelve or so, with matted hair and a very brown complexion much marred by scratches and bruises. She moved about very quickly on all fours like a dog, which she in all respects resembled. Her teeth were bared and she snarled and whimpered, resisting all attempts by the gathered household to subdue her. Caitlin suddenly reached down and placed her breakfast on the flagstones. The creature sniffed the air greatly, spied the dish, and thrush her face into it, devouring the eggs with a snap or two of her jaws. After that the gardeners managed to chase her back into her quarters with a broom and rake.

The handmaidens vanished. Nurse sat and drained a cup of hot wine. Milo pushed his popovers away and began to play with the salt and pepper shakers.

Caitlin had almost spoken when she remembered she was supposed to be keeping a vow of silence. Instead, she tugged at Milo's sleeve imploringly, making a question of her eyebrows and hands. He sighed and spoke.

"You see under what a bitter enchantment she suffers. We found her as we found you, during a hunt. Some sorcerer had worked a spell on her, so that she believed herself to be a wild creature. The dogs traced a wolf to its den, and when the hunters went in after it, they found this child living among the brood as one of them."

Caitlin was weeping. The tears rolled down her chin and spotted the tablecloth. She made no attempt to stop them: She was thinking of Abagtha. However terribly the old woman had treated her toward the end, it was thanks to her that Caitlin had not met a similar fate. Her tears were not wept out of sentiment. Rather, they were wept out of fear of what might have been.

Milo saw them solely as the mark of a sweet and gentle soul. He took her hands in his. Nurse watched him lose his heart and called for another cup of wine.

Even Ulick was asleep. He had been quiet all evening, since Nix had brought him a message scrawled on a wrapper. Fowk and Dice had seized happily on the fresh slivers of pear the boy handed through the bars. Now they, too, were fast asleep.

But the Badger couldn't close his eyes. He was thinking about the mysterious message concealed in Asaph's missal. Whatever the secret to the riddle was, it must be something valuable. For it, a man had been driven mad or, as the Badger feared more and more, murdered.

He kept thinking about the sugar they had found outside the barrow on the night of the fire. The horse had not so much as whinnied the whole time the culprit had been setting the trap: sealing the trapdoor, lighting the rags. Motley, the horse he would trust with his life above any man, had not made a sound. It made the Badger wonder if, given a chance, he might have found some sugar around the stables, where the missal had been left in the woodbox. Or if the hunter-bandit's pockets held any sugar-lumps. Had the same person poisoned Asaph, set fire to the barrow, and set him up as a poacher? The Badger feared the prison was making him a little mad. He also feared his crazy theory might be true. But it seemed the real answer lay in the riddle in the missal.

He sat up on his straw pallet, sweating and chilled, and went and knelt by the spot where Fowk lay sleeping.

"Fowk. Fowk. What's a Spellkey?"

Fowk opened his eyes and yawned, not seeming to find this midnight conversation at all unusual.

"Not sure. I've heard of them, it's true, but I don't know anyone who's ever seen one. Legend has it they were forged long ago in a lake of fire in one of the lost kingdoms, before Chameol, even—"

Ulick grunted in his sleep, and rolled over.

"—and that anyone who possesses one can open any lock, any prison, any chest. You see how it is."

"Yes. Such a person could rule the world." The Badger sat back on his heels and thought about that. Then he seemed to come to himself again, and blinked. "Good-night!" he whispered, and went back to bed.

Dice was awake. His eyes glittered in the dark: It could have been glee, or it might have been greed. There was no telling. His hands toyed with his teeth on their cord for a long time before he slept.

Nix stumbled through the palace grounds. In his hand he clutched two marbles, one green and one blue.

They were his prize possessions. He had owned them for ten minutes now. The man had given them to him through the bars. "Find her," he had said.

The little boy halted, clutching the edge of the marble wall. The stone was nice and cool beneath his feet. He would find her and give the marbles to her. Then maybe she would give him a nice drink with ice in it. He had seen people put ice in good things to drink. Or she would give him cake, and a kiss.

But he would find her.

The astronomer, who was Milo's old tutor, was in his laboratory, mixing periwinkles, earthworms, and leeks into a love-powder.

"Though I can't fathom why," said Nurse. "I should think that was the last thing we needed. He means to marry her! Then where will we be, I ask you? All our expectations depend on his dying without issue."

The astronomer slowly ground the worms in the mortar. "But what can we do, my pet?" he asked with a sigh. "If he means to marry her, he will marry her."

"To come so close and lose the crown! We must do something. We must say he is insane. We must say he is unfit. We must say *she* is unfit."

The astronomer put down his pestle in agitation. "Oh, my love, how it distresses me to see you this way!"

"He means to present her to his subjects during the Harvest Festival, when they parade the wicker men. I tell you, we are lost."

"My sweetmeat! Calm yourself. It is not good for your digestion, overworking your nerves so."

Nurse reached out, picked up the astronomer, and placed him on her knee. "You are too good to me."

"You are my life," he said.

The mermaid had died, and Milo was inconsolable. He hung around the summerhouse, taking neither food nor comfort.

Caitlin had finished one of the shirts. One sleeve was longer than the other, and surely no head would fit through the opening she had left for it, but it was done. Caitlin took it to where Milo sat brooding under a pear tree. He looked at it, smiled wanly, and drew her down on the lawn beside him.

"Oh, Emeralda! All I wanted was to learn the speech of the animals, to learn a little of the ways of magic. My father had no use for it. What was invisible was of no use here on earth, lest it was the breath in your lungs."

Caitlin stroked the flowers in the little shirt. They were faded with longing for the branch, but smelled heady still.

"I dined on it, the heart of the fox," Milo said, "but the barking

of the dog mocked me still. They say it is a marvelous thing, the speech
of animals. They say it can be passed on by a kiss."

And, against her better judgment and instinct and all her long
history with the ways of men, Caitlin kissed the king. It seemed to
improve his mood substantially.

When Nix found her later that day, the handmaidens were measur-
ing her for a dress, and Caitlin was growing suspicious.

"He told me to give these to you," said the boy.

Caitlin took the marbles in surprise. Then she let him take her hand
and lead her away.

"Badger!" Her voice at the grate woke him, and he hauled himself
up.

"Where in the name of sweet heaven have you been?"

"At the palace of the king. I can't tell you more now. Are you all
right? What are they going to do with you?"

"Let me rot, I suppose. Look, can't you charm the lock, or something?"

"Not unless you have the legbone of a roan mare on you. But I can
manage it eventually, if you'll keep. And there's something else. I think
the king means to marry me."

"Well, let him. The abbot can't confine you in a convent if you're
married to one of the High Thirteen, can he?"

"Then who will get you out, goose?"

"Do that first. What's a Spellkey?" He told her about the missal.

She shook her head. "I don't know. But there are a lot of books
at the palace; I'll take a look."

"Hurry. I've been thinking about things, and the more I think the
less I like all this. Get me out soon?"

"As soon as I can."

Nix lived in a barrel outside a tavern in the heart of the town. He was napping when he overheard the men. They had rested their tankards on the barrel-head, and Nix could hear them very well.

"During the Harvest Festival, we'll do it."

"How?"

"The wicker king. We'll fill it with our men, and when the king steps out to put the torch to it, we'll have our chance."

The men went away. Nix knew them. The first had given him a note for Ulick. Nix was climbing out of the barrel when a man came up to him. He was tall and thin and had red hair. He put his hand on Nix's shoulder.

"I'm looking for a girl. One blue eye, one green. Dark hair to here. And a youth, not tall but not short. Fair. Do you know where they are?"

"Yes," said Nix.

"Take me to them."

But Nix ran away.

Caitlin was asleep in her garden. She was having a dream, and as she dreamed her fingers ripped out the stitches in the shirt of flowers in her lap.

She dreamed of a magpie that had a tree to itself. It gathered around it brilliant objects: silver combs plucked from behind the ears of queens, coins snatched from fountains where lovers had tossed them, snuffboxes snatched from windowsills. But it gathered no food, and grew weak. It was soon too weak to fly, and the other magpies drove it from the tree and killed it.

Caitlin sat up, a cry in her throat. Nix was sitting beside her in the grass. In his hands he held a little man woven out of willow branches.

"Hello," she said softly. "What have you got there?"

"A wicker man."

Caitlin went to the palace and found what had once been the old king's library. Among a great many books on the hunt, and the building of waterways, she found a book on magic.

She ran her finger down the columns: *Speir . . . speke . . . spelch . . . speld . . . spele . . . spelk . . .* "Ah, here it is."

But the facing page, with most of the entry, had been torn out, and the next page, and the next.

6

A WICKER MAN

ix shivered in his barrel. A wealthy woman passing through the town had stopped at the tavern for a quick lunch, fastidiously trimming the crusts from her bread. These Nix had cunningly seized, and now he was eating them very slowly in the bottom of the dark, dank barrel.

It was harvest time in the countryside, but in the city it was merely an excuse to overindulge in drink. There was little of a harvest to celebrate. The best of the crop went to the king's table, and the rest—silver-edged lettuces, milk-fed veal on the hoof—was sold to merchants who would find eager buyers across the sea.

So it was that most of the wheat in Milo's kingdom was milled into cakes, not bread, cakes that would never fill the mouths of urchins like Nix. But as he ate his secondhand crusts he was glad he had them. Tomorrow there would be the bonfire and he could warm himself at it. And the giants would be there.

They were built of wickerwork, taller than the belltower of the temple. The giants seemed to move through the mean and dirty streets as if they had will and life of their own. Nix knew there were men and some of the older boys inside them, working the ropes that made the giants move and bob their heads. But knowing the secret of the giants didn't stop Nix from shrieking as loud as the next boy at them. They were a sight to see, moving down the streets, through the wild holiday crowd to the bonfire that flared in the distance. Thinking about it made Nix shiver again. That, and the two men talking: "During the harvest festival, we'll do it."

The crusts were gone. Nix felt for the little willow man in the dark, clutching it while he waited for it to grow dark, for the men to leave the giants and go home to bed. Then Nix knew what he would do.

Whether it was because of the cat amulet, or because of her eyes, or because her heart was full of confusion, it seemed that magic plied the needle, and not Caitlin's impatient fingers. The seven shirts of aster flowers were almost finished. Only the right sleeve on the last remained undone. What might have taken her seven months had taken eleven days.

The handmaidens had almost completed the gown. All it lacked was its buttonholes, and the left sleeve. The veils were done. There were seven of them, fashioned of sheerest net, light as cobweb. Everything was nearly ready. Still, Milo put off asking her.

He had tried many times. Breathlessly he watched her walk through the orchard near the summerhouse or drowse over a book. And each time he opened his mouth it was as if he were mute instead of she.

Caitlin wondered if you could refuse a king's offer of marriage. How easy it would be to stay, she thought, a little surprised. It was not that she fancied the rich life at court. But the circle of Milo's fashionable and devoted followers viewed nothing about Caitlin as extraordinary. Not once had anyone stared at her, or made the sign of the Pentacle out of fear, or remarked on her seer's eyes. They were too used to Milo's collection of grotesques and curiosities to look twice at a mere witch. So she dreamed dreams, did she? Well, who didn't, these days? Everywhere you went there were people setting out carpets and offering to tell your fortune for an outlandish price.

It would be easy to stay, except for the other enchanted princess, and the dead mermaid. It made Caitlin very melancholy to think of the mermaid, and wonder whether it might have lived if she could have somehow gotten it to the sea. But the memory of the wolf-girl, nose to the ground like a beast, drove all sleep from Caitlin's weary limbs, all dreams from her brain. In the morning, she would go once more to her silent task, swiftly threading the fading flowers onto the silken thread. She could look out the window of her room and see where the dark hills met the air. There was something in her that needed to walk and meet those dark hills. Then, too, there was Ninthstile, and the Badger. I must get away today, she thought, and go to the prison.

Why hadn't she come?

The Badger lay on his pallet while Ulick paced, Fowk dug, and Dice napped. What if she married the king? There would still be a price on his head even if he did get out of this hell-hole. After that it seemed he could choose between muleskinning and the gallows.

"Stop pacing," he said to Ulick.

Ulick ignored him. He was thinking of his sweetheart. Two summers ago Milo had spotted her in the marketplace and had brought her back to his palace to spin straw into gold. Ulick saw her now and then, from a distance, amid the king's party at a play, or a country outing to sample the new wine. She wore an elaborate wig now, and rouge, and applied a false mole to her cheek. When they met she looked right through him.

After tonight, she would have to come back to him.

Dice seemed to have lost all interest in his relics. They lay in a forlorn jumble on his tray. He slept and snored a little, but whether sleeping or waking, he seemed intent on something wonderful, smiling faintly to himself. If Fowk had not been digging, or the Badger brooding, or Ulick pacing, they might have heard him mutter to himself between snores: "The Spellkey!"

The royal goldsmith had finished the ring. It was a moonstone, an opal, set in a wreath of laurel leaves wrought in gold. Milo had been very specific with his instructions to the gemworker. An opal wrapped in laurel leaves was supposed to confer invisibility on the wearer. It was a very large ring, for it was an exceptional stone. On Caitlin's hand (which though finely made was not small), the ring reached the first joint of her finger.

The astronomer had seen the ring, and he and Nurse were having a conversation in the old king's study.

"It is worse," said Nurse, "than the time he kept that white mule in the court, convinced it was a princess under a cruel enchantment."

"Worse even," said the astronomer, "than the time he went hunting for emeralds in gryphons' nests."

They settled into a gloomy silence.

"Sugarplum," said the astronomer, hesitating a little. "I have an idea."

Nurse looked up.

"I shall make a love philter and give it to him so that he shall become enamored of you."

Nurse thought for a moment. "But what of you, pet?"

A feeble gleam entered the astronomer's eyes. "I shall always be one of the king's closest advisors," he said.

Nurse began to giggle.

Caitlin stared at the ring on her finger. She opened her mouth, but remembered in time to close it. Wildly she pantomimed to Milo, who beamed up at her from where he knelt. She shook her head firmly, removing the ring and pressing it into his hands. This only made him smile at her more tenderly still.

"I know your every objection, my love! Do you think I haven't thought them all to myself a thousand times? Do you think that before I first saw you I ever thought to marry a princess under a vow of silence? A wife who, night and day, must work at her task of selfless love? Do you think I have not said to myself, 'Fool, how can she have thought or care for a husband's caress as long as her dear brothers labor under such a cruel sentence?'"

If I remain with him another second, Caitlin thought desperately, I will be lost. This simpleton will convince me.

"Tomorrow night is the harvest bonfire. I have had a gown made for you, that I may show you off properly to my subjects." He took her hand and replaced the ring on her finger. Quite overcome, he kissed her, and through the kiss Caitlin thought, At the bonfire I can steal away and free the Badger.

That afternoon she crept away from the summerhouse while the handmaidens were drowsing and retraced her steps to the prison.

The Badger was uncheerful.

Caitlin saw him look at the ring. "I'm sorry I didn't come sooner," she said. "I couldn't get away."

"Neither could I."

Caitlin was annoyed, even a little astounded to feel herself blush. She told him about the pages torn from the book of magic.

"I don't like it," he said. The Badger was annoyed, exhausted, less able to quell the creeping terror inside him. "Why haven't you gotten me out?"

"I'm sorry—it's just that he's such a child, and I have to pantomime everything. Every time I try to make him understand, he thinks it's another tale about ravens and enchantresses. Besides," she added, "have you ever thought perhaps you're safer where you are?"

The Badger had not forgotten the redheaded stranger who had killed the stag.

Through the grate Caitlin closed her fingers around the Badger's arm. "Take heart," she said comfortingly. "I haven't dreamed about you yet."

Milo was very fond of oyster soup, and his favorite way of eating it was to have it served in a golden soup-plate shaped like an oyster shell, garnished with real pearls he would dissolve in his wine and drink for good luck. (He had read this in a book on the practices of the ancients, but Nurse maintained that it was a test that had been devised by the old king to see if the court jeweler was honest, since real pearls dissolve in wine.)

On the night that the king was accustomed to having his favorite soup, the astronomer made up some of his love potion into a pearl and placed it on the king's soup-plate. Nurse hummed, applying her womanly secrets: chewing on a clove and tying her second chin up in a piece of pretty silk.

But it was all for naught. Milo didn't even drink the pearls, but put them in his pocket to make into a necklace for Emeralda. Nurse's fine lace sleeves trailed in her soup, which she ate without savoring. Nothing the astronomer could say afterward was any consolation.

That night the stars were thick in the sky, and no one could sleep. Ulick's sweetheart lay awake, thinking of her family left behind. The wolf-girl shuffled swiftly around her room on hands and knees, whimpering and growling by turns. And in her own room in the summerhouse Caitlin twisted the heavy ring on her finger.

The king, too, was awake. Milo went to the window and looked out to where the summerhouse gleamed in the night. He had not undressed yet; he had stayed up later than usual to read his fairy tales. They did not entertain him as they once had. The king sighed and rattled the pearls in his pocket. Perhaps they would help him sleep. He poured himself a cup of wine. How pretty the pearls were in the dark, slipping into the wine as if into the sea. He could always get more pearls to make

Emeralda a necklace, after all, and nicer ones at that. Yes. It would help
him get to sleep. He drank the wine and looked out the window again.
The wolf-girl had escaped. There: She scampered across the lawn, and
there! she reappeared by the arbor-seat. How happy she seemed out of
doors. Milo was wide awake now. The love-potion began to work
through his blood like a bee sting. He would build her a run, so she would
get plenty of wholesome air and gain the strength she needed to fight
her enchantment. Perhaps they might even teach her to eat with a
spoon. He would ask Nurse in the morning. Milo went to bed, and the
wolf-girl loped through his dreams.

From the moment the sun rose the next morning Ulick willed it
to set.

"Set! Set on the day, and on the king's life!" he muttered.

Dice had put his teeth in. He was suddenly very interested in
Fowk's tunnel and offered a great deal of advice on how it might be
finished more quickly. Fowk kept digging steadily and silently while the
relic-seller fidgeted at his elbow.

It was dusk when Fowk broke through to the other side. Then they
had to wait while the guard brought their evening meal. As soon as the
guard had gone they all flung their bread aside and began making the
opening of the tunnel larger.

"Where's Nix?" Fowk wondered aloud, mopping his brow.

The Badger rocked a large stone back and forth to loosen it. "He
hasn't been around for a day or so."

Ulick pushed him aside. "Better leave the hard work to the men,
boy."

The Badger opened his mouth to retort, but caught Fowk's eye.
Without a word he began to hide the rubble in his mattress.

"It's an improvement, at that," he said under his breath. He wondered what sort of bed they gave Caitlin to sleep in. Goosedown, probably, and wide as a barn door.

Dice sidled up to him. "I have a business proposition for you," he said. The relic-seller looked as if he would like to take his teeth out, but kept them in.

The Badger kept putting the chips of stone into his mattress. "What's that, Dice?"

"Your friend, the one who comes to the window. She wears a charm. I would like to purchase it."

The Badger laughed. "What, the ring? I don't think she'll part with it, my friend."

"No, not the ring. The charm around her neck—a little cat—I would be willing to make an exchange. Any one of my relics for the charm she wears."

"I'm afraid it's not mine to sell."

"But you will ask her?"

"All right, I'll ask." Foolish old man, he thought. We'll never see each other again.

The Badger as usual was wrong on both accounts. Dice was no fool, and they were to meet again.

When the handmaidens went to dress Caitlin they could not find her. She was with the wolf-girl. A bit of bread soaked in a little beef blood had brought the wolf-girl in from the grounds, where she had been terrorizing the gardeners. Now she lay with her head in Caitlin's lap, licking the last traces of the treat from Caitlin's fingers. Caitlin saw that the girl was covered with hundreds of small scars and scratches, and her hands and knees were heavily callused from traveling on all fours.

"Was that good?" she asked softly, stroking the wolf-girl's coarse, matted hair. The wild creature bared her teeth a little, yawned, and was asleep.

And do you dream, I wonder? Caitlin asked herself. Watching her sleep one would never imagine this was anything but a slightly dirty child.

The handmaidens knocked and entered, bearing the dress and its veils wrapped in silk tissue.

"If you please, we have been sent to dress you."

She nodded her consent, but thought, Is it time already? and gave herself over to be dressed.

Night transformed the town into a weird and fantastic place. The air was full of something intoxicating, yet laced with fear and danger, something part carnival revelry and part nightmare. As the flames of the bonfire rose higher, they cast huge, grotesque shadows along the sides and roofs of the ramshackle buildings. The flaring fire cast the alleys into the deepest of blacks, picked out the glittering, dripping dampness on the gutters and rainspouts, and turned the familiar into objects from a world that ran on rogue magic, a world in which the laws of kings and nature were set aside until the fire went out and the sun rose again on the dour and the real.

The giants circled the town seven times before approaching the wickerwork altar where Milo sat with Caitlin. The light caught the thousands of pearls on her dress, drenching her in myriad sparks that cascaded down the length of her hair. It made Milo's cheeks rosy as a little boy's, and shone on his magnificent crown. From afar they could see the giants' heads above the rooftops as the wicker king and his court approached through the din in the streets.

Milo pressed Caitlin's hand. It was the hand with the ring, and the heavy moonstone pressed into the soft part of Caitlin's hand painfully.

When they crept out of the prison it was dark. Ulick was the first to leave the others. Then Fowk said his good-byes and went in the other direction. Dice hung back with the Badger, who was in a spot.

He had arrived at the prison slung across the back of a horse, and now he had no idea where he was. The old relic-seller made him uneasy, but he had to find the way to the palace and to Caitlin.

"Will you take me to the town and show me the palace?" the Badger asked Dice. He wondered where Nix was. Looking at the relic-seller playing with his teeth on their cord, he couldn't help but feel that the boy would have been a better guide.

"Perhaps, yes, I might, for a trinket—"

It was getting cold, and the Badger was getting anxious about Caitlin. "Yes, yes, you'll get your trinket. Come on."

So Dice led him off through the town.

Ulick made his way to the middle of the throng, to the giants at its heart. It seemed the very fire was in his veins, he felt himself burning, burning and towering above the crowd, like a wicker man.

"A new world for wicker men!" he said under his breath. "And death to kings!" He spoke quietly, but his words pierced the wicker armor, and the ears of the shivering Nix. Why had he hidden himself here? He was only a boy. If they found him they were sure to thrash him, or worse. He must hide a little longer, until the giants had come up to where the king was waiting.

But he must not wait too long. After his audience with the wicker men, Milo would set a torch to them and usher in the harvest.

The once merry crowd grew ugly. Some knew of Ulick's plot, and even if they didn't agree with it, none had any great quarrel with the outcome. With the king dead, the army would be thrown into confusion. Many would desert, or loot. It would be a thieves' holiday, and there was nothing wrong with that. Caitlin felt the hairs on the back of her neck stand on end. She knew a mob when she saw one. Oh, for my barrow, she thought.

Milo beamed, his arm around her waist to pull her close. "Look, dove. See how excited my subjects are. Look what a stir you have made among them. They can see what a queen I have chosen." In the firelight Emeralda seemed to him some enchanted being. Why, then, did his thoughts keep returning to the poor wolf princess?

His strength was no comfort to Caitlin. *I have only traded an iron ring for one of gold*, she thought. Why is this one so hard to cast off? Why was the crowd making her so nervous? It was more than the edge of violence, sharp and dangerous, beyond the shadows the firelight. The women who had dressed Caitlin had tried to take the catstone from her, but she had hidden it, reknotting it around her neck once they were gone. Now she fingered it lightly, and it seemed to the king that her green eye gleamed greener, and her blue eye bluer. Surely that was firelight, nothing more.

Elric slunk through the crowd, swearing as he tripped on a jagged piece of pavement. The stableboy had seen him. His foot was killing him, and the last thing he needed was a chase through streets full of drunks with daggers and high tempers. He ducked into the shadows to catch his breath. It was all because of that dratted snare in the woods. It was more than just twenty years' hard work, he reminded himself. There was much more at stake.

The Badger got a stitch in his side and had to stop. He hung onto the side of a tavern, heaving with exertion, until the pain subsided. The man with red hair was gone. Worse, so was Dice. He could tell he was near the palace. The streets were full of people carrying torches and shouting. The Badger was swept up and carried along for distance before he saw the giants.

He had used to wonder, as he daydreamed in the orchard at the Abbey of Thirdmoon See, what marvels and wonders were to be seen out in the wide world. Never had he imagined anything like this. The torch eyes of the giants sent shivers up the Badger's back: These were the dark figures of his nightmares. For a moment, he was again a boy of six, screaming in his sleep, with Asaph shaking him awake, walking him through the darkened courtyard to the dairy, where he gave him hot milk and a story about a poor man's youngest son.

He had lost the stranger with the red hair, but this occurred to the Badger only feebly. His thoughts were all for the giants. This was fear, fear as strong as that he had felt waking in the barrow, but a fear edged with something else. Danger, and excitement. The giants were very close.

Ulick was wishing that he were inside the wicker man, so his could be the hand that thrust the knife home. But he would have his consolation. With his queen he would take the crown, the throne, the kingdom.

Caitlin's hand was on the catstone, which was sending tremor after tremor of fear through her limbs. She could not move, she was held firm by the dreadful gaze of the advancing giants, spellbound as a creature frozen in the beam from a hunter's lantern. I must do something, she thought. I must act. But it was as if they were thoughts she had had very long ago when she was a young girl. Her hands and feet would not obey.

Just then, inside the wicker king, the assassin working the giant's head with a pulley drew an evil-looking knife from his sleeve.

Nix uncurled and launched himself from his perch, landing on the man's head.

The knife flashed through the wicker armor of the giant. The crowd gave a single shout, and the simmering riot came to a rolling boil.

The Badger caught sight of Caitlin but was quickly buried in the crush of the crowd.

Milo, who had been about to pluck a bunch of flowers from the wicker shield of the giant, felt himself shoved roughly to the ground. To his astonishment and dismay he heard Emeralda cry, "Milo!"

So Ulick's plot came to nothing, and the expectations of Nurse and the astronomer were dashed. Undone also was all the good of the aster flowers. Caitlin made Milo take back the ring. He took it without seeming to grasp what she meant. When he was presented to the king, the Badger was more than a little puzzled to hear himself addressed as one of the princess's brothers.

"You managed to save one of the shirts, at any rate," said Milo. "Although it was the one that lacked a sleeve. See where your poor brother has a raven's wing for an arm."

The Badger's arm, cut with a broken bottle during the mayhem, was tied in a sling of black muslin.

They left the king and walked in the garden. Caitlin told how Nix had taken the knife instead of the king.

"The soldiers came out of the confusion with the assassin and this tiny creature, like a little white dog run over by a cart in the road."

"Will he live?"

"If he does, it will be no thanks to the astronomer. He's put leeches to him."

But Milo's diviners and toothpullers put their wits together and between them managed to stop the bleeding. A clean bed and plenty to eat worked wonders and Nix grew stronger.

Milo put aside all his books of fantasies, boarded up his palace, and went to live in the summerhouse with Nix and the wolf-girl. The three of them made a cunning picture in the evening, walking along the brow of a hill at dusk, the tiny boy, the broad tall man, and a creature like a herd dog scampering at their heels. Only if you were to look more closely, you would see the boy was the wolf-girl, walking upright, that it was Nix playing mascot behind them.

With Milo constantly absent from court, Nurse once again had hopes of ruling. The courtiers, however, had left to find other livings, and one morning she found even the astronomer had gone, taking his telescope with him in search of another situation.

The moneylender, the hangman, and the rat-catcher, being the wealthiest men in the town, decided to form their own council, but to their chagrin the old king's huntsman and Fowk, the lockpick, soon joined them, along with the toymaker, the bookbinder, and the soapmaker—the poorest men in the town. Between them, they managed not to rule badly, if they didn't exactly rule well. The town still stank, but everyone ate a little better, and the pickpockets only came out after dark.

Some months after the Badger and Caitlin had left the kingdom, a fisherman's youngest daughter pulled a mermaid from the sea. Her father was in bed with influenza, and her brothers were all at a fair in the next town, so it fell to her to tend the nets.

It would be hard to say which was more surprised, the mermaid or the girl. They stared at each other for a long moment, each thinking the other a marvel of ugliness, and then the girl unfastened the net, and the creature slipped into the cold autumn sea and was gone.

7

the court of love

heir horses were nowhere to be found, and the Badger was inconsolable. He and Caitlin continued to Ninth-stile on foot.

As they reached the edge of Milo's kingdom, they met Dice, the old relic-seller. He was carrying his tray of scarabs and charms, and his teeth on their dirty cord swung to and fro like the bell on a goat's neck.

He fell in beside them. At first, he didn't remember the Badger, but once reminded of him was glad enough to see him. He put in his ill-fitting teeth in order to favor Caitlin with a smile, remarking at once on her amulet.

"A pretty trinket." His eyes glittered beneath their cataracts like filmy gems. "An heirloom, is it?"

"No, just a luck-piece." Caitlin put her hand to the catstone.

That made the old relic-seller wheeze and laugh. "Where are you journeying?" he asked when he had recovered a little.

"To the coast," said the Badger.

"And after that?"

"To Ninthstile."

Behind their cataracts the old eyes smouldered. "Ah. The good sisters! You must give them my regards." And he launched into a yarn about a wonderful relic, the teeth of a nun that, when shaken and spilt from a cup, spelled out the answers to weighty questions. This story lasted for the next mile.

At last Caitlin broke in gently. "You know so much of relics. Have you ever heard of a Spellkey?"

Dice removed his teeth and ran his tongue over his tender gums. "Well, well. Where did you learn about such a thing as a Spellkey?"

"Every child is lulled to sleep with such tales."

"I have heard there are indeed such keys of power. Keys that will open any door, unlock the truth from any man's lips. I suppose it is true enough, but I have never seen one. But then, there are so few true artifacts left since the Necromancer outlawed guildhalls and levied a tax on relics."

Caitlin fell to musing on magic. It occupied a curious place in the kingdoms where the Pentacle and its tenets were kept. Reasonable people saw nothing wrong with having their fortunes told at the fair, or buying a trifling spell to make it rain on the turnip crop, but they harbored a deep-seated fear of spellsmiths, seers, and other unsavories deemed dangerous to the public health. Magic was a fine thing, as long as it was licensed and practiced by people who had undergone a proper apprenticeship under a necromancer or apothecary. If you started letting changelings and simpletons and unmarried women meddle with spells, where would it end? So there were laws banning the study of the old rune tongues. You couldn't copy a map without a permit from a sub-necromancer. The sale of certain substances and objects was closely guarded; spinning wheels, swords, mirrors, tinderboxes, cauldrons—all could too easily slip over the threshold from household commonplace to object of magic. And cash bounties were paid on all cats with suspicious markings, goats with two heads or three legs, and dogs with forked tongues.

Bribery ran rampant, as might be expected, and spells were to be had on any and every street corner, if you knew whom to ask. All the same, if your fine, squalling baby just happened to have a beautiful star in the middle of its forehead, you didn't shout it in the streets at noon, and you might pay the midwife a little sum each month not to say anything about it.

Caitlin was very quiet as Dice finished a tale about the oracular tortoise's head. She shot a sidelong glance at the Badger. Intent on the old man's tale, he seemed for all the world as though he liked nothing better than a tale, no matter how unlikely, no matter how disreputable the teller. Did he just like a good story, or did he believe some of his Thirdmoon lessons still? Caitlin wondered.

They had crossed into Fifthmoon, and still there was no town in sight. It was agreed that they should make camp by the roadside, each taking a turn at watch while the others slept.

None of them had eaten, but it was an unspoken agreement that none should mention the fact.

The Badger took the first watch. It was really quite cold, he thought, pulling his blanket closer and stirring the coals with the toe of his boot. He was starting to worry about the crossing. Storms sometimes came early to the straits, making crossing impossible until spring. Then what will I do, the Badger thought, with this witch-girl on my hands (for so he thought of Caitlin, when he was tired and underfed), and a bounty on my head? Old Dice snored a little, but Caitlin only tossed, clenching and unclenching the amulet as she slept. *So dark,* he thought. *What is that old saying about eyes like hers? Otherworld daughters, that's it.* To his surprise the Badger saw how high the moon had risen. He would have to wake Dice in a moment.

The next thing he knew it was morning, and Caitlin was roughly shaking him awake.

"He's gone, and my amulet, too."

They breakfasted on regret and silence and went on down the road.

A short distance away, hidden by the swell of a hill, Elric watched them go. When they had gone far enough down the road he began to follow, riding Motley, Maud in tow.

Old Dice ran through a field of ripe corn. His teeth on their cord had fallen from his mouth; now the string snapped, and the teeth were lost between the rows of corn. The old relic-seller panted in his terror, whimpering and casting wild glances backward as he ran, but never letting go of the amulet. He clutched the catstone so hard it made a welt in his leathery palm.

"They shall never have it!" he muttered. "It is mine, it belongs to Dice the Wise, the Keeper of Relics." Here the old man got a stitch in his side and paused for breath beside a scarecrow, leaning a little on the bundle of rags and straw. But the arm beneath his hand was warm, and before Dice realized the dummy hid a man, the knife had done its work. Dice crumpled under the thrust like a withered stalk of corn under a sickle. The stone flew from his hand and vanished.

Elric turned the old man over to make sure he was dead. After closing the relic-seller's eyes, he pried open the hands, and swore under his breath. The amulet was gone.

"Damn!"

To his credit, he thought of doing something with the body. But there was no time to even cast a glance about for the amulet, much less dig a grave in a cornfield. Someone was coming toward him through the corn, and he was forced to leave Dice to the crows and run for it.

At first Caitlin attributed the dreams to thirst, hunger, and exhaustion—surely, they would otherwise have ceased with the disappearance of the amulet? But soon she was forced to allow that the dreams were coming as strong and as clear as ever, catstone or no catstone.

Wherever she looked now she saw the birds: reflected in the water of a ditch, perched on the Badger's shoulder, or diving so close to her that she leaped aside with a cry. At last the Badger turned and looked at her with concern.

"Let's stop and rest," he said.

But that would not do, no, not at all. She saw the birds so clearly when she was awake that she could only imagine how they would terrorize her sleep.

They were no magpies this time but shrikes, butcher birds impaling their prey on thorns. There were no thorn trees as far as the eye could see in any direction, nothing at all on either hand but corn and rye and barley. But Caitlin saw the birds all the same, the vicious shrikes at their grisly work.

"There's no shade," was all she said to the Badger.

He insisted on wetting his neckerchief at the ditch and tying the wet cloth around her forehead. She suffered him the gesture.

"Thank you," she managed.

To her puzzlement, he didn't answer, and looked away.

He was not at all certain they were on the right road, now that Dice was gone. They had little money, even if they did pass a farmhouse where they could buy some milk and bread. Caitlin must rest, that was plain enough. To watch her disturbed him: She was beginning to look like the hunted, haunted thing he had first met in the square at Moorsedge.

Just then they came upon a horse and rider in the middle of the road. The rider was dressed in splendid armor of white enamel with a pattern of blue knots worked in sapphires. The heat inside the armor was doing nothing for the rider's temper. He swore and spurred his horse in the ribs, the way a child will kick its parent's shin for spite. The animal rolled its eyes and laid back its ears, skipping in the road and making a distressed wickering.

The Badger dropped his gear in the road and ran up, taking the reins and calming the horse. It sensed his manner with relief, gratefully allowing the Badger to examine it. The Badger quickly found the problem, a sharp stone wedged into the tender part of the horse's underhoof. "Well, there's your trouble," he said. "There's a pebble in the middle of his frog."

A voice issued crossly through the slit in the knight's helmet. "A frog? Sir, I fear you have been in the sun too long. You hallucinate."

"No, his frog, the soft part, here." The Badger gently wedged the stone free with the point of his knife. "There. It must have been paining him quite a bit."

The rider put up his visor, revealing a face between thirty and forty, worn with the weight of his leisure, with sherry-colored eyes. Now his anger had passed the knight curiously looked the Badger up and down.

"You have my gratitude. I never could manage this animal. My page was better with him, bribed him with clove. Or perhaps he had a charmed whip. Whichever, it does me no good: He left me this morning, to have his wisdom teeth pulled." The knight saw Caitlin. "Who is your companion?"

The Badger found himself lying out of instinct. "My sister. We are bound for the convent at Ninthstile."

Caitlin lifted her head where she sat by the ditch. Her look was more bewildered than startled, and for that, pitiful.

"Is she ill?" asked the knight.

"No more well than can be expected. We've gone a day and a night without resting, with nothing to eat. We were set upon by highwaymen and robbed."

"Then you must let me offer you my protection to the castle of the kings of Fifthmoon. It's the least I can do, after all. You will stay with me a few days until my page's jaw is mended."

That was how the Badger became page, for a time, to Sir Henry of Fifthmoon, and how he and Caitlin were brought to the palace, where she was given a draught that brought her blessed, dreamless sleep. The Badger got no tonic, and he dreamed greatly, of a long conversation with Motley and Asaph in the orange grove at Thirdmoon.

Just outside the town Elric was sitting on a haystack, lighting his pipe. He had only smoked for a minute or two when a messenger, Banter, came into sight, leading his horse across the field under cover of the tall corn. Silently he handed Elric a bundle, and when Elric didn't reach to take it, tossed it on the ground in annoyance.

"You haven't reported in for nearly two weeks."

Elric took the pipe-stem from his mouth. "I experienced a difficulty that prevented me. Did you bring the money?"

"Yes. Go ahead, count it. I won't have you saying I bought so much as an ale with it."

"Come, come, no need to be that way about it. I'm sure it's all there."

"What on earth do you need that kind of money for? You could outfit an army with a sum like that. I rode the whole way in a sweat, thinking of robbers."

Elric laughed. "What a surprise they would have gotten! A beggar with a king's ransom in his skinny wallet."

The messenger narrowed his eyes. "What are you up to, Elric?"

"I'm not sure—I may have to ransom back my quarry."

"Sometimes, Elric, I think you are ill suited for this work."

"How's that?"

"You have an odd streak. I think you look on all this as a game for your amusement and nothing more."

"Well, if they *are* going to hold their tournament, I might as well stay to see it, surely? I love a good spectacle."

Banter was unamused and folded his arms.

Elric counted the money. "All crowns present and, shall we say, accounted for? Now I must be off. I have to get into the kitchen and find out what's on the menu this week."

In the garden, the two kings of Fifthmoon were having breakfast. The great lawn was planted in a checkerboard of rosemary and thrift, paths neatly marked out in crushed gypsum. The brothers watched the gardener trimming the menagerie of animals wrought in quickthorn, holly, and yew. Here, he lopped with his great shears the overgrown ear of a dancing bear; there, he shortened the tail of a peacock.

The kings motioned the servant over to complain about the temperature of the coffee. Linus, who was the elder, took out a pocket thermometer and tested the contents of his cup.

"Unsatisfactory."

"Bring us some more at once," said Levander.

The fresh pitcher, when it came, soon grew as cold as the first as the kings continued to watch the gardener barbering the huge creatures of privet and wire.

"Jam?" offered Linus.

"Please, yes," said Levander.

The Badger opened his eyes that morning to find the tip of a fencing foil tickling the base of his throat. His eyes focused slowly on Henry.

"Ah, you're awake," said the knight, withdrawing the sword. "You can help me out of this getup. I was trounced, so be glad you were not present to witness it."

The Badger fumbled with the laces and buckles of the fencing suit, then helped the knight into his morning clothes, a marvel of false sleeves, jet beads, silver bugles, quilting, tucks, and a pendant snuffbox of mother-of-pearl. The Badger was at a loss to know which was the front, and he almost misbuttoned the vest.

"Well," said Henry, looking in the mirror, "you did fairly well. Considering your talents run to horses, you might have saddled me, and tied on a nosebag. Come; we'll fetch your sister and leave her with the rest of the ladies in the garden. The kings await in the hall."

Caitlin, recovered, held the Badger back on the way to the garden. "What possessed you to say I was your *sister?*"

"Was I to tell him you were a witch I was escorting to a nunnery?"

"But sister?"

"It was the first thing that came to mind." A smile tugged at the corner of the Badger's mouth. "It is a little farfetched."

"For all you know, I might be—a changeling, and all that. Go on, catch up with him. I promise I'll behave myself."

They left her in the garden where nine ladies in exquisite clothes were playing cards under the trees. The Badger felt a pang of misgiving as he left her and cast a glance over his shoulder. Caitlin had already been surrounded.

"Her clothes are dreadful, but at least she has sound teeth," said Margaret.

"The complexion isn't too bad," said Hilda.

"She has nice small ears, even if they're a little pointed," said Anne.

"Her feet are large, I'm afraid," said Catherine.

"The nose, too, is regrettable," said Magdalene.

"But you must admit," said the prettiest, "those eyes are extraordinary." This was Oriel, whose silver hair would have been the envy of any silversmith.

This won them over, and soon Caitlin was offered a pipe of clove and asked if she wanted to wager anything on the outcome of the card game. When she said she had no money for betting, they pressed into her hands a purse made of silver links, full of gold, the coins stamped with the ladies' own likenesses.

But soon the ladies had put their cards aside. "It's too windy," they said, and they were bored besides. They lay on the grass in their fine costumes, skirts tucked up, smoking. Some began a little contest of riddles while the others napped. Caitlin found herself seated under a tree with Oriel's head on her knee.

"Why are you going to the convent? It sounds a dreary sort of life. Are you very devout?"

"No more than is seemly." Caitlin felt she ought to keep up the Badger's fiction for a while, at least. "But my brother and I are poor—

he's only a muleskinner and cannot keep me, if he wants to take a wife."

"How uncivilized! Here we do not stand for such trafficking of lives in the name of love. It's better off the way we work things. The knights answer to Levander, while Linus rules the ladies. The men have their half of the palace, we our separate chambers. Neither may trespass on the other side without consent. We dine separately, except as the kings declare otherwise. The kings even ordered that two sets of coins be struck, one as currency for the men, and another for ourselves."

"Don't you even speak to the men?"

"Only as far as we are required, at tournaments and feasts. Each man must pick a favorite from among us, give her his colors to wear, cheer her at jousts—but it's no more than courtly love. We'd none of us dream of anything more. Most men," said Oriel, sitting up to emphasize her point, "are empty-headed, vain things. They can't play cards and avoid the garden for fear of wasps and sunburn. So they stay in the parlors, gossiping and drinking sherry. We have no use for them."

"So I gather," said Caitlin.

"Then why do your brother's bidding, if it isn't what *you* wish?"

"It seems I need correcting. They say I have seer's eyes and ply a witch's tricks, and steal babies."

Oriel's eyes widened. "Babies! Are there babies where you come from?" The other ladies overheard and gathered around.

"Of course! What a strange thing to ask." Caitlin was beginning to think much about Fifthmoon was more than a little odd. "Aren't there babies everywhere?"

"Oh, and wells where you can draw nectar, and fields where rubies grow like strawberries!"

"Tell us," said Magdalene, "are they really born without teeth?"

"And without ears?" asked Hilda.

Caitlin looked from one to the other. "Where do you all come from, to have never seen a baby?"

Catherine spoke for the rest. "From the farther moons—their majesties bring us here when we are thirteen, and we must leave when we are thirty. We are coached to be forgetful of all we have left behind."

"And, too," Hilda broke in, "all they give you to eat the first week are poppyseed sandwiches and sleepwort tea. After a while, you're not sure what you remember."

At last they all began to gather up their scattered shoes and hairclasps. Soon, the kings would dismiss the knights, and it would be their turn in the hall. Caitlin and Oriel were left behind, picking up backgammon pieces.

"There was a baby at court once," Oriel confessed to Caitlin.

"Where did it come from?"

"Oh, we found it," Oriel said vaguely. "But it got sickly, and died."

"Why, what did you feed it?"

"Oh, cake, I think, and wine from a dropper."

"Oriel!"

"What? Don't give me that look. It was sickly from the start, I tell you." Oriel started for the castle without her, and Caitlin had to trot to catch up.

In the great hall, while the kings played chess, the knights loitered, playing dominoes or eating pistachios and spitting the shells into the great fireplace. Henry and the Badger sat a little apart. The Badger had learned of the peculiarities of Linus's and Levander's court.

"Oh—it was not always like this," said Henry. He and the Badger had claimed two armchairs apart from the others. "Not so long ago we were like other courts: We wooed and suffered like the rest, we swooned and swore our troth and wore our hearts on our sleeves. There was no energy, no industry; the looms and harps mouldered, and the horses grew fat and lazy, and the game in the wood went unmolested. We were quite content, you see, to lie abed all day. And, too, there were such rivalries between us, such jealousies, and duels. So we outlawed love."

"And no one complains?"

"Oh, we have our diversions." Henry glanced over to the corner where a particularly beautiful and petulant young knight was doing his best to ignore the knight at his elbow. "Our greatest entertainment begins tonight. You will see your sister, for we all dine together. The kings are announcing their champions for the tournament."

It was a custom of long standing for the champions to be announced at dinner, and each year the course was varied. Last year it had been done by soaking two of the puddings served with brandy. Everyone was required to touch a match to his or her own plate, and the two whose puddings flared up blue knew they had been chosen. Another year there had been chessmen in the dinner rolls.

All the court, knights and ladies alike, stood awaiting the kings' entrance into the hall. Caitlin was dressed in one of Hilda's castoff getups, a snapdragon-yellow silk that had not suited the other's fair complexion but set off Caitlin's black on white coloring splendidly. The Badger noticed it, and so did Henry and Oriel.

Henry had lent the Badger some of his clothes, a linen shirt faced with blue silk. There was a bit of paper stuck to his cheek where he had cut himself shaving. The young knight, who earlier had been petulant, had cheered a little and was now only beautiful. He noticed the Badger, and remarked loud enough for all to hear, "Where is Henry's page?"

"Having his teeth out," said someone.

"Where did he get this one?"

"In the road, I think."

"Did he?" The young knight sat up a little straighter. "What was he doing in the road?"

"Taking his sister to a convent, if you must know, Torquist," said Henry.

Only Caitlin, whose hearing was sharp from necessity, heard Torquist murmur, "Has he a sister? Is she so fair? As flaxen perhaps, but never so fair."

"You're never from any court," Torquist declared, "for no one has taught you enunciation and certainly not conversation. Yet you're no bumpkin. Where are you from?"

The Badger, who was now quite red, said, "Thirdmoon."

"Ah, yes—there is a temple there, I think. But you are no novice monk. No, a charity case of some kind, but you're not outwardly misshapen nor, I think, inwardly: You are rough-hewn, but the wood's not wormy. That leaves only orphans and . . ."

"*That's enough.*" The Badger had meant to hiss it, but it left his mouth a cold shout that rang in the hall. Even Linus and Levander looked up for a moment.

"Ah," said Torquist. "I thought it was that."

"No," said the Badger, "you didn't think. I may not have been born with a silver spoon in my mouth, but I wasn't born with my foot in it, either!"

There was a gasp around the table. Caitlin's eyes snapped, and Henry howled. Oriel leaned over and whispered in the Badger's ear, "Well put!"

The soup was brought out in golden plates. All the court leaned forward as the kings lifted their first spoonfuls to their mouths. Linus swallowed and said approvingly, "Turtle."

But there was nothing in the soup, no royal coin to signal the kings' choices for champions. The plates were cleared away and the next course brought in. It was a savory, devils on horseback, a dish unknown both to Abagtha and the cooks at Thirdmoon; both Caitlin and the Badger undid theirs a little to see what was in them before eating them a little cautiously. There was nothing beneath the bacon but a prune, nothing inside the prune but a little chutney—no jewel or other happy pit to the dish. These plates, too, were cleared away.

While Torquist and the younger knights displayed an intense interest in the courses, Henry sat back spinning his knife and enjoying his dinner. His eye roamed over the Badger, fell briefly on Caitlin, and wandered over the rest of the court. He felt himself safely out of the running at thirty-five. I am quite content, his look said, to savor this company and the extraordinary wine Levander produces from his vats year after year like a conjurer whose pitcher is never exhausted.

The next course was fish, trout in fact, carried in by the pages on great salvers and dispatched by the diners in record time, except that

Linus choked on a tiny bone and had to be patted on the back by his brother.

And so it went, course after course, through crown roast of lamb, two more savories and a pudding.

Finally the coffee came, pages following behind the urn with jugs of cream and a loaf of sugar, cutting lumps for those who liked their coffee sweet. Many refused a cup in favor of wine, or better, a double brandy. Henry took coffee with three lumps, as did Oriel. Linus and Levander each had a cup.

The whole court was whispering and looking at the kings with puzzled expressions. Perhaps they had been mistaken about the night. Perhaps, too, the cooks had made a terrible mistake. Or perhaps some uncourageous one among them had chanced on a pearl among the peas and decided not to speak.

Linus and Levander appeared unconcerned, even jovial. They ordered the fiddlers sent for, sent back their fingerbowls three separate times before they were satisfied, and finally fell to quarreling about the quality of the clove supplied for their pipes.

All of the sudden Oriel sat down her cup with a cry, holding up a brilliant the size of a sugar-lump. Not a moment later Henry began to cough and choke, and retrieved from his cup another diamond of the same size.

Linus and Levander began to applaud, crying, "Your champions!" Slowly, the rest of the assembly began to applaud. Torquist was the last to join in; he trembled, and his mouth was grim.

Henry himself was smiling nervously, while Oriel was pink and white with pleasure.

Someone else in the hall was not applauding. A tall knight stood apart against the wall by the steward and the boy turning the spit. He had thick black hair, worn long, and a heavy beard. As she clapped, Caitlin thought to herself: What is it about him? There was no place set for him at the table, and when Caitlin turned to ask Hilda about him he had disappeared.

8
tilting at the ring

he Badger found Caitlin in the corridor, sprawled in her silks with the palace cats. She did not look up as he approached, his boots sounding on the uncovered stone floor, but kept her eye on the littlest one, a black kitten. When the Badger had come quite near, it put out a paw and covered the toe of his boot, as if pouncing on a shrew.

Caitlin raised her head. As always, the sight of her eyes startled the Badger. He put it down to the color of the silk and the torchlight in the hallway, and the cats ranged on her skirts like a witch's familiars.

"Henry will give us horses and money enough to reach the coast, if I stay until the tournament," he said.

Caitlin looked down at the kitten for a moment before she spoke. "If you asked him he would give them to you tonight, I think. But no —it would not do to win your favor at the cost of your company."

"Why would a knight want to win the favor of a page?" the Badger said peevishly, purple as beets.

"You know the answer better than I," Caitlin said coolly. "I like it here, you know. I wonder if Ninthstile shall be like this. I think not."

He sat back on his heels beside her and picked up the kitten. "How could the abbot stop you from staying?"

She gave a soft exclamation that was almost a laugh and took his hands, the kitten still in them. "Badger, have you learned nothing at all? Not a glimmer in that thick head of yours, for all these weeks and miles we have traveled? Think back over your catechism: my barrow, Asaph, our hunter friend. Does it strike you odd that the abbot would take the trouble to have a third-rate witch escorted to a convent and place a bounty on her head?"

"It's only the bounty that would be on his own head if word got out the abbot of Thirdmoon harbored witches."

"But a price on your head, too? A stableboy is hardly in the same league as a witch."

"I suppose he thinks I need an incentive to deliver the goods, rather than sell you into slavery, which seems a better idea all the time." The Badger's words were a little hot; that "stableboy" had stung.

"Badger. Do you *really* believe that if we stop our journey now we will live undisturbed until a ripe old age? We may be no safer if we travel on, but at least we will know our enemy." With that she thrust the kitten back into his hands, leaped to her feet, and ran down the corridor.

Henry's training for the tournament consisted mostly of tennis. He claimed that it was good for agility and balance, eyesight and strategy. The truth was Henry was frightened of horses. The Badger sat in the penthouse behind the net while Henry hit a ball off the sloping walls, over the net, and into the court of his opponent. Henry's explanation of the rules and scoring had evaporated from the Badger's memory the instant play had commenced. The other player hit the ball with great force into the gallery where the Badger was sitting. A net stopped the ball, but the Badger still flinched. A bell tied to the net rang sharply, signaling the end of the game.

Henry paused in the low doorway and tapped the bell.

"Not an enthusiast of the chase?" he asked, wiping his face and neck with a towel.

"No."

"Or an enthusiast of another chase entirely? Your friend who looks so well in yellow? Oh, yes; I've guessed. Never my color, yellow, but those eyes are remarkable, I must admit. What do you know of jousting?"

"Nothing. I was raised in an abbey; the closest thing we had to jousting was knocking apples from the trees."

"An abbey—hmm. *'Is he chaste, then, as well as natural? No, it is too much.'* Do you know how they degrade a knight who has fallen from grace?"

The Badger did not.

"They strip him to his shirtsleeves in front of the entire company and cast his broken armor at his feet and his shattered sword on the trash heap. Then his shield is dragged through the crowd by a mule, and everyone parodies his coat of arms. Three times the jester calls out, 'Who is there?' and three times the women call back the name of the knight. And always the fool shouts back, 'No, it isn't so. I see no knight there, only a despicable coward.' Oh, I exaggerate, I grant you, but it is bad I tell you, very bad."

"And they will degrade you that way, if you lose the match to Oriel?"

"Worse! Here we are not so humane, and practice another sort of degradation altogether—marriage and expulsion, or, as I like to call it, banns and banishment."

Oriel insisted on practicing her tilting at night, although Hilda chided her, saying she would surely break her neck. Caitlin went with her, to watch, and watch after her.

"Why must you battle with Henry?"

Oriel laughed; she was saddling her horse at the edge of the titling field. It was just dark out. "You *are* from the provinces, aren't you?

Thirdmoon, isn't it? I don't mean to laugh, but you really seem such a bumpkin sometimes. I must fight Henry if I am to keep my freedom."

"And if you lose to him?"

"He gets to choose a husband for me. And if he loses, I get to name his bride." Oriel straightened the harness, making the bit jingle. "When I was seven years old," she said, "my parents gave me the dearest little suit of armor. It was leather and gilt, and the helmet and shield were of wood, and the lance was made of whalebone and parchment. How I loved that suit! The servants used to come to the door and call and call me to come in to supper, and finally they would send the houndsmaster, and he would find me in some hideyhole, slaying dragons."

And more than that Oriel would not say.

Caitlin had to light the torches on the tournament grounds so Oriel could see. Around the edges of the field the trees were ghostly in the darkness. From her perch on her horse Oriel leaned down to speak to Caitlin.

"It will be nothing like this tomorrow," she confessed. "Then my lance will be a good bit longer, and my aim will be to unseat him, not to snare the ring. We are in this for honor, not blood. Here—see how short the lance is."

"But what are you running at?"

"Do you see that post at the other end of the field? It's very dark, so it's hard to make it out, but it's there. There is an arm to one side of it, and a ring on the end. The aim is to snare it with my lance."

Oriel turned her horse and cantered to the far end of the grounds. Then, lowering her visor and couching her lance, she charged. Horse and rider thundered past Caitlin all in a blur, casting up clods of mud and tufted grass.

Caitlin couldn't see a thing, but she heard a muffled shout. Oriel posted back triumphantly, holding her lance aloft so that the ring shone in the torchlight. Deftly she tossed the ring from the lance into the air, and Caitlin caught it.

"That," said Oriel, putting up her visor once more to reveal a flushed and dimpled countenance, "is called tilting at the ring."

Off across the field, behind the bleachers where Oriel's groom had nodded off, the knight Caitlin had noticed at the banquet stood alone. He wore no crest or ring, but there was something soldierly about him, noble, and yet cruel. He watched the jousting party in the middle of the damp and chilly field, regretting that the smoke and coal of a pipe would give him away.

On the morning of the match, Oriel breakfasted early, and in bed. Rather, in Caitlin's; Caitlin awoke startled to see an outsized bird's head beside her, and sat up in fright before she saw it was only Oriel's helmet, nestled on the breakfast tray.

"I've changed my mind. I was going to wear my mother's arms, you know," Oriel said as she climbed into bed, "but her family crest is conies, and when I took the helmet out of its wrapping this morning I saw these ridiculous rabbit ears on it. Now, I ask you: You don't think they'll grant me the match if Henry falls off *laughing?* Father's arms are rather dull —I never knew much about birds."

"Oriel, it's still dark outside. What hour is it?"

"Oh, about four. This way we'll have plenty of time for breakfast. Breakfast should never take anything under two hours, that's my rule. Hand me a pillow, will you, and have some of this toast before it's cold."

The horses stirred restlessly in their stalls, but the grooms, who had found some wine that afternoon, were fast asleep. Carefully someone lifted a bridle from its hook, and another, and stole away with them, swearing at the horses to be still.

A few minutes later the tall knight quietly lifted the latch and stepped over the sleeping grooms. He knew from watching the jousting practices that Oriel was the better rider, but there was no sense taking chances. He passed Oriel's gear by and paused at Henry's. He scored the girthstrap with his knife so that with a little hard riding it would be sure to give. Even a practiced eye could not have spotted the mischief.

"Though it's beyond me," muttered the knight without a court, "why I can't use the knife a little more directlike, without all this pussyfooting. Never did like pussyfooting." This was an unheroic utterance, but the knight had only the height and breadth of a hero. He had the petty brain of a thief, and the soul of a pawnbroker. But then the knight's name was Conundrum, and he was a riddle.

"Conundrum? What's that?" he asked the man who had hired him. This same man had given him the name.

"A little joke of mine," the other replied, counting out silver pieces into the knight's hat. A joke that could just as well have been on him, Elric thought, if he hadn't kissed a pantry maid and made her tell about the sugar-lumps.

It was a twofold shock when the Badger entered the kings' stables. It was neither their size (three times that of Thirdmoon Abbey), nor the luxurious appointments (stalls of brass, troughs of ebony). He was overcome first by a wave of homesickness for his simple loft over the smithy's forge and for Asaph and lazy naps under orange trees. It hit him with such force that he held onto the doorframe. Henry, following behind, stopped and muttered under his breath, "The natural child, brought to court, reverts to his origins."

The second shock was to his sense of order, already in disarray from his sojourn in Fifthmoon. The Badger looked at the saddle, wheeled, and said accusingly, "There's no cantle on it!"

"What is a cantle? No, before you tell me let's go in. They usually keep some hot rum around here somewhere."

"Is that a good idea before the contest?"

"No, but if I fall—and I shall fall—it will be painless. Ah! As I thought. Now—what is a canticle?"

"Cantle. The back part of a saddle. There's no back to that," said the Badger, pointing to the first in a row of saddles.

"That is because the aim of the whole business is to unseat the rider."

"It sounds unsafe."

"There are nicer ways to be killed. Choking on a trout bone, an unstoppable nosebleed. I had planned, before today, to go in my sleep. For the love of heaven," Henry cried, looking at the Badger, "what have I said?"

The Badger's face had gone a deathly grey, imagining the many modes of Asaph's possible death. He forced a smile.

"No more talk of dying," was all he said, and he began to help Henry into his armor, fastening the arming-points, which after all were only laces, if laces of leather and silk. The Badger had spent a lot of stolen hours off in his loft with jousting manuals, making a litany of the mysterious terms.

It occurred to Henry he had nothing to lose by a little cajoling. "You really ought to stay."

The Badger turned away and began to ready Henry's charger, a nervous horse that did not often go tilting, if one were to go by the way the animal shivered when the Badger put on the trappings. Henry would not let the subject die so easy a death.

"I can hire someone to take your sister or cousin or whatever she is to her nunnery. There is no reason in the world you might not have a brilliant career here at court."

Though his words were meant for Henry, when the Badger spoke he could only look at the horse. "Torquist was right. My mother was the unmarried daughter of the village tanner. That's a good enough pedigree for a stableboy, but not for a knight."

"Here we do not live by such prejudices."

Henry put a hand on the pommel of the saddle, so the Badger had to duck under Henry's arm.

"No, but if I can find fault with someone who has been so kind to me, your customs are surpassing strange."

"That is by far the most elegant speech I have ever heard issue from your mouth. Very well—I will molest you with my supplications no longer. I could, if I wished, release you from your obligation, but only if you wish to be released—?"

The Badger reddened. "It's not that. I'm charged to go with her. I can't just give that charge over to someone else."

"No need to explain, I quite understand: love or duty or something of that ilk. They are the same thing so often, don't you think? Here; we ought to go. We'll be late if we tarry like this."

By noon the grandstands were full of courtiers, and the townfolk pressed to the gates by the paddock, little children perched on their fathers' shoulders, vendors threading through the crowd selling chestnuts and beer in bottles.

The Badger was a little disappointed. He had been accustomed to trading a bottle of the abbey's renowned wine to the knifegrinder for picture books of jousts. Though the books were only unskilled copies, the pictures were engraved in his head: maidens leading young men by golden chains into the arena, knights splintering their lances on each other's shields. The Badger had spent many a sleepless night over one spectacular colored woodcut of a knight who had taken his opponent's lance through the eye.

There were to be no masquers or jugglers today: A nervous Henry had persuaded the kings to keep the program short. As far as Caitlin could see, the whole business would consist of Oriel and Henry, decked in armor several times their own weight, riding horses at full gallop toward each other on either side of a barrier of wooden planks. The lances were padded, so there was no danger of mortal injury. The champion won his (or her) freedom, and also the right to name the bride or groom of the loser. That was as much order as Caitlin could make of the proceedings; she would not go as far as to say she made *sense* of them. In her mind she saw the shrikes of her dreams, and Oriel's helmet, and wondered: How does it fit?

What could be seen of Henry through his visor was very pale. Oriel was rosy and held her helmet until the last moment, so her silver hair streamed on the breeze like a banner. She rode as close to Henry as the rules allowed, saying cheerfully in his ear, "Death to bachelors! Long live cuckolds, and long may your horns grow!"

It was to be the best of seven. Caitlin and the Badger retreated to the sidelines to watch. All that ran through the Badger's head was a catalog of gruesome deaths from the knifegrinder's tournament books. Caitlin stood still and wished she had eaten breakfast when it had been offered. I could eat a horse, she thought, armor and all.

Oriel was an excellent rider, and she had on her side as well an intense desire to keep her freedom. For his part, Henry had a dread of marriage that unnerved him completely, so that the Badger even had to adjust the knight's hands on the reins.

"And keep your heels down, or you'll lose your stirrups."

Henry nodded, his throat too parched to reply.

All this ought to have thrown the contest to Oriel, but Henry had in his favor luck—and an unpredictable appearance of madness as he rode unevenly toward her, which caused Oriel to lose her concentration. And the girth strap, by some miracle, held.

Thus it was at the end of six passes that neither had been unseated. When Caitlin ran out onto the field to bring her champion refreshment, Oriel thrust up her visor, her dimples out of sight, eyes full of uncertainty and high feeling.

"I am lost! I ought to have unhorsed him ages ago. I don't under-stand—it's as if I'd been *charmed.*"

"Charmed by too big a breakfast, perhaps, but nothing else," Caitlin said. Her words convinced neither of them.

If there had been a charm, it soon broke. A little drunk with his incredible luck, Henry become overconfident and lost his air of deranged purposefulness. Oriel recovered herself and unseated him. He landed on the turf with an awful crash.

The Badger was the first to reach him. "He's broken a rib," he said to Caitlin. "Help me get him off the field."

They had no sooner gotten Henry to his feet when the crowd, which had been on its feet cheering Oriel, became oddly quiet.

A single knight on horseback had entered the arena and ridden to the stand where Linus and Levander sat. Reining in his horse, the solitary rider raised his visor, and Caitlin's heart leaped as she recognized the knight she had seen at the banquet.

The knight rode a black horse, and his armor was dull black, his beard was coal black, and in the shade of his visor his eyes, too, seemed dark as the undersides of two stones. When he spoke his voice was black and silvery, the sound of a sword leaving a scabbard.

"I challenge your champion."

The courtiers, townfolk, and sweetmeat vendors turned to one another and exchanged worried whispers and uneasy looks.

"Present your name . . ." said Levander.

"—and your arms," said Linus.

"And then we shall see what the tournament book tells us," they said together.

The knight scowled, and his horse skipped beneath him. "I am Conundrum of No-Moon," he said, "and my arms are as you see them on my shield, a crescent moon on a black field, and a wolf rampant."

Deep in Caitlin's heart a misgiving hatched. Oriel caught Caitlin's hand in a nervous grip.

"Oh, let them not allow it!" she cried under her breath. "They can't let him ride against me. It has never been done."

The Badger was busy strapping Henry's ribs; Henry put up an impatient hand.

"That can wait. Move aside; I want to see."

Linus and Levander were poring over the great tome that was the tournament book. After several minutes with their grey heads together the kings drew apart, clapping their hands and crying, "Let the contest begin!"

Oriel went ashen. There was no padding on Conundrum's lance, and the tip of it glittered like a bad omen. Somehow she managed to get into the saddle once more, although Caitlin had to point both horse and rider in the right direction. Caitlin felt the fledgling misgiving in her breast grow another inch. The way the black knight held his lance was very strange. It was as if he were going to pitch hay with it. Granted, he had armor, a horse, and a mysterious coat of arms, but in spite of it all he was an oddly unknightly knight.

The misgiving grew into full suspicion.

It was hopeless from the start. However poorly the knight held his lance, his size and bulk bearing down on her at full speed shook Oriel so badly she had not even the spirit to lower her lance. As the apparition of Conundrum grew rapidly closer, Oriel dropped her lance with a cry and threw her hands over her face. The lance grazed Oriel's shoulder, but she managed to stay in the saddle.

As Oriel was helped from the saddle and led off the field, Linus and Levander pondered their dilemma. Having completed the tilt without being unseated, Oriel was still champion, but she was clearly in no condition to continue the contest.

In this case, the tournament book had an answer, which Linus read aloud.

"In the event that the champion should become incapacitated and unable to ride, yet not be unhorsed fairly in the course of the tilt, the contest shall be completed by the champion's second."

The Badger looked at Caitlin.

"That's you."

Soon Caitlin found herself in a suit of armor that was too big for her, the Badger adjusting her stirrups.

"For the love of heaven, keep your head up and your heels down. And hold the lance level."

"Please shut up," she said, "and help me into the saddle, or this will never be over."

There were no charms for this. Caitlin ransacked her memory in vain for the simple thwarts and path-bending spells Abagtha had taught her. The cold weight of the armor reminded her of her barrow, which was, in an odd way, comforting. As she trotted to the end of the lists Caitlin realized what the butcher birds of her dream meant.

The horse knew this game better than she did, so that before she even heard the trumpet blast the animal was moving beneath her, the rough gait and armor making her teeth rattle in her skull. She could barely see through the slit in the helmet. Caitlin closed her eyes, and her lance wavered, for there were the shrikes at their grisly work. The Badger hid his face.

"Ah, she's going to kill herself—" he muttered.

But then something extraordinary happened. Conundrum's horse abruptly veered to the right. For, underneath the blinders and half moon of straw padding covering his chest, beneath the plugs of wool in his ears and the heavy bard and trapper was Motley, who had caught the scent of his beloved master, and headed for it with a cheerful neigh.

If the Badger had recognized his horse, this whole tale might have ended very differently, but just then the Badger had eyes for nothing and no one but Caitlin. Conundrum swore and tried to right his course. Caitlin seized her chance. Her lance splintered on the black knight's shield, and Conundrum fell thundering to the turf. The crowd rose to its feet with a single roar, hats and children were tossed in the air and caught again. The Badger felt his knees turn to jelly, and he sat on the ground and said a little prayer.

Motley was seized and led away, and the grooms who led him off were touched to hear how pitifully the animal wickered for its master. Conundrum, unhurt, stood before the kings. His fate now rested in Caitlin's hands.

Caitlin's helmet had been replaced with a crown of lilies. She addressed the knight before her.

"It seems I have the right to name your bride."

Conundrum shook, for this was indeed something to fear.

Caitlin lifted the knight's visor and gave a cry of surprise.

"You have black eyes!"

Conundrum glowered. "And what color did you wish them to be, milady?"

"Grey," she said in bewilderment. "By all that's right and reasonable, grey." To the kings she added, "I give this one his freedom."

Just then it was discovered Henry and Oriel had taken their own freedom a half hour before. They had been brought to the same dim stall to recover, and the grooms had left them alone.

There was no telling what made Oriel do it, or why Henry capitulated. Perhaps it was the look on Henry's face as he leaned on the bar of the stall. Perhaps she confused the throbbing of her shoulder with the throbbing of her heart. Whatever the reason, they embarked on a different sort of passage at arms altogether, and when the kings sent to have them fetched all that was found was a heap of armor, and a note that read, "Match forfeited."

Linus and Levander were disappointed, but not out of reason. After all, the tournament had been a grand success. Conundrum rode off with his page and was never seen in that kingdom again. When they had reached the border Conundrum swung down from the saddle and turned the reins over to the page, who in turn reached into his purse and counted out an alarming sum in silver.

"The balance, as we agreed," said Elric.

Conundrum scowled and tried to remember how you carried numbers in addition. He couldn't, and it raised his temper. "It ought to be twice this, for the broken crown it cost me."

"Ah, but it's nothing to the broken crown it cost the kings," said Elric. He spurred Motley down the road and soon vanished from sight.

Some time later there fell into the hands of the court an exquisite miniature on a round ivory tablet of the very sweetest face any of them had seen. It looked something like Oriel, and a little like Henry. Its lips were closed, however, in a small and inscrutable smile, so there was no way of knowing if it had teeth.

9

four letters and a map

aitlin had caught up Oriel's gloves of mail and wore them out of an unaccountable sentiment as they rode off on their new horses, parting gifts from Linus and Levander. While she found the sentiment troubling, it was a very good thing for both Caitlin and the Badger that she wore the gloves, or they both would have been lost. For the reins, so splendidly trimmed with gold, were soaked in a subtle poison, a drug that worked its way into the rider slowly through the hands. It took three days for the Badger to sicken. His decline was so gradual that it was late on the second day that Caitlin cast a sharp glance in his direction.

"You all right?"

He nodded, but the trembling hand he drew across his brow belied him. And still Caitlin did not guess. The next morning when she walked across the cold fire to wake him he would not stir. Panic gripped her as she felt for his pulse and laid an ear to his chest.

"Dead to the world, yes, but still in it," she muttered. She dragged him to a thicket of brambles and made a sickbed there out of the bedrolls.

She was too busy at first to fear the worst. There were herbs to gather, good clean drawing mud to dig from the bank for a poultice, and green twigs of broom to peel and burn for the healing vapor. But still she did not guess, and for all her efforts he worsened. When she had done all she knew to do she had at last a spare moment to sit and eat a heel of bread by the smoky fire. It was then that fear seized her in its steely grip, and she began to shudder with a noiseless crying, soundless sobs that shook her like a mighty fever.

"If you die," she said to the Badger's still form, dashing the tears from her eyes, "the ground's too hard to bury you, so think of that! Wild dogs will scatter your bones over thirteen counties . . ."

At last she thought to tend the horses, and it was then that she saw the gilt shining dully on the reins. Swiftly she slipped the bits from the horses' mouths, hobbling the animals so they would not wander, and carried the bridles to the fire and threw them in. The flames leaped up with a hiss and burned purple, then orange, then blue. Caitlin gave a cold, triumphant laugh.

"Yes! You thought you'd see if that trick would work twice! And it very nearly did. Sweet heaven, I've been a fool."

Now it was a simple thing to gather the right herbs, to roast a knobby root over the coals and grind it into a bitter powder. By the morning of the third day the Badger woke bathed in sweat and complaining of a headache. Caitlin only sat by the fire, her face streaked with soot, and smiled a weary smile. There could have been no better news to her ears than if he had awakened bathed in nectar, with a celestial melody and not an anvil-headache teasing his brain.

The Badger sat up, with no idea that he had lain near death for two days and nights. "It must be midmorning," he said resentfully. "You could have awakened me."

"I have been doing my best to wake you these fifty hours," she said, and told him as much as she thought he ought to know of it, but not enough for him to guess how gravely ill he had been.

But he did guess. As they were saddling the horses he saw her lean on the horse's broad neck, burying her face in the horse's mane, and while her expression was hidden from him, the way her shoulders relaxed in relief and exhaustion made everything clear to him. The Badger had a quick vision of her, still belled, lifting him from Motley's back and bringing him across the wide moor to her barrow.

"Put those away," he said, as she began to draw on the gloves of chain. "It's too cold a day for gloves of metal. Try these." He handed her a pair he had worn at Thirdmoon. Their hands were of a size, and they fit her as if made for her.

"They are warmer," she said.

But this only reminded them that it was much colder, and they had lost two precious days.

They rode along the main roads after that, and when they had to take a side track to save time it was with many a backward glance. As they rode they passed carts bringing the harvest in from the fields, and the Badger seized his chance to lighten the wagonload a little. They supped in the saddle, on apples, yams, and turnips. They stopped to sleep in snatches, for it was cold at night, and it was easier to stay warm riding quickly beneath the harvest moon along the empty highway to the sea.

Or nearly empty. Elric was still behind them, although this time he was not going to chance letting Motley get too close to his master. At night, as Caitlin and the Badger slept a fitful slumber, Elric stole up to their horses, distracting the animals with lumps of sugar while he pressed their hooves into a box of powder ground from blind cave salamanders. As the horses went down the road they left phosphorescent hoofprints Elric could follow easily hours later by moonlight. He would wake late, light his pipe, and wait until nightfall before taking up the chase. He had much to occupy him, notably the writing of a letter.

RECEIPT, or an Accounting of Monies Received for Expenses and Services—

ITEM, one suit of armor, enameled and jeweled, black and silver, one thousand silver pieces.

ITEM, one bard and trapper for a horse, also black and silver, five hundred silver pieces.

CONTRACTED, the services of a mercenary, one Hawker Mubrie of Twinmoon, one hundred silver pieces prior to performance of said services and a like sum to be paid upon their completion.

ITEM, enough stoveblack to cover one horse, thirty-seven coppers.

ITEM, one pair of boots, seventeen silver pieces.

ITEM, one loaf sugar, cut in lumps, five coppers.

P.S. I know, Banter, that you will say I have been extravagant. Well, you are right. A new pair of boots was overluxurious of me. I could have had the old ones mended for far less, and doubtless I might have won over the horses with an apple just as easily as with sugar. However, I am confident that if there is an audit you will be able to explain everything satisfactorily.

"Everything is going according to plan."

Elric was not the only one writing a letter. The same morning the abbess of Ninthstile woke, looked out the window, and said to one of the sisters, "Has the messenger come from the coast?"

"He has not."

"He has been held up, then. The storms must have started across the straits." The abbess looked out of her fourth-storey room at the nuns in their dull brown smocks digging potatoes in the convent fields.

"Bring me my writing things," she said, without turning around.

A lapdesk containing paper and a steel pen appeared silently beside her, and the abbess began to compose her letter.

Convent of the Sacred Pentacle
Ninthstile, Ninthmoon

Abbey of Thirdmoon See
Thirdmoon See, Thirdmoon

My dear brother in faith,

The unfortunate young woman you wrote me to watch for has so far not arrived. I am holding a room for her here, and as there are several women in the town who would like to make a living with us I must urge you to communicate with me hastily and tell me whether I may expect her by the year's turning, as without extra hands the onion crop will freeze in the field. I know you will give this matter your prompt and scrupulous attention.

Yours in the Pentacle,
Clovis

Thus it was that, no sooner had one carrier pigeon arrived from the south, another was sent with this urgent missive for the abbot of Thirdmoon See. The abbot was suffering from an earache, and had been in bed for a week. The abbess's letter did nothing to succor him. He read the letter grimly and sent for his secretary. "Take a letter," he snapped at the harelipped monk.

The Abbey of Thirdmoon See
Thirdmoon See, Thirdmoon

Convent of the Sacred Pentacle
Ninthstile, Ninthmoon

My dear sister in faith,

You shall receive by sea an allowance large enough to hold a place at the convent for my charge until such time as she arrives. You may feel free to use it, if you feel so compelled, to hire a maiden from the village to pull up onions until that time. I impress upon you the extreme displeasure that will be brought upon you by the Necromancer should you fail in this office, a displeasure against which I should be quite unable to shield you.

"Yours in the Pentacle, et cetera," said the abbot, applying a compress to his ear.

Upon receiving this letter the abbess went out into the garden herself, pulling up each onion as viciously as if she were twisting off the abbot's head.

There was a fourth letter, which the Badger had never unsealed, and of whose existence Elric and Caitlin had no inkling. It was the Badger's letter of introduction to the apothecary. Upon his brief rise in the world at the court of Fifthmoon, the letter had arrived at the royal laundry via the shirt in which it was pinned. A shortage of bluing had led to a pileup at the laundry, so that the Badger's shirt was not laundered until long after the Badger had left Fifthmoon. It was then that the abbot's note was discovered by the illiterate presser. Dutifully, he pressed it, admiring the handwriting:

THE SANCTITY OF THE PENTACLE DEPENDS ON THE DEATH OF THE BEARER AT ALL COSTS.

One morning the Badger woke and tasted salt on the air. They must be close to the coast. He counted the days swiftly on his fingers: When he had left the abbey the leaves had just been starting to turn after a long summer. It was now seven weeks since he had first ridden out the gate so cocksure and joyful, to become an apprentice to an apothecary. It seemed seven years. Still, it was good news: The earliest a storm could close the straits would be in a week or two, and even that would be freakishly early. They had made good time; if they were lucky in their passage, and had no more adventures, they could expect to reach Ninthstile in a few weeks.

Having made these calculations, the Badger saw no need to rise early, so he rolled over, hugged the bedroll to him, and drifted off to sleep again.

Caitlin's eyes were wide open, and while she had made no calculations, she felt a dire foreboding and a distinct need to start their journey again. No dreams this time, but an uneasy feeling that they were being closely watched. She rose quietly, so as not to wake the Badger. As she pulled on her boots she looked at the shock of tow hair that was all that showed of him and felt a severe helplessness. What a little boy, she thought. What am I to do with him, a total innocent? If things go on as they have he'll kill himself.

She walked to a clearing and her heart beat faster, the blood loud in her ears. There was someone watching her and listening. It was so still, no bird called, not a cricket offered a chirp to the morning air. Listening with all her might, all Caitlin could hear was the distant crop of the grass as the horses grazed.

Caitlin didn't know that she had spoken until the words were already hanging in the frosty air.

"Why are you doing this? What do you want of me?" she asked of the cold and still. Her words, and the thought that someone or something might really be listening, made her turn and run.

She shook the Badger awake roughly. One look at her face compelled him to hold his tongue and saddle the horses.

"Dream?" was all he said, when they had gone some distance down the road.

"Yes. No, I was awake."

In the clearing Elric had had a nasty shock. Her sneaking up on me like that, he thought. His hands shook as he lit his pipe, and he wondered whether he was feeling his age. In this occupation, it wasn't uncommon for men to retire early. Like the Badger, he had thought to sleep in, but now, like Caitlin, rest eluded him. Still, he knew something the Badger didn't, something that would throw all the Badger's calculations to the four winds: that the sailors who took passengers across the straits were a highly superstitious lot, and the sum that could persuade them to give passage to a young woman with raven hair past her waist and seer's eyes had not been minted.

They reached the port of Little Rim that afternoon. The horses, used only to an occasional hawking outing, took the scent of the sea immediately to heart and trotted toward it with heads lifted to the salt air, ears up like signals of good weather.

Caitlin and the Badger stopped at the first good-sized inn. Because of being followed, it had been some days since they had dared light a fire, and it was longer than they cared to remember since they had eaten a hot meal. They ordered a great mess of sausage and apples and potatoes and ale, and while they were waiting for it the Badger made inquiries about a ship for the crossing.

"*The Golden Mole* sets sail tomorrow," the tavern keeper told him, "and *The Wavetrimmer* two days after that. The next ship won't weigh anchor until late next week."

"And after that?"

"Oh, well," said the tavern keeper, "after that you'd best settle in until spring, or find a way to walk on water."

The Badger returned to their table to find Caitlin had made great inroads into the supper. He took the knife from her, scraped a third of what remained onto her plate, and began to devour his own meal straight from the serving platter, talking all the while.

"It doesn't seem as if we'll have any trouble at all getting passage to Ninthstile."

Caitlin didn't answer, and the Badger set down his knife.

"Look, Cait. You had better speak now. If you don't want to go I won't take you. I'll say you cast a spell over me and left me wandering around the docks with the net menders. And you can go where you will."

"And the bounty hunters?"

"I can be back in Thirdmoon by the first of the year to explain myself."

"I have come to believe with all my heart, Badger, that if you return to Thirdmoon with me undelivered, the abbot will not go easy with you."

"But better muleskinning for me than Ninthstile for you." As he said it the Badger felt the crimson creep up from his collar to his crown.

No," Caitlin said firmly, "you must deliver me, and on time. I begin to see a pattern in it."

"Pattern?"

"Only that there is more at work in this than one stableboy and a village witch with mismatched eyes can account for."

The blush was gone and he met her gaze evenly and with growing suspicion. "You know a great deal more about all this than you're letting on. Have you dreamed the end, is that it? It is, isn't it? You know what's up, and you're not telling! Sweet heaven, but you'll drive me mad before this is over!"

"That is the one thing of which you can be sure," Caitlin said. "But you'll find, I think, a serenity in lunacy. At least, I have always found it so."

They settled their bill and went in search of *The Golden Mole*. As they went, a man approached the tavern keeper.

"Were they asking after passage to Big Rim?"

"What if they were?"

Something gleamed suddenly in the man's hand. It was too dark to tell if it were money or the blade of a dagger. In either case the tavern keeper thought it prudent to answer, and civilly.

"He asked about ships making the crossing this week."

"Did he say where he was bound?"

"No." To his relief the tavern keeper saw a silver coin appear on the barrelhead beside him.

"Obliged," said his questioner.

"Don't mention it," said the tavern keeper.

"You had better not, if you know what's best for you, and if you don't, by the Pentacle, I'll teach you!" And with that he made his exit. The tavern keeper suddenly wanted nothing to do with the coin and handed it to an overwhelmed serving girl.

Reaching the street the man saw Caitlin and the Badger headed to the dock where *The Golden Mole* was moored. Satisfied, he stopped a passing vendor and bought a bag of steaming mussels. Before long Elric came into view.

The two men greeted each other silently, with a sign each understood. The other handed Elric the bag.

"The Golden Mole," he said.

Caitlin and the Badger had already been turned away. The ship's first mate took one look at Caitlin and refused to let them aboard.

"And if you come around here again with that evil-eyed thing you'll both make the crossing tied to the keel! Sainted Pentacle! I've never seen a petrel black as that!"

The Badger was shaken, Caitlin only sullen. When the Badger started to ask directions to *The Wavetrimmer* she protested.

"Where's the use in it? You'll never find a ship willing to take me on, not unless you can find a way to make my blue eye green."

As it turned out, there was no need for that: *The Wavetrimmer* had sustained considerable damage from rats, and it had been discovered in routing the beasts that many of the ship's timbers were rotten. *The Wavetrimmer,* they were told, had been put in dry dock, and would trim no waves until spring.

It began to rain, a cold, wintry rain. They pulled their cloaks close and bent their heads to the wind, walking back to the tavern. Suddenly Caitlin stopped stock still and stared. Almost hidden by a pile of rotting nets was an old woman selling eels. She could have been Abagtha, risen from the dead.

Caitlin's lips went blue, and she was so much more than usually pale that the Badger put out a hand as if to steady her. She shook off his arm and went up to the old woman.

"What a ghost you are!" she breathed. "As if you had come to take me back, or warn me."

The old woman merely narrowed her black eyes and held out a basket, lifting the lid to show a squirming mass of eels. Caitlin drew back with a shudder. Was it all a trick of the light? Now the old woman's eyes didn't seem so dark, and her face seemed younger, with something eerie about it.

"They are very fresh," said the old woman, shaking the basket so the eels slithered to the other end of it. "Or is it something else you are looking for, daughter? A ship, perhaps?"

The Badger stepped forward. "I don't like this."

Caitlin ignored him. "And do you know of a ship?"

"Something better! A way to walk on water, for a price."

"Cait, it's madness."

"Badger! Name your price, old woman."

"Your beautiful hair, my dear, and nothing less."

The Badger began to pull on her arm. "Come on!"

She shook him off so fiercely he let her alone.

"Show me, first."

The Badger made a noise of disgust and walked a short distance away, standing with his hands thrust as far into his pockets as they would go.

The old woman brought out a fish, freshly killed, and slitting it open with a knife she drew out a map. This she unfolded and presented silently for Caitlin's inspection.

It was beautifully made, the product of ancient skill, drawn on the finest vellum in colors that seemed to swim before the eye. Caitlin could clearly see the woods and streams over which they had just passed. But all the markings were in runes Caitlin had never seen, and half the map was missing—the half with Ninthstile. Before she handed the map back to the eel-seller Caitlin noticed a gruesome sea-monster on the part of the map representing the straits. Just a flourish of a bored mapmaker's pen?

"Where is the rest?"

The old woman laughed, a sound dry as driftwood. "You are thinking that it is little enough for the rich price! Your glory, your crown, for half a map in a tongue no one has spoken for seven times seventy years!"

Caitlin kept her gaze level, but her eyes were like two magnets, the blue one making the green eye greener, the green making the blue seem the thing they named the color for. She was not vain about her hair, but she remembered well the time it had been cut against her will.

The eel-seller relented. "There is a harpmaker who has the other half, and they say he knows runes from before the Pentacle."

"Even the Spellkey?"

The black eyes glittered, and the old woman reached out with a withered hand to touch the blue-black silk that tumbled forward over Caitlin's shoulders. "Perhaps. Your hair, first. Then I will tell you the way."

The Badger bit his lip as Caitlin bent her head and let the old woman saw off the thick rope of her hair with a rusty fishknife. The short pieces that remained began instantly to curl in the salt breeze, and the sight of her pale face with its dark halo made the Badger's throat go dry.

Caitlin seized the map and tucked it inside her belt. The hair glittered in the old woman's fist like strands of jet. "Where will I find the harpmaker?"

The old woman pointed. "On the cliff."

They left the old woman to her eels and baskets. Caitlin moved as if in a dream, deep in thought, not so much about the map and the promised Spellkey, as for Abagtha and the early days when the old witch's indifference had most resembled kindness. And she was hoping, too, that she had not surrendered her hair for nothing. She had let the eel-seller shear her in the hope that the map would prove all she guessed, but also that the loss of that seal of womanliness might drive from the Badger's eyes a certain look she had seen in them lately.

The Badger walked behind her, his eyes fastened on the bare nape of Caitlin's neck. He was greatly afraid that she was going mad, and he wanted both to run as far and fast as he could away from her and to seize and shake her to reason. For he had not even recognized his own symptoms, and he sickened more and more as the hours wore on.

The eel-seller sank back among the baskets and closed her eyes for a long moment. When she opened them again they were grey. Elric's calling was giving the beholder what the beholder wished to see, but this latest deception had called for a sorcery outside the boundary of his license and power. The mercurial potion he had drunk made him queasy, and he turned his head to retch. When he raised his aching head Elric saw atop one of the eel baskets the lively heap of Caitlin's hair. He let his fingers run through its silky mass and shuddered violently.

"Ah," he breathed, clutching a handful of the hair and holding it to his face, "that I could buy your eyes as well!"

10

a liar's tale

s they climbed the steep path up the cliff, they spied the wreck of a ship on the rocks, ghostly beneath the water, its timbers like bleached ribs, the broken hull a shattered breastbone.

"They must have tried to make the crossing after the first storm," the Badger said.

"Walking on water."

"What?"

"It's what the old woman said, about the map. I can't think what she means."

"She may not *mean* anything. What I don't understand is what she wanted with your hair."

"She may think she can get some sort of power from it."

"Well? Can she?"

"Don't be superstitious."

When they reached the top they were suddenly afraid they had climbed the wrong path, for there was no dwelling in sight. Then Caitlin pointed and laughed, crying, "How could I have been such a fool!" Up through the sod of the cliff rose a chimney, and from the chimney a plume of smoke. "Though it seems a much more mannered barrow than mine. A *chimney*—"

There was a trapdoor in the ground, and after looking for a bell (for some reason he thought there would be a bell) the Badger stamped on the trapdoor with his boot.

The door was lifted immediately, as if the harpmaker had been waiting for them (which he had). He beckoned them in, talking quickly.

"Call me Leier," he said, "as in one who tells untruths, or as in a kind of harp."

Leier looked glued together out of driftwood and catgut, all sinew and weathered grey. He wore what must once have been a bard's uniform of bright green; now it was a harlequin pattern of varnish, wine, and gravy stains. The room was crammed with harps, the smallest no longer than your thumb, the tallest seeming to hold up the roof. The single table was crammed with music, newly glued harp frames drying, and skeins of uncut harpstrings.

Leier gave them cups of hot bogberry juice, laced with gin, to warm them from the inside out.

"You have come looking for a map, and hoping to find the Spellkey but you haven't been told what it is. So you are frantic to know, and you have sold your hair to find out. Did it mean much to you, your hair?"

"No more than it weighed."

"Ah, but hair can weigh a great deal, you would be surprised. A young woman not far from here drowned, washing her hair in the river. Sank like a stone. Perhaps that is what you meant, after all, that your hair meant a great deal to you?"

"It was no sacrifice. How do you know what we have been sent for and told to do?"

"It's my calling to know such things. I am no seer, mind. My eyes are of a color. But I am a storyteller, and a storyteller must have an eye for detail. I have had signs all morning and afternoon of visitors: Part of the cliff fell into the sea, and I saw a little cloud the shape of a cat chasing its tail. Which is an odd thing, for it's dogs that chase their tails.

But it was a sign nevertheless, and here you are. But wait." And Leier disappeared among the harps, reappearing with a scroll tied with string.

"The other half of the map?" the Badger said.

"He is quicker than he looks, isn't he? Well, we'll put the halves together and see." Leier unfurled the map on the table. Once the corners had been weighted down with gluepots it was clear the parts matched exactly. Caitlin's eyes fastened immediately on something penciled faintly in one corner, in runes she knew.

"Chameol!"

"Then it's real after all," the Badger said.

"Who ever said it wasn't? Don't tell me you're a Pentaclist!" Leier peered at him closely.

"But it's just a map after all—we can't sail across the straits on it."

"Just a map? Who said it was anything *but* a map? But it is a very good map, perhaps the best in thirteen kingdoms. Believe me, it is worth the best you have to give." Leier's eyes went to Caitlin's shorn head. "And you have already given your best, or very near to it."

"Well, that settles it. Let's go, Cait. Heaven knows we haven't got anything to give for it." In truth the Badger still had some money, but he didn't mean to spend the last of it on a crazy hermit who'd had too much gin.

"Oh, but you mustn't judge it by what you can see in it. It's what you can't see in it. But here—you have nothing to lose! You say you have nothing to give me for it. We will work it this way. I will tell you every tale I know; if you fall asleep before I am done, I keep the map. If I run out of tales before it is light again, the map is yours."

Caitlin considered. "Will you read the runes to us as well?"

"Ah, milady, you drive a bargain hard. The runes, too, and more, but only if I'm tongue-tied before day is broke."

"Cait," said the Badger, "we've got to get back to the horses."

"Then go to them!"

"And leave you here, to kill yourself on the rocks in the dark?" The truth was that the Badger did not relish making his way to the inn alone.

"I had managed to keep myself alive without your help before you came, and I shall manage when you are gone," she said tartly.

"Brute luck, that's all." Then he and Caitlin drew their chairs away from the fire, so they would be a little chill, and emptied their cups into the jug, so the gin would not make them nod. Then Leier reached for one of the harps hanging overhead and let his fingers skim its strings.

"Long ago, before the Pentacle, for there are some things so old, before things became as they are now and there was still magic abroad in the land, an old woman had a field of enchanted potatoes. As there was no Pentacle, and no Pentaclists to tax her for growing enchanted potatoes, the old woman grew as many as she wanted, without having to give half to the temple.

"Now it happened one fine autumn that the crop was larger than she could ever remember, and the old woman had a very good memory indeed. She had calluses on her hands the size of soup-plates from digging up the crop, her cellar was overflowing with potatoes, and the barn, and the corncrib, and the house, until the potatoes threatened to fill the chimney. At last the old woman threw up her hands in despair. Much as she hated to do it, she loaded the cart with potatoes and drove it to the rubbish pile on the edge of town. Then she went home and had her supper of ordinary potatoes: for enchanted potatoes are unpredictable things, and the old woman wanted a good night's sleep, and no surprises.

"But enchanted potatoes are full of all sorts of arbitrary magics, and even in the dump pile they waited in their jackets of silvery brown, and before long there came a wandering soldier home from the wars, lame and ready to drop from hunger. He had been turned away from every inn in the town, and all he wanted was to curl up on the rubbish heap among the broken crocks and parings and catch a few hours' sleep. If he found a morsel fit to eat, or half fit to eat, the poor soldier was starving enough to eat it.

"Now, right after the old woman had dumped her load of enchanted potatoes, a sweep had come up with a cartload of live coals and ashes, so that when the soldier curled up on the heap he was surprised to find a warm spot at his feet. What should he discover but a potato, roasted in its jacket and piping hot! He delightfully devoured not one but seven—for he hadn't eaten in as many days, if not more.

"At first the enchanted potatoes had no effect except to plunge the soldier into a deep sleep, and he seemed bound for that in any case. But he had no sooner shut his eyes than he began to have the most extraordinary dreams—"

Caitlin was jolted awake by the Badger's elbow in her ribs. "You'd better do better than that," he hissed. He himself was an old hand at staying awake, having been awakened every four hours throughout his boyhood for prayers.

Leier told them the rest of that tale, and then another, and then he stopped. "Are you hungry? Can I offer you a bite? A potato? Well, if you're sure—"

He told them the story of a blacksmith's youngest son's great kindness to a cricket king, and the inheritance it won him; the curious history of a girl who climbed down a staircase under the hearthstone, and the strange things she found there; of a fisherman who pulled a locked box from the sea, and many more. . . .

"There was a simpleton who built a castle of butter in an icy waste, and there he ruled in summer, crossing the icy waste to the desert in the winter, where he built a castle of biscuit. And he made himself a wife all of butter, and a wife of biscuit, because he found the one of butter cold . . .

". . . upon a time there was a beauty whose father promised her to a beast. And living with him, she grew to love him, and loving him, changed into a beast herself . . .

"Once upon a time there was a dairyman, and he and his wife were childless. The wife was so jealous of their poor tabby that she drowned the cat's litter. Not long after the wife conceived and bore a small son with a cat's face, and they called him Catswhiskers . . ."

Leier paused. It was the middle of the night. He reached for another harp and began his seventy-second tale, when Caitlin stopped him.

"No, we've heard that one already."

"Are you sure?" Leier frowned.

"Yes." Caitlin yawned. "He kisses the princess, and when she wakes he finds she is his stillborn twin."

"Mmm." Leier put the harp in the pile of finished tales. The next harp gave out a weird chord that made the Badger shudder.

"A prince loved to ride in the fields outside his father's palace. He would leave his mare under the trees and go walking into the broad golden meadows, discarding his fine embroidered coat and glossy boots to walk unfastened through the bowing, fragrant hay. One day he met there a lovely girl, all mute, naked but for her red and golden hair and a skirt of straw and flowers. She beckoned him to the bank of a stream, and he followed her and lay there with her all day in delight until night fell, and she left him. He met her there for many days, neither of them speaking a word, she mute, he mute with desire for her."

Caitlin's eyes were narrowed as if in sleep. The Badger seemed hardly to breathe as the harpmaker's voice washed over him.

"She always was the first to leave, and the one demand she made, imploring him with her eyes, was that he never follow her to watch where she went. For weeks he was only too willing to comply, to admire her neck and rosy flank from behind as she left him.

"But as time went by the prince began to convince himself that she went from him to another lover. He hid his mounting rage from her, determined to follow her and catch her unawares.

"At their next meeting she seemed full of tenderness and sorrow, and kissed him upon parting as though sending him to his death. As soon as she was out of sight he struggled into his clothes and stole after her. The sun seemed willfully to blind him, the grass to reach up to trip him. She was in his sight one moment, gone the next. He fell, rose, stumbled after her. She had gone back to the grove of trees where he'd left his horse. He thought he saw her stepping from some ermine mantle, body gleaming in the last rays of the setting sun. Then the sun left his eyes and he saw she was stepping into a horse's hide, her human foot already knitting with hoof and shank and fetlock. Turning and seeing him, she rent the air with an inhuman cry of grief and vanished through the trees, leaving the prince to grieve forever the loss of his beloved roan mare."

Caitlin nudged the Badger, who seemed in a trance, and he drew away from her touch as if from something hot. He went to the pail of icy water by the door and splashed his face until some color returned to it. Out the single window carved into the cliff-face it was still dark: It could be one hour until dawn or six.

Leier strummed a gentler chord, staring at the ceiling.

"There was a young queen, newly wed, who rose every dawn while her husband was still sleeping and let a ball of wax fall from her taper into the basin. One day the wax formed the sign she was watching for, and the queen knew she was with child. Now, it did not sit well with the king's advisers that he had married a woman from a land so far across the sea. What was known about her? And did not women from strange lands work magic and devour their own children? The young queen had not been married a week when she overheard the king's advisers plotting to steal her firstborn and stain the queen's robe with blood, so that the king would have her put to death.

"Now the young queen did indeed work magic of a benevolent variety, and she used all her ingenuity and quickness of wit to devise a means for outwitting the royal advisers. So when the wax curdled tellingly in her basin, she lost no time going to the palace apiary, where she made a secret cradle of beeswax and said a spell over it. She visited the cradle regularly, with spells and flowers, and in the spring she surprised her husband with a daughter . . ."

When Leier finished this tale he could tell by the sound of the sea on the cliff where the tide was, and what hour it was. The pile of harps which had already given up their stories filled the room. Leier picked up a harp that had some strings missing, but he was unable to remember the ending, and Caitlin refused to allow it as a tale.

"There's still a harp in that corner," said the Badger.

"No, not really." Leier shifted in his seat.

"What do you mean? It looks like one to me. Either tell us that tale, or hand over our half of the map."

Leier looked at them a little wildly, his eyes glazed from a night's tale-telling, the cords in his neck standing out in concentration. He crossed the room and picked up the last harp. It was made from a different pattern than the others; when Leier picked it up the candle on the table guttered, and the pile of finished harps settled with a musical sighing.

"Once—" Leier cleared his throat, licked his lips, and started over. "Once there was a tanner's daughter's son—"

He got no further; the Badger had him by the collar, pinned to the floor, growling, "How could you know that, if you are any good thing?"

Caitlin dragged him off. "Stop—look, it's light—we've won."

But the Badger had paused, mind racing, hand on the purse of money in his pocket. To hear the rest of that tale—to know how this journey should end. But Leier had seized his chance: snatching up a knife, he cut through the strings, and for good measure threw the now mute frame into the fire.

Then he held the map over a candle.

"Careful," Caitlin said, her hand going to her bare nape, "that cost us much."

As Leier held the map over the flame, writing that had been invisible to them darkened by degrees until at last it could be made out: the figure of a key in the sea between the Eight Moons and the Far Five.

"The Spellkey?"

"No—but you are not far from the truth. It is the key to Chameol."

"That's uncharted water," the Badger said uneasily.

"Only if you have a Pentaclist map. A few nights out of the year it is shallow enough here at the ebb tide for you to wade across. Tonight is one of those nights. It will take you three hours to cross, and once you've begun there is no stopping and no turning back, or you'll be caught in the incoming tide."

"Say no more." Caitlin reached for the map and went over by the fire to study it. Leier seized the Badger's arm.

"Watch over her. She is the stronger of you, and because of that, she is in the greater danger."

The Badger nodded, then shook his head. "How can I protect her, when I don't even know what the danger is?"

"Only know it is in your power to save her, as she has saved you."

Caitlin came back with the map. "You promised to translate the runes."

Leier had barely taken the map from her hand when a knock sounded on the trapdoor. "Quick," cried the harpmaker. "This way!"

Under the rug there was a crawlspace as damp and unwholesome as could be imagined. "It leads to the beach at the base of the cliff, here," he said, showing the place on the map. "Go, I tell you. I know that knock, and they mean you no good."

So it was that when Leier opened the door to admit the bounty hunters, there was no one else to be seen. There was only one cup of hot gin on the table, and the two spare stools were being used to hold a harp frame while the glue dried.

"Two strangers traveling together? No, no, can't say I have. But there were two bodies washed up on the beach just last week, though it would be saying much to say they traveled together."

11

the devil's sieve

lric had lost them. They had gone up the cliff, he had watched them, but neither he nor anyone else had seen them come down. To go and visit the harpmaker would be too great a risk, exposing them both. It was when he stopped for a hot toddy that he overheard the bounty hunters.

"Washed up dead, the two of them, just like Flotsam and Jetsam in one of them romancers."

"But will they pay? That's the thing."

"I have them in sacks out i' th' front. I'm goin' to find the notary right after my dinner and get 'em notarized. Then it'll be back into the sea with them, with some lead weights this time, and a prayer if I can remember one."

Elric set down his tankard and went outside to where the sacks with their unlovely burdens leaned wetly against the tavern stoop.

He felt curiously light, looking down at them, thinking: Will I end that way, when it is my turn? And he could not really believe she was dead, that it was over, his job was done.

This was not how any of them had imagined it would happen.

Caitlin and the Badger had descended into the caverns that honey-combed the cliff. From the moment the trapdoor slammed shut above their heads they were assailed by an eerie moaning, deafening at times, but most frightening when it was barely audible, sending shiver after shiver up their backbones. Now it was low and mournful, now a raging wail that threatened to deafen them, shrieking and howling around their heads like a loathsome spirit denied rest.

The Badger, who was not insensitive, grew confused and dispirited. Caitlin, who was like a harp upon which all manner of otherworldly notes could sound themselves, was driven half mad by it. The Badger had never seen her so frantic, or looking less human. She was as a cat trapped in a burning house, so paralyzed with fright that she shrank against the walls of the cavern, incapable of moving forward or back-ward. At last the Badger blindfolded her with his handkerchief and led her along that way.

If you can call it leading, he thought to himself, *for a leader knows where he is going.* The darkness and the echoing, eerie cry of the sea drove his sense of direction from him. He felt, as he led Caitlin inch by inch through the chill, pitchblack caverns, as if he were an unwilling player in a giant game of Blind Man's Bluff. All that time Caitlin clutched his arm silently, shuddering like some poor mute creature. The Badger had never seen her so devoid of spirit, and it frightened him.

After wandering the caverns for hours they came upon a landmark —a curious projection from the ceiling of the cave oddly like a human hand. The Badger realized with a sinking heart that they had been this way hours before. His panic passed through his hand into Caitlin's like a spark, and she thrashed out, striking at him blindly, and making a terrible, catlike moaning. The Badger tried to calm her but ended merely parrying her blows. They kept up a silent, frantic wrestling for a moment in the dark before the Badger slipped and fell. They hit the cavern floor together. Caitlin, suddenly calm, took the blindfold from her eyes.

"We've lost our way, and ourselves with it."

The Badger had no answer for that, and only drew away from her, hiding his head in his arms.

"I must be going mad," Caitlin said, laughing ruefully. "I smell cooking."

The Badger suddenly raised his head with a cry. They had been surrounded by a dozen brown and wizened faces, all studying them with intense curiosity.

These were the Cavekin, sand-urchins who shunned the bright beach, descending from the caves only to scavenge among shipwrecks, returning with their booty to the Devil's Sieve. They were the children of sailors who had never returned from the sea and of country girls who had abandoned hope with their children and returned to the farm. Put to sea in casks, they had quickly been spat back on the rocks by the waves. Thus rejected by both the land and the sea, they took to the caves, which were half on the land and half in the sea but really neither.

Now they led Caitlin and the Badger to a chamber deep in the heart of the cave and spread a royal feast before them: crabs and oysters and mussels roasted in the shell, and all sorts of dainties from a chest tossed up by a storm—potted meats, preserved fruits, figs in wine, cake in tin boxes, cheese, and a lone bottle of wine from the captain's store that hadn't been smashed on the rocks. On one of the wax-sealed jars Caitlin recognized the seal of Milo's kingdom. This, then, had been part of a shipment bound for the Far Five. Caitlin and the Badger ate with the relish of relief, for while the chamber was smoky and sooty and smelled of fish and unwashed children, it was a boundless comfort after the hours in the catacombs.

The urchins themselves gorged on fish, largely raw, and on what the Badger greatly feared were bats, topped off with a quantity of weak and extraordinarily salty beer made from dune grass and sugar beets. Afterward, the urchins all fell asleep in a heap. "Like so many puppies," the Badger said, carefully stepping over them, torch in hand, to inspect the part of the chamber that lay outside the glow of the fire's light.

The walls were covered with runes and fantastic pictures of strange creatures: winged elk, and lions with human bodies. The Badger traced maps of cities lost in the clouds, or hidden beneath the waves, where women leaned from watery balconies, singing back to the whales their own songs.

Caitlin found, scattered among the sea chests and stray sailors' shoes, strange and wonderful pieces of workmanship such as she had never seen in any book: a clock that told not just the phases of the moons, but the procession of the heavens; an herbal in runish tongues that showed the healing uses of plants Caitlin had never seen, with names such as toad's eyelash and dwarf's fist. There were maps of the bottom of the sea, and fine instruments whose use they could not guess, steel such as the Badger had never seen.

"These are never from any shipwreck," said the Badger. "Look at this." He waved a hand. "Glass, pottery—none of this would have made it over the rocks in less than a hundred pieces."

"Mmm."

"Then where did it come from?"

"Here. It must have been here before these catacombs were formed, or when they served a different purpose." She pushed away the tattered flag of a ship long splintered into driftwood, exposing a niche in the wall of the cave.

"This was a fitting for a torch, once. Besides, you don't think the children carved these runes, do you? They probably can't write in any *living* tongues, let alone a dead one."

The Badger was studying intently the runes on the far wall. "Let me see the map," he said suddenly.

Caitlin took the halves from their waterproof packet inside her shirt.

"Yes," the Badger said. "See, they match the ones on the map, here, and here. They're the same as the *L* in Chameol."

"And there are three letters before, and three after—as in Spell-key." Caitlin's eyes were shot with gold from the torchlight.

One of the urchins woke and dashed the sleepy-sticks from his eyes. He was the eldest, and remembered something of the speech of men. The runes and "pretties," as he called the treasures, had been here as long as he could remember. He led them to a spot where part of the cave had collapsed. Through an opening they could see an ancient chamber, lined with what Caitlin guessed were stone biers, and here and there the glint of further treasures.

The Badger remembered their engagement with the tide, and the boy led them swiftly through the tunnels. As they went, the boy would stop and snatch a blind white salamander from a crevice, kill the creature with a quick bite to its skull, and sling it from a thong at his waist. By the time they reached the cave entrance a tassel of salamanders hung from the urchin's waist, and the Badger was feeling queasy.

It was a steep drop of forty feet to the narrow strip of rocky beach that had been left along the base of the cliff by the incoming tide. The boy lowered them to it by means of a rope, hauled it back up, and disappeared.

They found themselves alone on the beach.

"It won't be out again for hours," said the Badger to the tide. He squinted at the sea; the moon had risen, and there was a light wind. Caitlin settled herself on the sand.

"We ought to sleep," she said.

But although he was so weary and cold he was ready to drop, the Badger found he couldn't sleep. Instead he sat and watched Caitlin sleep, dreamlessly, it seemed, for she tossed and muttered not at all. She lay curled as flexible as a cat, the sea breeze stirring the roughly cut hair at the nape of her neck. The Badger closed his eyes, and when he opened them he was a little surprised to see her there still, sleeping so soundly.

This was no beauty he had ever been taught to admire. Beauties had winning smiles, shy glances, breasts ready to roost in the hand as a dove. Caitlin was as tall as he, or taller, probably stronger, yielding in nothing, contrary in everything, beetle-browed and stormy.

But for all that he was conscious of nothing so much as the desire to kiss her, and not very gently.

"God help you," he said to himself, "if you fall in love with that!"

But he already had.

She was awake now, rubbing the sleep from her eyes, pulling her clothing closer around her against the cold.

"How long have I been asleep?"

"I don't know. A few hours. The tide is almost out."

"We should wait another hour, don't you think?"

He nodded dumbly, and watched her stand and walk toward the surf.

"Where are you going?"

"I'm thirsty." She knelt, scooped up some water, and quickly spat in a completely dumbfounded manner.

"It's salty!"

He laughed. "And what else do you think it should be?"

It was a defeat for Caitlin, if a small one: She hated these confrontations with facts alien to her, common to everyone else. Most people do not live in oak trees with red doors; most children do not dream the future; the sea is salty. The worst thing was always thinking each humiliation was the last. It never was.

"Here," he said. "I saved us a bottle of wine. The children seemed to prefer that sugar-beet concoction."

She accepted the bottle from his hand, and as her fingers closed around the neck they brushed his own. The moonlight did not show the way he colored.

She handed back the wine, and he drank, too.

"I've never seen the sea, either," he confessed, "and if Asaph hadn't told me, I wouldn't have known it was salty. He was a sailor at one time, and he used to tell me—"

"Badger. I think I should go alone."

His heart froze. "What?"

"I want you to leave me now."

"And what will you do?" He spoke calmly, but his heart was hammering.

"Swim across on my own."

"Don't speak nonsense. And don't tell me half-truths, either! You've had a dream, haven't you? You had a dream just now, didn't you?"

Caitlin was silent so long he thought she wouldn't answer, when she said, "Yes."

"Cait—"

In the moonlight a tear ran down her cheek unchecked. "Don't you see? I don't want you killed over nothing."

"Over you is hardly over nothing."

"I don't want you killed at all."

"Well, I don't plan on dying, don't worry. I think we had better start out." He began to take off his boots, then his jacket. "You'd better do the same. When these get wet they'll be like lead weights."

They waded into the shallows with their teeth chattering. Hands shaking with cold, they held the halves of the map together.

"Yes," said Caitlin, "this is the place we're supposed to cross."

"All right." The Badger watched her go out into the waves, and then, with a heavy heart, he went after.

Leier stood in the cliff gazing out to sea. The breeze made sails of his cloak and shirt. He paced to the edge and back, muttering under his breath.

"Not good! Not good, I fear, not good at all!"

The Badger had miscalculated the tide, and a storm was coming.

The map was folded and pinned in Caitlin's shirt, and as the water came higher she took out the packet and clenched it in her teeth. They were not halfway across when suddenly Caitlin could no longer feel the bottom.

In front of him the Badger saw Caitlin flounder as a wave hit her. Sweet heaven, he thought, she can't swim.

So this is how I die, she thought. It was not at all as she had dreamed it; she was so numb with cold she hardly felt it anymore. The salt was bitter, but now the water seemed to her as warm as tears.

The Badger fought through the waves toward her. There was no way he could swim to either shore and manage to hold her head above water. He might gain the shore alone, but he did not think of it. He reached her and pulled her head out of the water, but a large swell drove them apart.

When the Badger broke the surface she was out of sight.

"Cait! Cait!" His calls were lost in the empty sky more quickly than an albatross's cry. Then the water was over him, and he remembered nothing.

The first bounty hunter paid the fisherman. As he got out his wallet he made rather a show of the dagger he carried. "And a little extra, eh? for the wife and babby, and because you're a man what knows how to hold his tongue."

He and the other bounty hunter pushed the fishing boat into the waves.

"There's a storm coming," said the other. "I don't like it."

"Well, neither do I, but it's a damn good thing I thought to check her eyes, isn't it?"

Gently, gently, the dolphins nudged the still forms. Working in pairs they kept their burdens steered toward the island that lay before them, shrouded in mist and ringed with rocks. They chattered between themselves of the coming storm, still a distance off, and to the north. On the shore someone was waiting with a lantern, for the storm had made it dark again. There would be mackerel for them, and their warm, watery pen. Closer and closer they nudged the two forms.

Although the coming bad weather had made it dim, there was enough light to show the gold collars the animals wore, and the strange runes upon them.

On shore the two were put on litters and carried off to the building, white as coral, that rose above the others on the island. As the procession of lanterns and hooded figures wound toward the fortress, the storm closed in.

Caitlin woke in a wide bed in a shuttered room. *Am I in the convent, then? No, I'm dead. This is heaven, or hell, or some such place.*

A woman entered the room bearing a tray. Caitlin could not tell, looking at her, whether she was angel or fiend.

"Where am I?"

The woman did not reply, but placed the tray on the table beside the bed. She held a cup to Caitlin's lips, and gratefully Caitlin emptied it of a liquor, clear as water, thick as honey, fragrant as lilies and evergreen. No sooner had she finished it than Caitlin felt strength coursing through her limbs and, too, a profound weariness. Her eyelids shut of their own accord.

When they opened once more there were two women in the room, the one who had ministered to her before and another—taller, her hair hidden by a headdress.

"Am I in the convent?"

The woman looked at each other and laughed, but did not answer her. They helped her out of bed and dressed her in clothing that was light and soft yet marvelously warm.

They led her down an open corridor with arches facing the sea. To her right Caitlin saw a low orchard and fields falling away to a bay. Then they turned a corner and the women led her into a room.

Lost in the bed at the other end of it lay the Badger, his head bound, his cheek cut.

Heart beating swiftly, Caitlin thought, no: *He isn't dead, or they*

would have covered the mirrors, and put coins on his eyes. There—the
sheet moved—he had breathed.

"Leave me with him."

When they had gone she went and undid the dressing with trembling hands. Satisfied they had treated the injury competently, Caitlin turned back the covers. She meant only to feel for broken bones, or at least that was what she told herself as she ran her hands lightly over the Badger's limbs.

"How cold you are . . ." she whispered. There seemed nothing wrong in slipping in beside him, ". . . to warm him," and press her cheek to his.

All of a sudden she realized he was awake.

For a long moment, she lay tensed in his arms, pretending to be asleep. But his arms tightened around her. He shook her gently and said in her ear, "Cait—"

When he remembered it later, it seemed to him he had moved from deepest sleep into the throes of an agile, fevery passion quite unlike waking. He had imagined what loving her would be like more often than he liked to confess, but never the way it happened: halting questions, to learn whether she was in the bed by design or accident; the first shy kiss, careful of the bandage, then a needy one, in which all the breath was drawn from his body through the top of his head, as though a fire had been drawn through him, leaving him light as ash. The first shock, and then abandoning themselves to it, like burning and drowning and falling all at once. Who would have guessed that a tongue of acid could taste that sweet, that one so rough could be so tender? Bewildered but content, he pulled her shorn head close and kissed the top of it softly.

Caitlin let herself be lulled off by his heartbeat, silently reciting her surprise: The sea is salty, and this is sweet. Sure now this was neither convent nor hell, and that they were safe for the immediate future, Caitlin slept, for tomorrow was all she looked to.

12
the island

n the morning they woke to find a breakfast set out for them on the end of the bed: fresh fruit in winter, melons and strawberries that seemed hot from the sun, steaming cups of wine, bread and butter. Two sets of clothes, identical except for size, had been laid out as well; as she had the longer legs, Caitlin got the longer trousers. A basin had been left, and a razor, and the Badger let Caitlin barber him. She didn't cut him at all and, when finished, bent her head and quickly kissed him under the chin. She got lather on her nose doing this, and while they were still laughing the door opened to admit a woman.

She was taller even than Caitlin, and unlike the women they had seen the day before she wore no headgear but her hair. It spilled in a bronze riot over her shoulders and down her back. Her clothes, too, lacked the restraint of the sicknurses' uniforms: a full-cut gown of black velvet and turquoise silk that fell to her knees, and under that black trousers and boots. She went to the window and threw back the shutters.

"Good morning! I trust you spent the night well." Mischief leaped up in her eyes as she said it.

"We did, thank you," said Caitlin coolly.

"Good, good. I am your ambassador and interpreter, Iiliana. Now, tell me your names and how you came to be in such a cold sea in such a nasty storm."

"We couldn't afford passage to Big Rim, so we thought we would wade across at low tide," Caitlin said.

"And why did you need to reach Big Rim?"

"Our parents wouldn't agree to our getting married," said the Badger.

"Why didn't you stow away?" asked Iiliana, opening her eyes very wide. Caitlin shifted uneasily; the eyes were very blue, and very knowing.

"If we'd been caught, they would have put us ashore again in Little Rim, and then our parents would have kept us apart forever."

Iiliana burst into scales of laughter. When the hilarity had subsided she put on a pair of glasses and examined closely some papers she drew from a pocket.

"Matthew Tannerson, bastard, born to Margaret, daughter of widower and tanner by the name of Thomas in the town of Moorsedge, Thirdmoon See. Remanded by maternal grandfather to the guardianship of the abbot of Thirdmoon See to be apprenticed as a monk or else taught a trade. Apprenticed briefly to an apothecary in Moorsedge but returned in semi-disgrace."

She looked at the next page. "No given name, familiarly known as Caitlin, abandoned as a child in the forest known as the Weirdwood, raised by a recluse and spell-seller named Abagtha. Little known of intervening years until the death of the old woman. At about the age of seventeen the girl left the wood and went to live in a burial chamber on the moor. During this period she may have suffered abuse at the hands of local men (this is undocumented). Allegations of witchcraft, and so on."

Iiliana looked at them over the rims of her glasses. "Shall I continue? There is more."

Caitlin could only shake her head.

"What do you mean to do with us?" the Badger asked, an arm stealing around Caitlin's waist.

"Only what it is my duty to do," Iiliana said, pocketing her glasses. "Show you our beautiful island."

"No one else has spoken to us," said the Badger as they followed Iiliana through the gardens to the street. "Is there some vow of silence?"

"Not exactly. The women attending you have been with us a short time, one less than a month, the other not yet a year. They cannot speak to outreefers until they have been on the island a year. It is one of the things we are most severe about." Iiliana burst into laughter. It was hard to imagine her severe in anything, or to feel that they were in any danger on this island.

For it was very beautiful. On the low hills in the distance they could see flocks of goats and scattered cottages of thatch, and behind that a mill set against the gnarled trees of an orchard, the dark green of a vineyard.

Iiliana took them away from that peaceful beauty to the sea's edge, where hundreds of crested lizards sat basking on the rocks, diving into the rough surf to fish, looking for the world like old men taking a cure at the mineral wells. Iiliana seized one and scratched it under the chin, so that it seemed to fall into a stupor.

In the distance on the far end of the beach they could see figures in grey smocks moving around the sand with wooden hoes.

"What are they doing?" the Badger asked.

"Sweeping the sand back into the sea," said Iiliana. "Combing the seaweed to dry, really, but that doesn't have the same appeal."

"Is the seaweed used as fuel?"

"Heavens, no. There's peat for that. We call this sea-flax, and we weave a fine linen of it."

"I can't imagine it," Caitlin said.

"Oh? You're both of you wearing it."

There were surprises for them all that morning. For one, there were cellars of cheeses and other stores that stretched for acres beneath the town, the sea kept out by a system of pumps and locks. Then there were the guildhalls where the sea-flax was woven into everyday fabric and intricate tapestries on enormous looms.

"Wouldn't it be simpler," the Badger shouted above the racket of the looms, "to import things? Surely good Fourthmoon wool would be cheaper than weaving your own linen this way,"

"It would be—if we had a port."

"Do you mean to say," said Caitlin, "that you make everything you require on this island?"

"Correct."

"If you have no port," said the Badger, "how did you bring us ashore?"

Iiliana turned from the bank of looms to the doorway. "Come. I'll show you."

She led them to an inlet that widened into a lake, its surface paved with lotuses. On its shore Iiliana stood and lifted a whistle to her lips. The Badger heard nothing; Caitlin held her hands to her ears as if against a painful sound, and six beautiful creatures broke through the carpet of waterlilies with ease and grace, leaping in arcs and falling back into the water.

A woman appeared, hauling a pail.

"G'morrow, Iiliana."

"G'morrow, Haana. Is that their breakfast? Allow me."

"You'll get fish on your clothes."

"Yes, I will, won't I? It will be like old times, when I went around smelling like a baitbox. I used to do this, if you remember, Haana."

"I had forgotten."

"Well, it was a long time ago. Here," she said, turning to Caitlin and the Badger, "give this to them."

The creatures, gentle and curious, pressed up to the bank, making a strange and happy music, turning somersaults for the fish.

"We used to pen them in the bay," Iiliana said, "thinking they needed the salt to live. But we found again and again that they made their way here, to the lilies. At first we drove them back, afraid they would get caught and drown."

"How can a fish drown?" the Badger asked.

"They aren't fish. They breathe even as you do. See that one over there? She's nursing her calf. For some reason they like it here, inland. It's a mystery."

As they walked back to the palace, the Badger tried to learn more from Iiliana about the island and its inhabitants. It was like trying to pry apart a clam.

"You've shown us all the island's natural features, but none of the artful ones."

"Not true. You've seen the waterworks, the flax beds, and our greatest industry, the cheese. I am fond of cheese," Iiliana said aside to Caitlin.

"I meant your culture—history, and government," said the Badger. "How did you come here?"

"Is it really as late as that?" Iiliana exclaimed, pulling out a pocket watch. "I've missed all my morning appointments."

She strode ahead without them. Bringing up the rear Caitlin and the Badger had a chance to put their heads together.

"What do you think she means to do with us?" said the Badger in Caitlin's ear.

"I'm not sure—nothing bad, I think. We've been treated well enough."

"Yes—but to what end?"

Caitlin only shrugged. Iiliana had stopped a little distance ahead.

"Come along, you two gossips! Yes, gossips! My ears are fairly buzzing with all you're saying about me, oh, and none of it true, none! That is what pains me." She stood gripping her side as if she had a stitch, then broke out laughing.

That afternoon Iiliana summoned a young girl to take the Badger to see the horses. He was reluctant to leave Caitlin, and it made Iiliana smile to see the struggle written so plainly on his features. In the end he didn't say anything, but turned and went with the guide.

"Now," she said to Caitlin, casting down her napkin and pushing back her chair. "I have more yet to show *you*. Follow me."

Whatever Caitlin expected to see on the other side of the door Iiliana opened, it was not the sight that confronted her: a dozen pairs of eyes, merry and shy and sullen, blue and brown and grey, hair tawny as wheat and neatly bound, or the color of hazelnuts and tumbling everywhere. The girls stared at Caitlin, whispering, and giggling, so that the woman who was giving them lessons had to clap her hands for order. She apologized to Iiliana.

"The day is so unusually warm, and they will sit about as still as midges in the spring."

"It's all right, Iirena. I'll take over for a while."

"Now, you there," Iiliana said when the door had closed again, "wipe that fresh look off your face and stand up. Tell our visitor why you were laughing at her."

"I'm sorry, but she looks so peculiar."

"Define peculiar," Iiliana shot back.

"Strange, queer, odd, uncommon, or unusual—that which is different in its nature from others."

"Please," Caitlin burst in, "don't be harsh with her. I'm afraid she has described me very well."

"She has, hasn't she? Don't misunderstand: I was not punishing her. Thank you, Mara, you may sit down. Here we teach that a breach of conduct must neither go unexplained nor unforgiven. Punishment would teach her merely to be silent, to keep her opinions to herself. A method used in the best schools in thirteen kingdoms, and see what a multitude of wisdom there is in the world to show for it!"

The catechism continued.

"Saasha. Why is class taught in the round?"

"So that the speaker may always see and be seen."

"What else?"

"So that no one may be behind or forward of anyone else."

"Very good. Paetrel, tell me why we work in the fields in the morning."

"Because it is not so hot then as in the afternoon."

A smile tugged at Iiliana's mouth. "Yes—and the other reason? Yes, Taara, help her."

"We must exercise our hands as we do our reason."

"And?"

"Because you can't make dinner out of sums."

"Nor a poem from a potato, and so we study in the afternoon. What has Iirena got you studying lately, mmm?"

"Natural history."

"What is your field work?"

"We took nets to the inlet and painted what we caught."

"Ah—you see," Iiliana said aside to Caitlin, "how wrong I am. They *do* make their dinner out of their lessons. First they paint the prawns and mussels, then pop them in the kettle for lunch."

Iiliana returned the pupils to the care of their instructor, and took Caitlin along the corridor to a suite of rooms. Once inside the ambassador kicked her shoes across the room and collapsed onto a couch.

"Ah, ah, ah! Look what you have done to my feet."

"If it's balm to you," said Caitlin, "mine feel no better."

Though she said this, Caitlin did not sit. Instead, she roamed the room's perimeter, examining the many curious things. She was reminded of Abagtha's pantry, the barrow, and Milo's conservatory at the same time.

There were wonderfully made books everywhere, most illegal under the tenets of the Pentacle. Walls not covered with books were covered with carpets, tapestries, paintings, and maps. The floor was bright with mosaics: women swimming in a circle with dolphins, the sea mirroring the stars painted on the vaulted ceiling. There were cases of stuffed birds, owls and dodos and puffins (Caitlin did not know their names, for all her birdlore); slabs of rock thick with silvery shells; coins with their portraits worn away to noselessness; urns and globes and a telescope.

When Caitlin turned again to Iiliana she found her host asleep on the couch, mouth a little agape, head to one side. The bed upon which she lay was fashioned from massive stone-grey bones too large to come from any animal Caitlin knew. Glancing out the window, she saw two figures far in the distance; Caitlin imagined the Badger in the tow of a girl barely out of her headdress, black locks tossing in the breeze.

What immunity did they get here, she wondered. *Do they bruise their hearts ever?* For lately her own was aching something uncommon, and Caitlin knew no remedy for it. Abagtha had put no faith in love-spells, thinking them good only for getting a week's dinners out of a lovesick farmer, and she had never taught them to Caitlin.

That I was nameless still, Caitlin thought. *That I had never met* him. She pressed the bone above her breast, as if to quiet her heart.

"That won't help."

Caitlin, used to her own uncanniness, found it disquieting in another.

"I know—but tell me any remedy for it," she said, turning to Iiliana.

Ankles crossed, arms folded beneath her head, Iiliana seemed still asleep, except that her eyes caught and threw back the light from beneath their copper lashes. "Time, and distance. So you must either have patience or a cunning, swift boat! Would you maroon him here with me, if I'd let you?" She laughed softly. "I think not. You were so busy cringing from the sting of the fang, you never felt yourself treading farther into the web."

"Yes—it is a web, leading inward, with no way out but dreamless sleep—"

"And you are already caught?"

"You yourself said it."

"Do you wish yourself free?"

Quite unwillingly Caitlin remembered vividly the long nights she had nursed him in his fever, hauling him from the tavern gutter, striking out at him that first day in the square, and clinging to him in the catacombs, so that remembering their nakedness in the dark, and his caress, it seemed the least of their intimacies. "I can see no good coming from it," she managed at last.

"You can't see any good, or you have already seen no good?" Iiliana's eyes were barely open.

Caitlin's heart began to beat more rapidly, and her breaths came ragged.

"Yes," said Iiliana, "I think you have already had a little bad dream, a nightmare, and it has frightened you badly. Are you so exalted an oracle that your dreams must always come true?"

"They tend to," Caitlin said unsteadily. She was whiter even than usual.

"I don't doubt it. But remind yourself from time to time that the mind is the greatest mystery of all, and that we sometimes make our dreams come true, whether we mean to or not."

Tears worked their way gently between Caitlin's eyelids, and she moved her mouth silently, in pain.

From the couch Iiliana offered her arms.

"Come! Come here, and tell me all. I know everything about you, everything. But come: I would hear it again."

The Badger followed his guide through field and marsh until at last the girl put up a hand and signaled for him to stop.

"There! Do you see them?"

Across the misty clearing a herd of mares, all white and grey, moved almost noiselessly through the shallow water.

"They're wild!" the Badger exclaimed.

"Of course. If they were tame I dare say we would have put the stables a little closer in."

"Are none of them broken to saddle?"

"The distances are too short on the island to warrant the violence it would do their spirit. We have no fields to plow, so their greatest usefulness to us lies in their beauty."

"Surely you don't come this distance often just to look at them, even in fair weather?"

"No, but they are here all the same, aren't they? The sun warms you, doesn't it, even if it is all day behind the clouds?"

The horses had stopped to strip the younger myrtle trees of their leaves, some stretching their necks down to nuzzle colts.

"How did they come to be here?"

"They are descended of survivors of a shipwreck, horses meant for the Far Moons, as breeding stock."

In the failing light of the winter day the horses seemed to him ghosts of his own life, or the part of it now irretrievably gone. As the herd turned and moved off through the mist the Badger felt he was watching something of himself move away from him forever.

"Come on," said the guide. "It will be dark before we get back, and the last ones to meals have to do the dishes."

In the herd the single stallion, a piebald, turned his head and whinnied in distress, but the eldest mare gave him a nudge, and he followed.

"Do you remember anything more?"

Caitlin nodded.

"Tell me."

"I can't."

"Yes, you can. You must."

"It hurts—"

"You have hurt before and will hurt worse than this, I promise you. It is a hurting business, life. But it will pain you a little less if you tell me—"

Caitlin turned her head as if to avert her eyes from the vision in her own mind.

Iiliana took her hands. *"Tell me what you see."*

The words came at last, in a whisper: "My own death."

The Badger turned to Iiliana savagely. "What have you done with her?"

"Put her to bed, that's all. Be still; she is unhurt, but she *is* exhausted. See for yourself. You may go to her, if you like."

They left him with her. She was cool to the touch, sleeping a bottomless sleep. He felt for her heartbeat, then pressed his lips lightly to her temple and felt her blood beat its faint kiss.

"Oh, Cait."

He had done a count of the days in his head. There were not many left.

When Caitlin woke she felt as if all her blood had been replaced with nectar and quicksilver. She sprang up in bed, a laugh in her throat. The Badger, asleep in a chair by the bed, woke startled and stiff-necked.

"Are you all right?"

"I feel wonderful. Why? Shouldn't I?"

"When I came back Iiliana had put you to bed and wouldn't tell me what had happened."

"I hardly remember myself. Oh. Yes. We talked."

The Badger felt a hiccup of jealousy leap in his throat. "Oh? Of what?"

"You, among other things."

"And you had only good to say, I trust?" he said a little coldly.

She seized him by the collar and hauled him onto the bed beside her.

"Look in my eyes, idiot, and tell me what you think!"

He was not to be put off so easily and broke away. "Where you're concerned, I sometimes think I know nothing at all."

"But I am such a simple book. Here, then," she said, more gently. "I'll show you."

Late in the morning they were summoned by Iiliana, led this time to a different room than any they had been shown, a long hall with an empty throne on the dais at one end. Iiliana sat waiting for them, in a chair below the throne and to the right of it, befitting an ambassador.

"You asked me about our history, and our government. I had hoped to introduce you to our head of council, but she has been unexpectedly called away. She did leave word, however, that I was to extend to you her most heartfelt greetings, and her sincere regret that she could not see you off at your departure.

"For depart, I am afraid, is what you must do."

They were led to the mist-shrouded bay and put blindfolded into a boat without a rudder.

"She means to kill us on the rocks, after all," the Badger said in a low voice as they were put into the boat.

"Nonsense," said Iiliana, standing a distance from them on the shore so that it was impossible she could have overheard. "There is a charm sewn into the sail, and besides, the boat knows its way to the far shore. When you have been put off at Big Rim, I daresay it will find its way home again."

"Home to Chameol," Caitlin said softly.

"Ah, you gratify me. I thought you would never guess."

"I'm sure I haven't guessed all."

"No, but I think you have guessed enough. The dolphins will stay with you, to nip at the heels of the sea monsters!"

As the waves got a grip on the boat's keel and steered it into the current, they heard the golden laughter of Iiliana, queen of Chameol, pealing in the salt air like a toll of fair weather.

*Legend has it there is an island where only women live,
working at arts men have long since put aside in favor of
sword and cannon. It is an island you cannot reach from any
direction, no map will lead you there, but if you think yourself
lost beyond all saving you may find yourself cast upon its
shores. There you will find many wonderful and mysterious
things, as visions in a dream, but you may only remain on the
condition that you drink a draught of forgetfulness: dolphins'
tears and lotus nectar. Then they will put you in a boat and
set you adrift toward the mainland, and when you tell your
tale none will believe you.*

13
ELRIC'S CALLING

lric might have never caught his mistake if it hadn't been for a rat-catcher's terrier. The dog was worrying the two sacks on the tavern stoop, where the bounty hunters had left them in their haste. In kicking the animal away Elric saw the sack had come untied. Feeling his gorge rise, he knelt to refasten it.

But the bodies had dried a little in their patient wait on the stoop, and the corpse in the open sack had the wrong color hair. With trembling fingers Elric undid the the other sack and began to laugh.

"By all that's holy!" he said, reknotting the sacks hastily, "I hope I am not too late!"

By the time night had fallen, he was safely stowed away on *The Golden Mole,* bound for Big Rim.

In his chambers the High Necromancer of the Near and Far Moons had received that morning a communication that ill pleased him. He crumpled the paper and fed it to the fire. Picking up the pigeon that had brought it, he held the bird a moment gingerly in his hand, weighing whether it would please him more in his annoyance to kill the creature, or serve him better to set it free. With a grim mouth the Necromancer opened the slit of shutter and released the pigeon. The creature settled in an apple tree, got its bearings, then beat home for Little Rim.

A monk came up and offered him another cup of wine.

"The fool!" said the Necromancer, waving away the pitcher. Not only had the abbot made the grave mistake of sending the pair off together to Ninthstile, he had tried to make up the miscalculation by sending incompetent assassins after them. The boy was not so important, the Necromancer mused. But the girl he must have alive.

He poured a quicksilver substance into a small cordial glass, floating a few black, pearly drops from a vial on the surface before tossing the drug down. He was sorry now he had let the pigeon go, but an alternative presented itself to his imagination.

"Have the fastest horse fitted out immediately."

Once in Big Rim, Elric went to the tavern, looking for a man with a thin wallet and no weapon but a small dagger. There were a handful that fit those specifics, but always Elric found some trait that made him turn away: The man was drinking on credit, or gambling, or talking too loudly, or had an outstanding physical mark—a broken nose, a boxy beard, a tattoo. At last Elric spied his man in the corner, back to the chimney, smoking quietly, talking to no one unless spoken to first, drinking modestly, and avoiding scrutiny of any kind. Elric was sure that if he turned his gaze away he would be hard pressed to tell what the man wore, or what color his hair was. Which was as it should be.

"D'you mind if I join you?"

"Not at all. There are two stools, and I have only one arse."

"What news?"

"None good," said the other.

Elric's heart leaped up. "Well, out with it!"

"Banter's dead."

Elric swore softly. "How?"

"It's not pleasant."

"I didn't think it would be."

"The harpmaker found him at the bottom of the cliff. He had been strangled with a fine cord—"

Elric nodded, not needing to ask the likelihood of misadventure. "What was he working on?"

"Last we heard, he had found the girl's amulet and felt he was getting close."

"Well," Elric said, lifting his tankard. "Here's to Banter."

They drank to the repose of his soul.

"What of you?" said the other. "I heard you'd found them drowned and had been recalled."

"I was wrong, for once! No, our pigeons have flown off again, and after that storm two days ago heaven only knows where they will come to roost."

"Well, they haven't been seen here. They may not yet have landed."

"Or landed to the east," said Elric, "and made for the forest."

"The silk forest? If they've reached it, we'll never find them."

"If they've reached it, we'll have to."

Elric left the tavern and went to a certain house in the town. After a night in the hull of a ship with the rats, he was in need of a bath and a meal not cooked in a tavern back room, and a pretty face and some conversation.

He got little enough of the latter. The woman who opened the door seemed to know him, for she let him in without a word, and soon Elric was bathed and seated by the fire with a fine dinner: a nice stuffed chop and a savory.

"Ah, Emma, you can still cook."

"And why would I forget? I get enough practice."

"Forgive me. You wouldn't happen to have any tobacco, would you?"

"You're broke, then?"

"Mmm."

Emma put her hands on her hips and shook her head at him.

"Don't worry," he said. "I have enough on me for the bath and dinner."

"Yes, well, it's the after-dinner I'm thinking of."

"I was going to talk to you about that. I think I'd better skip it this time."

"Suit yourself."

When she had gone Elric put his empty plate on the hearth. She had left a pouch for his pipe after all, and Elric lit the bowl with a coal from the fire. But glancing up suddenly Elric caught sight of himself in the mirror over the mantel, and it seemed to him his eyes had turned green and blue.

Hearing a curse, Emma came back into the room.

"It's just my pipe," he said, showing her the pieces.

Emma gave him a long, hard look, took the fragments, and set them down. Then she turned and began to unfasten Elric's vest.

"I told you, sweet," he said. "I'm bust."

"Never mind about that," she said, kissing him. In her mind she had calculated that the chop would not be missed, and no one would know the ring in the tub was his. In her mind she had already pocketed the money.

The next morning she let him sleep late, and he cursed her for it, but gave her a quick squeeze and a bite on the ear just the same. He walked off down the street without a backward glance, as was his habit. Emma watched him go without a pang. Strange egg, she thought, though handsome in a funny way. Wonder who the girl is, though. She had slipped him a sleeping powder in his toddy (she kept such things on hand), but even in his deep sleep Elric had called out a name.

By the time they had worked themselves loose from their token bonds, and lifted the blindfolds from their eyes, the island was already lost again in mist. On either side of the boat they glimpsed, from time to time, the flash of blue and silver that was a dolphin's back. There seemed to be little enough wind, but whether it was the charm sewn in the sail or the guidance of Iiliana's dolphins, the boat without a rudder seemed to be steering a steady course.

"Yes," said the Badger, "but where?"

Upon waking that morning Caitlin had felt as though the weight of a lifetime's nightmares had been lifted from her, and when she washed in the basin she was surprised to see that her eyes had not been changed in the night to a blessed, ordinary brown.

So it was with some startlement that she woke from a dream of the man with red hair and grey eyes. It was a dream that featured neither shrikes nor magpies nor any other kind of bird, and it was not in the least foreboding. He was standing on the shore in full sunlight, smiling a little smile, looking into the distance after something. Caitlin opened her eyes and looked into the Badger's blue ones. She frowned.

"What's wrong?" he asked.

"Nothing. A strange dream. Not bad, just—strange."

He had learned not to press her. "I think I see the shore."

They reached the Far Moons to the east of Big Rim, on a steep and rocky beach that rose to meet a stand of trees stretching as far as they could see. No sooner had the companions waded to shore than the boat began to drift back out to sea, against all logic, not to mention the current. The last they saw of it was the sun flashing on its sail, and the bright back of a dolphin leaping in a sparkling arc.

Iiliana had returned to them their own clothes, piecing out their gear with warm vests, cloaks, and boots to guard against the gathering winter, and as they walked up into the dark wood they were glad of them.

"Well, it seems you lost your hair for nothing, Cait," he said. "The map's gone."

"Well, we reached the other side, and that's all we hoped the map would do," she said.

"You go first, then, since you're so full up with confidence," the Badger replied.

Caitlin disappeared before him into the trees. Before he followed her, the Badger paused, afraid he was turning as uncanny as she, for his heart was full of foreboding. *What you should do before you take another step*, he thought, *is catch her up and run off somewhere, far away, to safety.*

But safety from what, and where? The red-haired man, and anywhere but Ninthstile.

And, too, he thought, she would never go with you.

It started to snow.

In the streets of Big Rim, Elric suddenly felt his pocket being picked. He whirled around and caught the offending hand in a beartrap grip; at the same instant he recognized the pickpocket. Elric let out his breath. He pocketed his property and walked on down the street without looking back. The pickpocket followed.

"What's up?" Elric said quietly, stopping to turn over apples in a stall.

"You've been recalled."

Elric spun about. "Recalled?"

"Here—" said the other uneasily, turning his back on Elric. "Eyes front, and not so loud. You're to report to the council tonight, an hour after dark, back room of The Mole and Toad."

"So twenty years, they count for nothing?"

"If it makes you feel any better, it has happened to the best."

Elric didn't reply. He couldn't.

At the appointed hour he made his way to the tavern and was shown to the back room. He knew every man seated around the table although some of them he had not seen since he was a boy of twelve.

"Sit."

Elric shook his head, arms folded. "I think I'll stand, thanks, while you tell me why."

"We have it on the most reliable advice that you are too closely involved in this case, and your judgment has been adversely affected."

"In ten words or less, please."

The speaker paused. "Iiliana herself has ordered it." And he pushed a letter across the table at him.

After a long moment Elric picked it up. At first the words scrawled in the familiar hand swam, and he couldn't read them. Then a single phrase rose from the rest, like treasure worked free of a shipwreck, rising up, up through the waves.

In short, my dear Elric, you can longer keep the vows you made to me, and I must call you home again—

He looked around the circle of faces, thought, *Banter isn't here,* and then, *Banter's dead.*

"You understand, Elric, that we can do nothing in this matter."

Elric clutched his head, for his ears had begun to ring.

"There is more to it," the spokesman went on. "The abbot of Thirdmoon See has been murdered rather spectacularly, and we can only take it as a warning: We have been found out. We simply cannot entrust this case to someone whose allegiance had been compromised."

Elric opened his mouth as if to say something, but thought better of it, or else the words refused to come. He turned wordlessly and left them.

For some hours Elric walked the streets of the town. His calling had been taken from him, and he, a man of all trades, suddenly had no trade. He had no family, no country, no wife, nothing to claim him and nothing to claim. Rather, the one thing he longed to claim was the one thing forever to be denied him. As the night grew deeper and he wandered into the part of the town where there were few street lamps, he saw before him always, always those eyes, a sapphire and an emerald, specters in the dark. He cried out, stumbled and fell, cutting his knees on the sharp pavement.

"Sweet heaven, help me!"

He sat a long time where he had fallen. When at last he picked himself up, Elric stood looking back on the lights of the port, where the ships rose and settled on the waves.

"All right, then. You have called Elric back, and Elric you shall have."

He descended into the town once more, rousing some storekeepers from their beds so he might make a few sundry purchases. At last he collared a small boy and gave him a package, and some instructions.

"Do you understand? Good! Here's a little something for you. Now go!"

The next day Iiliana was roused from her late morning nap by a knock on the door.

"What is it?"

"A strange thing. A boy seemed to be foundering in the waves—the dolphins went after him—he fastened this box to the collar of one, and swam to shore—"

After the messenger had gone, Iiliana sat looking at the oilcloth parcel for a long time, started once or twice to open it, but both times her hands fell back into her lap. At last, with an impatient cluck of her tongue, she seized the box and tore off the cloth and twine.

Lifting the lid, Iiliana collapsed on the bed in helpless laughter.

Inside, nestled in a wad of cooper wool sold for scouring pots, was a pair of grey marbles. There was a note.

> *You have recalled Elric, and he has come! Did you think I*
> *would give up my quarry after twenty years? Then your brain*
> *has gone soft as a bad chestnut. I will come home when I have*
> *done what you sent me to do.*
>   *Your servant,*
>   *E.*

"All right, then!" she said, wiping her eyes and holding one of the marbles to the light. "All right."

The silk forest was nothing like the Weirdwood where she had been abandoned and had grown up nor was it like the seedy deerpark where Milo had chanced on her. As the snow swirled and fell around her, Caitlin remembered the wood where she had spent her first seventeen years: stands of ancient oaks, and beneath them hemlock, everything chewed by rodent teeth, nights thick with the flight of owls. This place was nothing like that. The trees were smaller, and evenly spaced, as though planted long ago by a single hand, silvery in the dusking, snowy evening: birches arched in girlish yearning, black pears, darker, bent in wisdom.

Caitlin resisted the calling of the trees. Madness, she thought. Don't give in to it. But the Badger had fallen quite far behind her, and the speaking of the trees grew louder and louder. Stumbling in the snow, Caitlin clutched at one of the trees, and as her ungloved fingers closed around the smooth bark she saw clearly as waking a young man in springtime, bending down the catwillows and smiling, lifting up a young woman and laying her upon the bed of branches, while her fingers, silvery as birch twigs, undid the ribbons of his shirt.

The Badger's hand fell on her shoulder, and Caitlin started with a word on her lips. He looked at her curiously.

"What did you call me?"

Her eyes were full of wonder as she looked up at him. "I don't know."

"No, you called me something. What?"

"I called you—Tybio."

The Badger shuddered uncontrollably. "Don't go so far ahead next time, or I may lose you."

She nodded, and they went on together, side by side.

Everything slept. Where the owls of the Weirdwood would have been watchful, and Milo's deer nervous, everything in the silk forest slept. In the roots of the trees the bright-eyed things with their coats of winter fur were curled in a deep December sleep, waking only to bore a hole in an occasional nut while half conscious. If you had taken a spade and turned over the frozen mud of the creekbed, you would have found in it a fantastic, living lode: frogs green as emeralds, salamanders milky as moonstones, turtles faceted like onyx yet to be polished. The birds had all fled to southern islands, and those that had wintered over tucked head under wing. Deep underground, among the slumbering worms and the drowsy mole, the cicadas were halfway through their seventeen-year sleep.

Everything slept, except for the cat and the badger, stealing forward on human feet through the snowy night. The snow fell steadily, thick as a curtain, lacy as a wedding veil, and upon its silvery page they saw painted innumerable wintry visions, dreams upon the eyelids of the sleeping earth.

They felt they were the only living, waking things upon the earth, and then suddenly the snow stopped, the curtain was torn, and they saw before them a sight that brought them to their knees, and to their eyes the tears of speechlessness.

In the clearing they saw before them, entire, a hunting party, frozen in time, wrapped in a silky gauze transparent as breath, so that you could see at twenty paces the light down on a young man's cheek, the stubble on the chin of the gamekeeper, the delicate ivorywork of the saddles. They were all looking east, over their shoulders, with expressions of wonder and surprise, and everything about them, every look and gesture and inclination of the head, had been captured by the light silky stuff in which they were enrobed. As they watched, Caitlin and the Badger saw the silk was being mended and restored by a thousand tiny spiders, moving tenderly across eyelid, lip, and wrist. They remained for a long time kneeling in the snow, watching the wakeful spiders go about their ageless task.

"Are they living or dead?" the Badger said at last.

"Neither. Both. I don't know," she replied. "Look, behind them."

It was a hunting lodge, and they had to gently free the handle and hinges from the clinging silk and shoo the anxious spiders away as the door swung inward.

The air inside was itself like silk, clinging, warm as if it had just left the spider. At first they couldn't see very far into the room and made as if to brush the air from their hair and eyelashes. Then they saw, asleep at the spinning wheel, the spinner.

She was the one thing the spiders had not touched; everything else in the lodge wore a net of silk, and the thousand spiders, like the ones tending the hunting party, crept slowly from eave to eave, mending the silk. What they lived on Caitlin could not guess: Not a midge stirred.

While not old, the spinner seemed of another age; her hair was dressed in the ancient way, and her clothes were not merely old-fashioned but archaic: wooden sandals laced over painted leather leggings, a skirt and tunic of silken wool trimmed with bells.

But the face itself was not ancient, not a quarter as old as the clothes, no, not even as old as Abagtha. She was only just past that age at which women are still counted young, and time had just begun to carve its traces around her eyes and sleep-softened mouth. The spinner was a woman of means, her rank woven in the border of her robe and stamped in the signet of her ring. But wealth had not come easy; the hands themselves were callused by the thread, red from work they were used to.

Caitlin moved through the gauze of silk toward the spinner, not knowing she did, heedless of the spiders that scurried desperately from her tread.

Just as she was reaching out a hand to touch the sleeper's shoulder, the spinner's eyes opened.

"Ah, how I have been watching for your coming!"

14

the RIÐÐLESPINNER

o, ask no questions. I have little enough breath in me;
let me save it for the answering, for it is the answering
they tell me I have a gift for.

"You are wondering what I am, and how I came
to be here, and what befell those outside. They are
living yet, do not fear. Take a mirror, yes, and hold it to their lips. It
will mist even now."

Her voice was like nothing they had ever heard, neither a young
woman's voice nor an old woman's. The spinner hardly seemed to move
her lips, yet her voice filled the room, low and clear. It was the sound
of silence at dawn, when you are alone in the dark, waiting for it to be
light. They sat spellbound, listening to that voice, and found they could
not speak or move. Nor did they desire to. They wanted nothing but to
sit there in the lodge in the middle of the forest while the spiders spun,
and the spinner's breast rose and fell with her breathing, and outside a
fresh snow fell softly all around, fell silently and eternally on the hunting
party and the wood.

Everything she said to them was like memory restored, and as she spoke she began to spin, working the wheel so that it sang and whispered beneath her speech.

"Such a way you have come, farther than you even know. And you think that you are lost, and fear it may be past all saving. You, boy; what do you know of the swallowort?"

The Badger was tongue-tied.

"You, tell him."

Caitlin licked her lips before answering. The wise eyes, now young, now ancient, seemed to look through her, and then into her soul of souls. "It is a plant. When you place it on the forehead of a sick man, he will either laugh or cry. If he cries, you know he will live."

"Yes," said the spinner. "The saving tears. You must remember this, when you leave me. For you are not lost; I shall tell you the way, in a little while. But first you shall hear a tale. It is not my own story, but it is the story of one like me, who is now dead."

And this is the tale she told them.

"Long ago a brother and sister were born to poor parents. The boy was named Myrrhlock, his sister, Myrrha. One day a strange woman appeared at the door of the cottage and announced that she had come to take the boy away, for he showed a talent for the shifty arts. But the father wanted the boy to help him in the fields and said, 'Take my daughter in his place, we have no need of her: There is little enough food to cook, few clothes to mend. Besides, we have no dowry-money, and no man will ever marry her.'

"The woman was ill-pleased, but she took the girl, who followed behind crying quietly, frightened and stricken with grief at leaving her home, however humble.

" 'Don't cry,' the woman told her. 'They did not want you, so it must be that you are going to a better place.'

"Her mother had always told her that you went to a better place when you were dead, so the girl only cried harder. At that the old woman (who was a powerful spellcaster) picked her up, though the woman was frail and the child heavy, and carried her along as if she were a feather, telling her stories until she stopped crying and fell asleep.

"So the girl was brought away to a distant country and raised up in a fine house in the countryside, where she was set to the study of geography, botany, geometry, weaving, architecture, astronomy, cooking, and others of the arts her instructors thought fit to teach her.

" 'It is well you did not bring the boy after all,' they said to the old woman, 'for this child is so bright and quick and kind we can imagine no one better.'

"But the old woman regretted leaving him behind. Tilling and sowing, she feared, would not fire his mind, and when she thought of the matches there were for such tinder, she did not sleep well.

"She was borne out: Myrrhlock grew broad and strong from the hard work, but resentful of his father, for he well remembered the day they had taken his sister away. At first he missed her, but after a while he began to imagine the life she led away from them. As he dug potatoes in the hot fields he thought of her in a summerhouse, eating sherbet; while winter winds howled about the house, and his mother served up roast turnips and black bread, he imagined his sister in a featherbed, eating sweetmeats and roast pullet.

"And the boy's heart became poisoned with hate and ripened with it until it was so full it overflowed into his eyes, which became the color of quicksilver and just as changeable.

"One day ten years after she had taken the girl away the old woman returned to the house where the poor farmer lived with his wife.

" 'I have come for the boy as well, if he will go with me,' she said.

" 'You're a day too late. Yesterday while I was milking the cow he made off with my only drafthorse. I hope he's thrown and breaks his neck!'

"The old woman journeyed homeward, thinking nothing good would come of it. Indeed, the boy had not been gone a day when he fell in with a Necromancer, a magic worker who had betrayed so many kings he was an exile, welcome nowhere, compelled to travel the highways all the year, never resting. He took the boy as his apprentice, teaching him no art but magic, for it was in his eyes the only art, and then only dark magic, for he thought it crowned all the others. Since the boy's thirst was the thirst of hatred, he drank up these bitters greedily and never longed for the waters of knowledge.

"Myrrha his sister had grown up bright of mind and countenance, graceful and excellent in all things, fluent in seventeen tongues and renowned for her spinning. *Any fool can spin thread of wool, and even gold from flax is no great trick,* she thought to herself. *But silk! There is something to spin.*

"It was said she could spin a thread before the silk had left the silkworm. That is truth-pulling, but her tapestries were wonderful to look at: portraits of long dead kings and queens, none larger than an infant's thumbnail, and marvelously lifelike. She wove into the cloth all manner of animals and plants, and beneath them mottoes of their descent and use, and as she worked word traveled through all the kingdoms of her talent. Coopers wearing linen of her making were said to make matchless barrels, and the wine from these casks was said to taste as nectar. A cat that slept on a scrap of her weaving was rumored to be the best mouser the kingdom had ever seen, and its kittens fetched a pretty price in silver.

"At last word of the spinner reached Myrrhlock, and leaving the magician he went to the kingdom where his sister was living. There he inquired after her, pretending to be a lovesick admirer, and the townfolk smiled on him, and bade him welcome to the ranks of the spinner's army.

" 'Has she many lovers, then?' he asked, crestfallen.

" 'They are as stars in the sky, but the chief among them is Tybio.' "

"Tybio!" Caitlin cried.

"Let me finish," said the riddlespinner. "Then many things will be clear to you."

Caitlin sat back, subdued, and the riddlespinner went on.

"Tybio was one of the workers who gathered the cocoons from the silk forest and tended the mulberry trees, and it was there that the spinner had met him in springtime. They were not long falling in love, and often as she sat spinning Myrrha would smile, thinking of him, how he had bent down the branches of catwillow and made for her a bed, soft! unimaginably soft.

"Myrrhlock vowed his revenge should start with Tybio. One day as the young man came to the grove of mulberry trees the magician's apprentice fell upon him and killed him and hung his body from a tree, so his sister should see it as she came to meet her lover in the grove.

"For a time Myrrha would take neither food nor comfort, and it was greatly feared she would starve her body or her reason, for she ate enough neither to feed the one or the other. But one day the old woman came to her in her chamber and found the spinner once more at work, her tresses cut and coiled on the bed.

" 'They were what he treasured most,' Myrrha said. 'Bury them with him.' And she kept up her spinning, her hand steady on wheel, foot true to the treadle.

"Now her brother had taken up catoptromancy, which is magic-with-mirrors, and many of the other mancies, and such magics that were so dark that black was too light a color for them. And when he gazed into his mirrors and saw his sister at her wheel and loom, Myrrhlock became so enraged that his teacher, the magician, himself left the house, taking nothing with him, for he feared his pupil, and justly."

Here the riddlespinner paused, sinking back to catch her breath. A minute golden spider, no bigger than a honey-drop and as transparent, hung suspended from her earlobe like a pendant, amber earring. Then the riddlespinner opened her eyes and continued her tale, setting the wheel spinning faster just as it was about to slow to a stop.

"So Myrrhlock set out for the place where his sister was living. As he set off he caught up a lump of myrrh from the counter where his glasses and tripods were laid out, and mile after mile he worked the lump

in his hands, working the poison of his hatred into it, saying over and
over to himself:

> *Sister, know a brother's love,*
> *Everlasting as myrrh, and the grave,*
> *Sweet as a tomb-posy,*
> *This love portion shall you have.*

"Now it happened that not all that had been Tybio went with him
into the dark earth. Not long after he had been buried the spinner
discovered she was carrying a child, and before the start of winter she
bore an infant girl. And in the child was all the spinner's love of life born
again. Her eyes were full of light and gladness, and her laughter rang
once more in the marble hallways.

" 'Work your ruin!' she cried, as her daughter pulled the cloth from
the table, scattering the silver. 'Pull all the world down around its ears!
You will remake it, you will, my little world-maker.'

"On the road, Myrrhlock saw mother and child in his mirror, and
he saw the means of his sister's undoing."

At this Caitlin shuddered uncontrollably. The spinner beckoned
her closer, and although there was no fire on the hearth, Caitlin felt heat
warming her blood, heat that seemed to come from the spinning wheel,
or the spinner herself.

"One day the court and all the household went hunting. It was the
harvesttime, and they were on the luck-chase, to catch an animal and
let it go in barter for a good harvest, fidelity in love, and bounty in all
good things.

"Now Myrrhlock disguised himself as a huntsman and worked the
lump of myrrh into something like a baby, swaddling it and hiding it
in his saddlebag.

"The custom was, when the quarry was caught, to exchange a kiss
between neighbors instead of the first blood, and these kisses were
bestowed regardless of sex or station. It happened that when the deer
was caught and the garland placed around its neck, Myrrha turned and

bestowed a kiss on her brother, not recognizing him, but as their lips met she felt cold, and cried to the old woman, who rode near her. 'Where is my daughter, my prize?' The old woman reassured her, but as Myrrha watched them cut the luck-tuft from the deer's tail and present it to her, her heart was cold with foreboding.

"As they rode back to the palace Myrrhlock cast a spell so that they should lose their way and ride deeper and deeper into the forest instead of homeward. Myrrha became separated from the rest of the party and called out for her daughter and for the old woman and lastly for the huntsman. Suddenly she saw him before her, holding out to her a bloody bunting. With a cry in her throat the spinner reached for the bundle, and when she touched the myrrh-baby she was held fast and fell down dead.

"But her brother's victory was not without its price. As his sister fell dead at his feet, Myrrhlock's lip where she had kissed him split, and his hair went white.

"Now the old woman came upon them with the baby in her arms, and when she saw Myrrha lying dead she cried and said, 'I knew long ago no good would come of you. See what a thing you have done.' Myrrhlock spoke a terrible spell, but because his lip was cleft the old woman and the child were not killed, but the rest of the party was cast into an endless slumber, and the baby made deaf and dumb and blind. Having done his worst Myrrhlock left the wood.

"The old woman took the child to a lodge, and with her skill gave the child new sight and speech, giving her the eyes of creatures of the night and the speech of the whippoorwill and the ears of the owl. And knowing that the time of her own death was near, the old woman cast a last spell, a spinning spell, so that all the spiders in the wood came and cast a silky pall over all the wood. The child grew up alone in the wood with only the spiders for company, and it was they who taught her to spin. So she lived out her life under Myrrhlock's curse, spinning all winter, asleep all the summer, so as never to see the springtime, when love is abroad in the world.

"To this day they say that if the spinner in the wood is ever awakened, that murder of love and life itself shall be avenged, and the world set aright. The eyes of the world will be opened, and everyone will understand the speech of the birds, and the creatures of night and air, and the wisdom of the ages shall become the bride of the future.

"All this I say, but this is not my tale, but the tale of one like me, and she is dead these ninety-nine and nine hundred years. Child, are you yet cold?"

"No. Warm."

"Then you shall spin for me, and I shall rest. Here, the distaff, and the spindle. Ah, the thread has cut you already. Your hands are yet tender, though not unused. Is your heart so? You must put it in a box and have a key made for it." The spinner laughed softly, "Yes, you shall have a key made, or make one."

For the thread Caitlin was spinning was a little rosy with her blood, and it seemed to the Badger that Caitlin had slipped into some kind of trance. He rose with some words caught in his throat and fell toward the wheel. As his hand closed on Caitlin's arm he felt a shock and found he could not pull his hand free. The sensation hurt a little, but not greatly. One had only to give in to it. The Badger surrendered to the whispering of the wheel and let himself be drawn into the skein.

Scenes from his past and scenes beyond his imagination spun before his eyes: There was Asaph, hiding the missal beneath his cot and looking over his shoulder. There was his own mother, her face so lovely and full of the sorrow that half made it so, looking at him and weeping, and grandfather, angry. A young woman weeping as she hid a baby in a heap of moss in the wood, and old woman finding it. A young girl being led along a hillside by an old woman, the small hands clutching close something in a cloth. Then the child turned her face toward him, and he saw that it was Caitlin. He saw her putting coins on the old woman's eyes and fleeing through the snow, and then they were leading her out, tied to a pole like the spoils of a hunt. They cut her hair from her, and there, at the edge of the fire, the man with the red hair! And there was Elric again, in the field of corn, turning over a body, and it had the face of the relic-seller. But now it was Caitlin again, her clothes torn, her face bloodied, being held down by two of the toughs from Moorsedge, while a third stood over her, smiling. Then the scene changed again, and he saw himself lying as if near death, with Caitlin bending over him tenderly. And then, scenes of horror: Asaph's eyes, open in death—the Cavekin lying heap on heap, horribly slain—the waters of Chameol, the bay red with the blood of Iiliana's dolphins—and Caitlin herself, pale in death, decked with flowers as if for the grave, a man in a black mask bending over her with a slender knife.

With a cry the Badger wrested Caitlin from the wheel, and she collapsed in his arms in something between a faint and death. The Badger raised his eyes to the spinner's.

"Is this the future for her, then?"

"Some of it is the past, some the future. Some is what might be, some, what will be. You pulled her free before you had seen all. Some happy things—"

"Is this a happy thing?" he asked, over Caitlin's head, pressing her senseless weight to him. "You've nearly killed her."

"No; the vision passed through her into you. She will recall nothing."

"What are we to do?"

"You journey to Ninthstile. I will tell you the way there."

"No. Not Ninthstile. Tell me where I can find the Spellkey."

"And what will you do with it if I do? Do you even know what it is?"

"I know it is her life and death."

The spinner looked at him a long while. She seemed much older now, as if each word of her tale had aged her. At last she answered him.

"In the heart of this wood there is a cave, and in it a dragon. He is older even than I, and they ran out of numbers for my age long ago. Tell him his name, and he will have to answer you three questions. But do not ask him about the Spellkey first; ask him the two other things first, otherwise he may trick you of an answer."

The Badger nodded. "Whisper his name in my ear."

"No need—the spiders are discreet. He is called Ormr."

The Badger took Caitlin up in his arms and carried her out into the snow. The cold woke her, and before long she was walking through the deep snow without his help, except that she held his hand, tightly.

When they had passed out of sight of the lodge and the hunting party, an extraordinary thing occurred. The silk that covered everything began to take on a gloss and hardness, as if it were spun glass, and the whole grove began to ring like a tuning fork, a single exquisite note that shattered the silk coverings. Inside them there was nothing but some quicksilver motes and ash. Where one moment the hunting party had stood wrapped in their silky dream there was nothing but a dusting on the snow that was soon covered up.

In the lodge the spinner smiled and worked the wheel faster, so that it made the same pitch that could be heard in the clearing. Then she, too, was gone, leaving nothing but the wheel and the spiders. At first agitated, the spiders gathered in one corner, golden and quivering, and then they, too, began to die. At last there was only one. She crept to the highest eave and began to spin. When she had done, she hung herself upside down beside the new egg case and went to sleep, waiting.

15
ORMR

n the town where he had been a boy, before his grandfather had sent him away to live with the monks, there had been a widow whose husband had been killed by a dragon. At least, that was what they said. You used to see her at the well, being shunned by the other women drawing their water. It was bad enough, they said, that she was a dragon-widow, but she had stopped wearing mourning after a month or two, going about with her head uncovered, and when the mayor's wife spoke to her about it, she only laughed.

On the streetcorners, the Badger remembered, the spell-sellers sometimes hawked dragons' teeth, but you were never sure what you would get for your money, as this was also the name for a peppery, preserved-plum sweet given to children who were being weaned from the teat.

And there was a time, not long after they had sent him to live at the abbey, when they pulled a man from the bog. He must have been there for three hundred years, but he was perfectly preserved, his skin soft as a baby's. There was a noose around his neck, and he wore the death-sentence of a dragon-shirt: a black tunic emblazoned with a red dragon. No one sacrificed to dragons anymore; such barbarism had died out with the advent of the Pentacle. Besides, the dragons had all but vanished in the great drought, the population scattered to the distant mountains and caves to avoid the ravages of the settlements: chimney and plow, forge and mill.

The Badger didn't even believe in dragons; though, as they went farther into the forest, he began to. They walked through the snow, threading their path through the trees, from time to time watching the silent flight, quite close by, of an owl. Every once in a while the Badger would turn and look at Caitlin, as if he walked in fear of her suddenly vanishing in this strange forest that was so much more her province than his own.

Caitlin walked in a dream of dragons, the withered lizard soldiers that had been her accustomed playthings back in the oak with the red door, fighting battles for her, their queen, against Abagtha's rages, against the long, long darkness of the night in the Weirdwood.

She remembered the books Abagtha had of the natural history of dragons, what they ate (veal on the hoof, still nursing; young pigs and lambs; melons, when they could get them back to the cave without breaking them), where and of what they built their nests (from the roofs of caves, of their own scales, shed, and softest bat down), how they chose their mates and raised their young, and the songs they sang to one another in winter, when their thin blood was in danger of freezing, songs said to be more lovely than any birdsong, more stirring than any of the songs of men. When she had asked Abagtha why the trees lost their leaves in the winter, the old woman had told her it was the dragons' fiery breath on the wind that caused the leaves to turn brown and fall from the branch.

Once, when Caitlin had been very little, she was walking alone in the wood, gathering mushrooms for Abagtha, when she spied a man a little way off through the trees. This was before she had looked into the book with pictures of people kissing in it, and for some reason she did not connect this man with the farmers who visited the oak with the red door to barter for Abagtha's potions and powders. This may have been because the man she saw now was naked, or because he was cleanshaven, or because he had red hair. Whatever the reason, Caitlin hid behind the tree for a long time, watching the man take a bath with a cloth and a kettle next to the fire in the clearing. He did not see her, so Caitlin got a good look at him. He resembled her lizards more than he did either Abagtha or herself, so Caitlin decided he must be a dragon. Even when this notion had been dispelled, she continued to regard men with some of the awe, fear, and revulsion she reserved for dragons. Little of her experience of men since that long-ago day had changed her impression, so that once in the Badger's arms she had fought the urge to free herself, imagining in his kiss a dragon's tongue, scales on his back beneath her hand. From her earliest days, Caitlin had been slaying dragons, and harbored some still, in the farthest caves of her mind.

Elric had followed them into the wood, tracking them easily through the snow. Having them well in sight on the second day, he paused for a brisk sponge-bath. Melting some snow in a cup over a fire and using a nearby tree as his valet, he washed and shaved, hooting and singing, which might have been his ruin. It was only luck that he heard the rustle of a fleeing wood creature. He had the fire out in an inkling and hid himself inside the same tree. Too late he saw his razor in plain sight on the stump, but the bounty hunters thundered past without noticing it. Elric waited a long time before emerging to dress, cursing because the hiding place had undone all the good of his bath. He moved off quickly through the trees, and there rose before his eyes upon the black and white screen of the snowy forest a vision from the past: Caitlin being chased through the snow, the dogs at her heels. Elric's breath caught roughly in his throat; he stumbled and nearly fell.

"Let me have done the right thing! For her sake—"

The night didn't answer: the snow only fell, the owls looked at him, then over him, searching the snow for signs of life.

At Ninthstile, the onions and potatoes had all been dug, and the fields lay under new snow. The abbess stood at her window and looked over the white fields to the fringe of trees to the south, her fingers playing on the silver pentacle she wore around her neck.

After a time a bit of darkness detached itself from the darkness of the trees. It was not the pair on horseback she was hoping for, but a cart with a single horse.

It was the last day of the old year, which held a special significance for the villagers of Ninthstile. It was Riddance Day, a day for house-cleaning and cleansweeping, getting rid of unlucky encumbrances. It is unlucky enough to own a cat with one eye, more unlucky still to kill the cat—except on Riddance Day.

So it was this particular cold morning that the carter was driving a load to the convent. The single passenger was a girl of five, named Winna. She was the one mouth too many to feed at her house. Her parents scraped a living by gathering ends of tallow from inns and taverns and melting them down to make new candles. It was Winna's job to cut the wicks. But then her older brother had run away to be a soldier, and she had to pour the hot tallow. It was only a matter of time before she burned herself; the hand healed perversely, so she lost the use of it, and now her father had to hire a boy to pour the tallow, and her mother had to do the wicks and take care of the new baby, so it was off to the nuns with Winna. Her parents wept at the gate and handed up a meal for her in a box, and as the cart drove away her father swore that they would get her back, just as soon as things were paid up. But secretly, and he was ashamed to tell his wife this, he felt a burden lifted from his shoulders, the weight of loving this odd child with her one blue eye and one green one. Perhaps, he thought guiltily as the cart turned the corner and was lost from sight, perhaps now their luck would truly turn.

The carter reached the gate and gave a shout. Two nuns ran out through a little door in the high gate. Having ascertained the carter's business, they gave Winna a hand down from the cart. Winna slipped through the door into the convent. The carter turned his horse, one hand on the rein, the other exploring Winna's box-dinner; she had picked at it and given the rest to the birds, so there was nothing left. The carter grumbled, then sighed.

"Ah, she's welcome to it. God knows when she'll eat as well again."

The Badger had turned in the doorway in afterthought. "How shall I know the cave when I find it?"

The riddlespinner was already spinning once more and gave no satisfactory answer.

"Just go through the forest as if nothing interested you but getting to the other side. Then you are sure to fall into it, headfirst."

Which is what happened: One moment they were walking through the wood and the next the Badger had vanished from sight, and before Caitlin could cry out she had fallen after.

They fell along a passage not much bigger than a badger set, suddenly landing unhurt on the smooth floor of a large, long chamber. One of the tiles had come loose; Caitlin frowned, turning it in her hand. It shimmered in her palm, irregular and ever so slightly curved. She raised her eyes to the Badger's.

"Dragon scales?"

He shrugged, but in his brain he swiftly calculated the likely height and breadth of a beast with scales a foot square.

"What I want to know," he said, standing and brushing himself off, "is how it gets in and out. This place is smaller than your barrow."

"Perhaps there's another entrance," she said. She was thinking of a certain spider in the Weirdwood that builds its trap like a silky dungeon, a tunnel that gets narrower and narrower, ending in a web. She shot a look at the Badger and sent up a silent prayer to that sweet heaven of his that they would not shortly be food for worms.

At the end of the passage there was a low archway, and beyond that only darkness. If there was another way out of the cave it lay on the other side. While both saw the arch at the other end of the passage, each perceived the tunnel leading to it differently.

The Badger saw it black and sooty, the shadows crawling with large grey beetles—tomb scavengers. The pieces of an unfortunate adventurer's backbone were scattered up and down the passage like the tokens of a grisly game. As he neared the end of the hallway the Badger kept whirling around to look over his shoulder, a chilly sweat pearling his lip.

That part of her life not lived in the Weirdwood Caitlin had spent in a soldier's grave: none of the Badger's imagined horrors would have made her shrink; no, she saw the passage clean and well lit, and through the archway a light. She herself was suddenly garbed in a white gown and crowned with snow poppies from a mountain meadow. The Badger no longer walked at her side. With each step she took Caitlin knew she could not go backward, and that through the door lay her own death.

They knocked against each other and came to themselves once more. The Badger saw the tunnel free of terrors, and Caitlin found the white gown of sacrifice had vanished, and she was clad once more in riding clothes.

"Is this a dream?" the Badger asked, his hand tight on her arm. "Or is it real?"

"If it is magic," she said, "it comes from within us."

"Then we are mad," he said. "Though mad together."

"Hush." They had come to the archway, which was so dark now they could not see through it. Then they realized it was not darkness, but a heavy curtain of black velvet. Caitlin lifted it, and they entered.

The room was piled with treasure, piles of gold coins and gemstones, uncut, heaped carelessly as coals, but with a hint of the precious luster—scarlet, azure, verdant—hidden inside. The treasure seemed alive; it slid over and under itself like a seething cauldron, pearls tumbling over rivers of falling coins and medallions. Then the whole pile gave a great shudder and from the center there rose the dragon, the head all fiery eyes and dreadful teeth ranged like an army of spears. Then there were the wings, such terrible wings, clawed, and large enough to blot out the sky. The wind that rose from him tore their clothes, pressed their lips tight against their teeth, seared the buttons painfully to their flesh, forcing them against the wall. Then the fire came, hot as a furnace, singeing the breath from their lungs. But through their terror, through the sensation, they realized there was no real pain.

The illusion was gone as soon as they thought it. There was no pile of treasure in the room at all, and no dragon, only shelves of books and instruments of alchemy. Cages of rare animals and plants under hothouse glass lined the walls. A retort flared, shooting purple and orange sparks into the air, and the whole room was pervaded by a strong smell of sulphur.

Then they noticed a small horsehair couch with clawed feet, about the size of a dog's bed. On it there lay a creature no bigger than a spaniel, with black wings not unlike those of a bat. The trunk of the creature was a deep turquoise, and soft, without scales or fur or feathers, and it rippled as though some mysterious engine were at work within. The head had a muzzle like a dog's and huge golden eyes. The brow began in iridescent scales of black and blue-green, ending in a few rich plumes on the back of the otherwise naked creature. Besides the wings against its sides, it had an assortment of other limbs; sometimes there seemed to be six pairs, sometimes only four. One pair had human hands, another a beetle's pincers, one set broad paws, another neat cloven hooves. The creature's tail was long, slightly flattened, and pebbled like a turtle's.

The creature regarded them with a calm expression for some time, blinking its lovely eyes, two winking coins. It folded and unfolded its wings, and they made a funny sound, like someone working a bellows. The creature opened its maw in a gesture like a yawn and they saw that it was toothless. It coughed a little cloud of soot, crossed its hooves over its breast, and spoke.

"Who are you?"

"Badger of Thirdmoon See, and Caitlin of—of—Barrowmoor."

"Where are you journeying?"

"To Ninthstile."

The creature beat its wings, coughing again; this time a few sparks flew out. It ran a pointed, lavender tongue over its chops. "You can't get there from here," it said.

"We are looking for Ormr," said Caitlin, "so he may guide us."

"I am Ormr," said the creature.

"We were told Ormr was a dragon," she protested.

"So I am: Ormr the worm; also, wyrm, wirm, wirme, wyrme, virme, weorm, werm, werpe, wurm, wurem, wurrum, wrm, wourme, weirme, woorme, waurm, and vermis. As in serpent, snake, dragon; anything which crawls, insect or reptile. I am many things. I am one of the pains of hell (so they tell me). I am the grief that gnaws; I am your conscience and your madness. I am your most perverse fancy and desire; I am indeed a very worm of your own brains.

"The dragon you saw before was an illusion. You think I put it in your heads, but this is not so, not at all." The creature worked its bellows, then folded its wings neatly. "What you saw in the passage, the dragon, even the treasure within was what you expected to see. I did not invent it. Your brains were ripe for the breeding of brain worms when you were yet children. You labor under an infection of nightmares; they crept in too small to see through your eyes and ears and mouth and bored their way through to your brain, and there they slept, causing you neither pain nor discomfort, for many years. Then one day they hatched as dragons, and there is ruin in the land. Listen: There is the tap-tap even now, the egg-tooth on the eggshell. Be careful what you eat: Starve them out, as if they were a fever, yes." Ormr coughed, a shower of soot and sparks.

During his speech Ormr's voice had gotten quieter and quieter so that when he had finished they thought he had fallen asleep. Caitlin and the Badger looked at each other, as if to reassure themselves that the other had seen and heard the same. When they looked back at the dragon the golden eyes were open again, regarding them with a look they would have said was amused, if this had not been a dragon. Once more the creature spoke.

"She who told you my name," it said thoughtfully. "Did she also tell you that I must answer three questions of your choosing?"

The Badger nodded.

"Begin, then," Ormr said, scratching an itch under one wing with one of its paws.

The Badger remembered the riddlespinner's advice not ask about the spellkey first.

"Where is the way to Ninthstile?"

"It depends where you begin," said Ormr. "If you are lucky, it will be a long journey. If you are very fortunate indeed, you will never reach it."

"That is no answer," said Caitlin.

"True. Ninthstile lies a day's journey from here on foot due north."

At this they caught their breath and traded a glance; so close to the end of their journey—

"Who are the men pursuing us?" Caitlin asked.

The dragon closed its eyes and snorted, giving off a lot of sooty smoke. "I can tell you one, the red one, for his face is clearer than the rest. He is named Elric."

"Is that all?" Caitlin asked, dismayed.

"If you would know more, you must ask your third question," said Ormr. The black slits in the golden pools of its eyes had narrowed.

That one is foreasked, the Badger thought. "Tell us what the Spellkey is."

Ormr shifted its body on the couch, the beautiful turquoise body rippling. "The Spellkey," it said, "also spell-key, spaekey, key-of-hours, spell-kie, spell-kay, and spell-keie. That which unlocks a spell."

"That we know," said the Badger impatiently. "That doesn't explain how it can empty prisons without unlocking doors. And what is the lock of hours?"

"That," said Ormr, "is a fourth question." It closed its eyes and seemed to go to sleep.

The Badger went up and put out a hand as if to shake the dragon awake, but as soon as he touched the creature his hand was stuck fast. Caitlin took hold of the Badger's arm to pull him free and found herself held fast with him. Ormr opened his eyes.

"You will reach Ninthstile safely," he said, "but there all safety ends. You are in greater peril than you guess, and you must arm your-selves against it well." They found they were able to move again.

"We carry no swords," said the Badger.

"Such arms would be useless in this battle. You must go armed in fear, in human fear."

"You say we are in mortal danger and yet you speak to us only in riddles!" the Badger cried. "Why won't you help us?"

"There is help and help," Ormr said. "I could tell you all I know, and your peril would not be reduced, and many things would be ruined."

"Many things will be ruined if you do not!" said the Badger. "Our life, one, our happiness, two!"

"He is rash," Ormr said, turning his golden gaze to Caitlin.

"Yes."

"It may yet save you both. If it does not first kill you. Here, there is yet a little gold in the room, if you look. Gems, as well—take them, if you wish."

They could be persuaded to take nothing with them.

"Then take this stone from my mouth; it is lodged in the back and hampers my eating. Can you see it?"

The Badger stepped forward and looked. At the back of the dra-gon's mouth a heart-shaped stone glittered and winked.

"I can just reach it," he said.

Caitlin remembered something dimly from Abagtha's dragon book. "Badger—"

But he had already extracted the stone, which glittered in his hand, ruby red.

"His heart—" Caitlin cried. Horrified at what he had done, the Badger dropped the stone on the floor.

Ormr's breathing was labored, and the dragon worked its wings stiffly. "Pick it up and keep it. Think of the cost. It is done. Now I sleep." The dragon closed its eyes.

That was how Ormr the dragon died, head curled to its breast, its various limbs drawn up and the tail wrapped around them.

As they went out once more into the snow the Badger looked at the strange stone in his hand, bewildered, wrapping the thing carefully and putting it in his pocket.

After a short time they came to the forest's edge and looked down on the town of Ninthstile and, a little way off, on the convent itself. The Badger looked gravely into Caitlin's eyes.

"How is it with you, love?"

She shuddered, turning away from the sight of the snowy nunnery.

"I'm thinking of what Ormr said." If they were to go forth armed in fear, she was well armed.

16

ninthstile

inna had been roughly wakened at dawn, given a harsh bath with stinging soap and icewater, and dressed in a robe too big for her. A nun came to inspect her once she was dressed: She had a kind face and eyes blue as cornflowers. She placed a lead pentacle around Winna's neck, ". . . for you *are* lead," she said softly, "basest lead, but in a year's time, if you have learned your lessons and worked hard at the tasks given you, you will have earned one of tin, and the next year, copper, then brass, and if you persevere, one of silver. Think of that!"

Winna was then given her breakfast. She was not allowed to sit with the nuns because of the impure influence of her eyes, so she took her milk and bread in the pantry, with the cats. While they all ate, one of the nuns read to them from *The Five Points of the Pentacle* and other holy works, exhorting them at intervals to "chew slowly, and contemplate your mortality."

After breakfast Winna was led to the windowless cellar of the convent and set to making sacks out of string.

"When they are finished, you can start filling them with potatoes from that heap," the nun told her. She was left with a lamp of mutton tallow.

Winna took up the string and began to make a sack, but soon she had made a cat's cradle instead. Staring into the web stretched between her fingers, Winna was soon intent on a vision: two people kneeling in the snow. She tried to see what they were saying, but she could not make out the words. Then she noticed through the white and rosy web of string and fingers, a chink in the opposite wall. Pressed to the gap was an eye. Winna inhaled softly, out of surprise rather than fear, for the look of the eye told her there was no need to be afraid. Winna went up to the wall, and as she approached the eye disappeared and was replaced by two fingers of a hand. Winna touched the fingers, and immediately pictured the man on the other side of the wall, not the gaunt figure he was now, but as he had once been, standing laughing in a grove of fruit trees, wearing a funny hat. Through the stone she heard him weeping.

Winna took out the heel of bread from her breakfast and passed it through the crack. The man passed it back.

"No, it is your ear I am hungry for; press it to the crack, and listen!"

"What are you stopping for?"

Caitlin had halted in the road, standing stock still, staring at the grouped buildings of the convent which lay directly below them along the snowy road. She turned suddenly and buried her face in the front of the Badger's coat. He put his arms around her.

"I'll take this as a sign, then, that you have had a change of heart and mean to go off with me like any sensible woman."

"Sensible? I'm all numb. I can't feel a thing. No, I mean to finish what I have begun. Only allow me a little reluctance."

"I only wish you had more of it, reluctance. Or less, where I am concerned."

Caitlin broke away and stood looking at him with dismay and

sadness. "Is that what it must always come down to, where *you* are concerned?"

The Badger's heart began to beat swiftly.

"Isn't that natural, considering what you are to me?" His voice left him huskily.

"Yes, what *am* I to you? A wolf-girl you found living in a barrow, that you have taught to eat with a knife and fork, and to imitate the speech of men. You have cut its collar off, and the law says you may keep it."

They stood and stared at each other, both appalled at what she was saying, but unable to prevent the words from being uttered or taken in. The Badger could hardly see: The blood rushed to his head and he saw only a looming blackness. Caitlin watched him go a deathly white and thought: Sweet heaven, go to him, you're killing him. But her marrow was frozen in her bones, and her limbs would not obey her.

"Perhaps it's as you say; what if it is? I never meant you harm, Cait. You know that."

"Do I?" The words were out of her mouth before she could bite them back, and the taste in her mouth was bitter.

The Badger dropped the pack he had been carrying and sat in the middle of the road, folding his hands over his bowed head. At last he looked up, eyes brimming with undisguised pain and love, and the sight of them cut her to the quick.

"Why?" he asked suddenly. "Did you mean to end it this way, from the start? If this was the way you felt, why did you ever save me? If it was for this, it was no kindness."

She could only shake her head.

"Look," he said at last, "you have to tell me what you're thinking. I'm not the mind reader."

She was beside him in a heart's beat, speechless, tearful, kissing his face and mouth, pulling off his glove to kiss his hand. For a long while they held one another, kneeling in the snowy road.

"The Weirdwood. They would never find you there."

"No."

"You could go alone." He did not look at her as he said this. "They would never track you by yourself."

"They would find me. Maybe in a year's time, or in twenty, but they would find me."

"Chameol, then. You would be safe there."

"I have to go. I must finish this."

"I don't understand—"

"But it's too simple!" She stood up, and pointed toward the gates of the convent below. "Once I am through those gates, I will never see you, or hear of you again, unless I dream of you, or say your name myself, when I ought to be praying." She laughed. "I don't even know how to pray. Abagtha used to tell me to always greet the sun and the moon, out of courtesy, and that when there was an eclipse, it was because someone somewhere had forgotten."

The Badger turned her toward him, hugging her fiercely, but there was no undoing the words, or the past, or, it seemed, the near future. They divided the burden between them and started down the steep road to Ninthstile.

"Send him in."

While the novice was out of the room, the abbess removed a mirror and comb from their hiding place and combed her eyebrows smooth, tweezed a hair from her upper lip, and rouged her cheeks with pinching. When the rabbity monk entered the room, the mirror and the comb were gone, and there was a slight scent of anise seed.

The abbess was annoyed. "I was told to expect the Necromancer himself."

"I am his messenger."

The abbess found this difficult to believe, but on the outside chance it was the truth she held her tongue. "What is your business?"

"You yourself. May I say that you are a most pleasant business to behold?"

"I am sure I don't know what you mean."

"Only that such outward beauty must evidence surpassing beauty of the spirit." The monk ran a finger through the fine film of talcum on the writing desk.

"I am as a crystal vessel only, and any pleasing aspect is that of the Pentacle, any beauty its own."

The monk licked his harelip surreptitiously. "Quite so." The abbess looked at him expectantly.

"Your business . . . ?"

"The Necromancer himself sent me ahead to settle matters with you about the foundling girl, the one from Moorsedge. Has she arrived?"

"She has not, but if being looked for counted for anything she would have arrived here before she left."

"Your dedication does you credit. The Necromancer did not send me here to discern that alone. I must tell you that the abbot of Third-moon See has been murdered."

The abbess didn't blink. "Tell me what is expected of me."

"The situation is now so grave the Necromancer sees that he himself will have to right matters. To this end he has sent me ahead as his emissary, for he trusts me as he trusts himself. And you know by now, madam, that this is a delicate business. A barleygrain here, a barleygrain there, and—disaster."

"I know your meaning well."

"Then you will see it as your duty to honor what will seem an odd request."

"Assuredly."

"There are on the grounds, I understand, underground chambers, outfitted for certain ceremonies?"

A shutter was slid to one side in the high gate, and an eye pressed to the opening. The eye had a tendency to drift, which distracted the Badger as he stated their business.

"Badger Tannerson and Caitlin Barrowmoor. We have an appointment with the abbess."

The gate opened and the wall-eyed nun regarded them with interest. "You have been expected these six weeks."

"Yes. We have been detained unavoidably, I fear." Caitlin turned to the Badger. "The shearing is next, I believe."

"Yes." He looked at her, afraid to even take her arm with the nun watching. The nun took Caitlin by both ears, turning her head this way and that and frowning.

"Hardly your crowning glory, now, is it? Well, there'll be that much less to cut. You, boy: Don't go. The abbess would speak with you as well."

Caitlin and the Badger exchanged a startled look.

"What can she have to say to me? I'd rather be on my way again."

"I am hard of hearing," said the nun. "Did someone ask you your druthers?"

"What's up, I wonder?" Caitlin whispered as they followed.

The Badger didn't answer. His heart was brimming with a peculiar mixture of dread and ecstasy that left no room for speech. Ecstasy that he had not been sent away; dread he soon would be. This is torture, then, he thought, never to know which look, which word between us will be the last.

The abbess was alone. She rose and greeted them, if the cool civility with which she met them could be considered a welcome.

She went up to Caitlin and examined her closely: first her eyes, as though they might be counterfeit. Then the abbess's gaze moved deliberately over the cropped hair, wind-roughened complexion, stableboy's clothing.

"You have traveled together as man and wife, or something not as good," said the abbess at last. "That is regrettable. I will leave you with him a moment, so you may say good-bye. Tell him, for me, that if he tries to meet you, or climbs these walls it will go hard on you both, but

hardest on you." She turned to the Badger. "You are to return to Thirdmoon at once. The new abbot awaits your arrival."

"Why, is the old one dead?"

The abbess paused with her hand on the doorlatch and looked at the Badger strangely. "Yes. Quite dead. I will return in a minute, to show you out."

"I have nothing to give you—" The Badger felt in his pockets for some token, but there was only a stone.

She took the abbess's scissors from a table and cut a piece of his hair, hiding it in her shirt, a piece of gold, and gave him his change, a kiss. "Listen to me. Do not go to Thirdmoon; go anywhere else . . . but you must not go back."

"You can't stay!"

"I do, I do stay. This is what happens, there is no changing this."

"No, the spinner said—"

The abbess had come in, had heard the word, *spinner*. Their hearts beating wildly, Caitlin and the Badger turned to meet her gaze.

"Farewells all said? Come along, then, you. Do not keep my gatekeeper waiting."

The wall-eyed nun reappeared and showed the Badger the way out. He did not glance back; there was no need. Caitlin's face would not begin to fade from his memory for a long time to come.

When the door had closed on him, the abbess turned to Caitlin.

"It is usual with us here at Ninthstile to attend first to the cutting of the hair. As you have taken that into your own hands, let us walk in the garden."

The wall-eyed nun led the Badger out a different way than they had come in. As she led him through the convent the Badger took in the drabness of the place, the timber buildings with walls of daub and straw. The only building of any beauty was the temple, whose belltower rose

pink and silver in the winter afternoon. To this the nun led him. As she opened the heavy door, the Badger protested.

"Look here; this is not the way out, and I am in no mood to tarry in prayer."

The nun made the sign of the Pentacle and plucked the Badger's sleeve. Her breath was unpleasant, and that eye would drive him wild. He wanted to shake her loose, but something about her checked him.

"What do you want with me?"

"I have something to show you, concerning Brother Asaph."

She led him into the temple, through the great hall and up a winding staircase to the choir stalls. From the bottoms of the wooden seats carvings of grotesque figures leered at him, the same hideous faces that had haunted his childhood, taunting him, keeping him from sitting down during the night-long vigils of hymns and prayers. It was to just such a place as this he would be returning, to a life empty of anything he loved. It was that thought that made the Badger follow the nun up into the vaulted timbers of the temple. Surely, she could not really know anything about Asaph, though it was odd she should know of him. The Badger followed her merely to postpone the moment he would be on his way again toward Thirdmoon, and ever away from Caitlin. Who was he, now, to care where he went and what he did?

Ahead of him the nun walked with more speed than you'd guess she had in her, bent over, sniffing like a rat after cheese. She stopped now and turned from him, busily adjusting her habit. The Badger realized suddenly they were quite alone, out of earshot of the rest of the convent. It occurred to him that the nun could have no good reason to know about Asaph's disappearance, no holy reason for leading him here.

"Enough of this," he said uncomfortably. "What do you have to tell me?"

To his horror, the nun turned to him, seized her left ear, and seemed to tear off her face. Beneath the mask of putty and gum was the face of Elric.

For a long moment they stood and faced each other, rooted to the spot. Then Elric realized he had made a miscalculation: Suddenly, this was no ex-stableboy or failed apprentice before him, but a person far more dangerous. What's more, the Badger had a knife.

"Easy," Elric said, backing up. "Give me a listen, first!"

"Easy! Easy!" The Badger punctuated the word with thrusts of the knife. "Who should know better than you about Asaph's death? You killed him! And if you didn't fasten the bells around Caitlin's neck, you watched whoever did, you filthy—"

"Hear me out!"

"Hear you out—! Hear you out, you—no, I won't libel dogs for you, that's too good for you. You're worse than a bastard, and that, believe me, is not a word I use lightly."

"I'm unarmed, man!"

"Then arm yourself, or watch me cut out your liver before I take your eyes!"

Elric caught up a candle-mount, its massive candle held in place by a sharp spike. But this proved heavy and unwieldy, and after a few parries and thrusts Elric had to abandon it, vaulting over a row of stalls and sprinting up the aisle. Elric had speed over the Badger, but was hampered by the habit. They reached the rail of the gallery together and Elric found himself using a prayerbook to fend off the Badger's jabs. Who would have guessed a stableboy to be good with arms? Again Elric had to retreat, this time over the railing, swinging down a few flights faster than the Badger could follow on the stairs. By that time Elric had shucked the robe and was lost to sight among a thousand glowing tapers at the altar. It was too dangerous to swing here, and miss, thought the Badger; he would set the whole place on fire. He stepped forward cautiously. Was that a footstep, or his own steps echoing? His breaths, or Elric's? But no, there he was, a galley above, moving up, ever up, to the belltower.

By the time he reached the staircase to the belltower Elric was nowhere in sight. The stairs rose out of sight at a dizzying angle. There was nothing for it but to climb them, even though it meant leaving himself open for attack from above. If he jumps from that height, the Badger thought, he'll kill us both. The Badger moved up, climbing ever to the left in an unending spiral, prepared at every turn to duck a pikestaff, or a falling block. At last there were no more landings, only a trapdoor leading to the bells themselves, a skeleton of scaffolding and ropes.

It was all striped light and shadow. Nothing stirred except a barn swallow, which darted gracefully into the open air of the courtyard. The ropes rose up out of sight, and the Badger could see the dim gleam and swell of the bells above him. It's so peaceful, he thought. The knife slipped in his moist hand.

"Give it up, Elric. You won't get past me, not without wings."

All he got by way of answer was the padding of feet on wood high overhead, and the single, sleepy toll of a bell. Something fell from above, and the Badger turned it over with his foot, keeping a wary eye on the bells as he bent to pick it up. It was a drawstring bag; inside it was a braided circlet of hair—Caitlin's hair. Suddenly the bells began to toll, and the Badger looked up.

Elric landed on the Badger's back, the force driving the Badger's chin into the landing with a terrible crack. The knife skated across the sawdust of the floor. The Badger reached it first, seizing Elric by the collar and pressing the point of the blade to his throat. Elric did not plead for his life; he gazed calmly at the Badger, a fox with human eyes. But from the stairs below someone pleaded for him:

"Stop!"

It was Asaph.

There were white roses in the garden. The abbess paused at the entrance to the yew walk and cut one with the scissors that hung from her waist by a ribbon. With tenderness or care she placed the rose behind Caitlin's ear. Caitlin trembled, for she remembered the dream of snow poppies and the vision in Ormr's chamber. The abbess had not trimmed the thorns from the rose, and they pierced Caitlin's temple.

It was not a yew walk into which the abbess led her, but a maze. Caitlin started to protest but with each step she felt fainter. As the snowy rose behind her ear grew a little rosier, Caitlin's skin became as white as wax.

They came to the heart of the maze, and the walls of thick yew fell away. In the clearing there was a design worked in black and white and red marble: thirteen moons circling a five-pointed star. The pentacle itself was painted on wood: a trapdoor. This the abbess lifted, and as Caitlin was now too weak to follow (the bloom behind her ear was blood red), she took her by the hand and led her into the gloom beneath the yew maze.

At the bottom of the stairs the abbess made the sign of the Pentacle and let go of Caitlin's arm.

"The Necromancer himself has asked for you. Wait here until you are fetched. There is a gown over there; put it on." The abbess's foot was already on the first step when she turned back.

"It will go easier with you if you do not resist." Then the trapdoor opened and shut, and Caitlin heard the bolt being shot home.

Outside the abbess made the sign of the Pentacle and shuddered. She hurried along the path, concentrating on the turns of the maze. The old abbess had been lost in the maze, and when they finally found her she was quite mad. The present abbess did not mean to meet the same fate, so she put Caitlin and the Necromancer from her mind.

Caitlin was too weary to put on the gown. She put her hand to her throbbing head, and it came away bloodied.

This is the way I die, she thought. After a short time she fell into a delirium, and in it she saw a figure coming toward her, the face obscured and uncertain.

"Badger?" she said, and then: "Abagtha? Oh, Batha, have you come for me after all?"

The Necromancer came up to her carrying a wand. Now he struck the ground with it, and it flared up blue and silver and showed his face.

He wore a mask of black obsidian that made his eyes and mouth black holes. His hood slipped back and she saw he wore a skullcap of goblinstone, silver-shot blue.

"You do not fear me," he said.

"I have foreseen this."

He nodded and put out a black-gauntleted hand to touch the milky pallor of her skin.

"It is past time," he said, and plucked the red rose from Caitlin's ear.

She fell at his feet as if dead.

17
the heart of the maze

aitlin woke to see her old cat amulet swinging slowly in front of her eyes. I am in the nut cellar, she thought, but it was not so. Gradually the things that lay beyond the amulet's arc swam into focus: cages of animals and shelves of books such as she had seen in the dragon's chamber. But the clasps that bound the volumes had no keyholes, and the pages were sealed forever beneath a film of gilt. Then Caitlin saw the plants ranged beneath in bell jars: foxglove, hemlock, buttercup— all deadly. She realized she was not alone. Her eyes focused again on the amulet, then on the hand that held it. At the sight of the mask, glittering black, she gave a cry and wrenched her head to one side.

The Necromancer went to one of the cages and removed the animal inside. As he stroked the badger's fur, the Necromancer's mask was streaked with silver, spitting light from a flame that blazed up, consuming some gassy fuel.

"Consider the badger," he said. "The feet and eyes of the animal are supposed to confer invisibility, though it is not specified whether the parts are to be ingested or worn as an amulet." His voice was unmuffled by the mask; rather, it seemed louder and clearer for passing through the absolute, fire-born blackness of the obsidian.

"They are also said to make a powerful charm for instilling fear in and persuading one's enemies. This I have not witnessed. It may be true. It is also said to be a love-charm, which may be hearsay, but I like to believe it. What is love, after all, but the persuasion of the enemy?"

The badger squirmed in the Necromancer's arms, but did not bite. It was as if it struggled against the jaws of a trap and knew the end of its struggle was nigh.

"Don't hurt him." Caitlin meant, and did not mean, the animal in the Necromancer's arms.

Set your fear aside. Go armed in fear, in human fear. The black mask glittered, seamless, flawless. It revealed only pale, ancient eyes, the white flare of a tooth, the purple ghost of a tongue when the Necromancer spoke.

He turned and returned the badger to its cage, picking up a mortar and pestle, from which there carried such a reek that Caitlin turned her head into the table where she lay.

"Romantics say that if you cut open a lark you will find its tune scrolled there, like the works of a music box. It is not so, but lovers will cut the birds open, anyway, out of fancy. But if you open a swallow, you will find a stone, the swallowstone, also called chelidony. This must be pulverized with some few other things: resin and a gum; orpiment, which some call arsenic; tortoise bile; white of egg; a certain purple dyestuff. And what do you think it becomes when it is snatched from the fire?"

She could not answer. Like the badger, Caitlin knew death, or something good as death, lay around the edges of the room and hour, expectant.

"It is not the answer you suppose." He set the mortar down. "It is only a paint, a compound for labeling glass vessels. Did you think it would be an elixir? A love-potion? Or perhaps a poison, sold to lovers in a play of circumstances?" The Necromancer paused, gazing down at

Caitlin. "They thought boiled honey and barleysugar were powerful medicines, once."

"Who are you?"

"I am the Necromancer."

"If that were all I would not fear you as I do."

The eyes clouded behind the mask, moons suddenly obscured. "You may call me Greykys."

Though she could not see him smile Caitlin knew he had. She shook with the same cold terror she had felt falling in the snow, hearing the dogs behind her.

"You have been drugged, otherwise you might have injured yourself struggling. For my purpose you must be unmarked. A delicate procedure: A bruise would ruin it."

Caitlin struggled to remember what she knew of the old rune tongues. *Greykys. Grey kiss*— She raised a hand, as if she would have removed the mask, had she the strength. Her hand fell back. "Elric—"

"You are trying to puzzle me out, are you? Where is the harm— no one shall ever learn it. Here is half the riddle, then. When I was a boy, long ago, the old language was still spoken, and *grey* was the word for hare. Consider it your wedding gift."

So that was what he meant to do with her. She had borne it before. But if he meant to keep her here . . .

He read her look. "The idea repulses you. That surprises me. You have lived in such a chamber before, indeed you chose it, and I flatter myself enough to say I would make a better bridegroom than a corpse in a barrow grave.

"But that is not the marriage I mean to make with you."

It was only then that Caitlin saw the velvet cloth he had laid out, and upon it the silver knives.

🙶🙶🙶

The abbess saw the three figures running through the snow to the maze, one tall and thin, red head like a match; the second shorter and broader, hair light as dun; the third a shaggy madman.

"Good. To it, gentle men! By springtime we will send the little ones in after, to gather up your bones."

She frowned. Deep in the flesh of her thumb was imbedded the thorn of a rose.

Heaving with effort, the Badger fell to his knees, clinging to a stone seat, afraid he would break his ribs with breathing.

"Hold on—we've lost Asaph."

They drew ragged breaths of the frozen air.

"How will we ever find her?" the Badger said at last.

"We'll have to, that's all. Perhaps she managed to break off twigs as she went."

"Perhaps she's already dead."

"No." This was said by Winna as she was carried up in Asaph's arms.

For Elric, it was as if he were once again a boy of twelve, beholding the child in the wood for the first time, seeing his hope, her seer's eyes, the saving of the age.

"Here," the Badger said to her, kissing the top of her head. "You know your right hand from your left, don't you? Tell me, as we go, where to turn."

Elric started to protest but the Badger silenced him. "No, it must be me—someone must stay with the child and Asaph is too weak. Yes," he said, more to himself this time. "It must be me."

"The drugs are wearing off. That is good; you must be sentient when the cut is made. 'In full knowledge,' the old text says. It will take some minutes yet: The abbess was overzealous with the dose. While we wait I shall tell you what I am.

"Have you guessed my little riddle yet? No? You surprise me. You have such a talent for surmising things. It has cost me much, more than you know.

"I stumbled out of the wilderness, looking like an old man, though I was young. Only lately the wilderness had been fertile land, and I wore upon my face the singular mark of my misfortune. Those who found me made of it the mark of a prophet. I was glad to oblige them. Taking up a stick I drew a pentacle in the sand. I needed a heaven myself and was glad enough to invent theirs for them.

"As the new faith attracted more followers I became a high priest, and a rich man. I filled my apartments with the apparatus of alchemy, for I had found my home-made heaven hollow and was searching for another immortality.

"Others have documented the quest—I trust you are familiar with it? Then I need not repeat it. I brought metalworking in the kingdom (for it was a single kingdom then, the moon yet unshattered) to a high art.

"I had become a skeptic, disbelieving in everything, when I made a discovery. Through long work with poisons (quicksilver, mostly, and some arsenic) I had become impervious to them. I could boldly eat them as if they were sweetmeats, for I had unwittingly taken in so much of them through the years I suffered no effect.

"Have you guessed it yet, that riddle of mine? Well, I will go on.

"I took up my studies with a new enthusiasm, for I had stumbled on a provisional immortality. While the temples spread across the kingdom, I spent the gold from the temple coffers to buy every manner of killing drug known to surgeon and cutthroat. After a while I began adding other ingredients to the mixture: the tears of the tortoise, yew ash, dust from tombs.

"My age became so great that I declared myself Necromancer and in a year's time announced my own death, appointing myself my own successor. I kept up this fiction for lifetimes, so that now time shrinks before me. Your own journey, a winter's span, for me lasts only an eye's blink . . ."

His voice was lulling Caitlin to sleep, but as her eyelids tugged shut, the silver knives would wink and she would jerk awake again. In its cage the badger paced. Caitlin fixed her gaze on it, and, unused as she was to praying, began repeating a little prayer: *Go armed in fear, in human fear.*

"I did not age; rather, as my age increased so did my knowledge and my strength. This drew many to me, both men and women. I had no need of them; my secrets were my own, what need had I for the companionship of inferiors? My only mistress was my work, and there was no earthly woman to usurp her. Until—she—came.

"Her name was Tỳbitha. I saw her first at the temple, stealing offerings from the plate. How to tell you how I felt, seeing her kneeling there, slipping the coins into the lining of her blouse? Her face was in shadow, and the only parts of her the candlelight showed were her bowed head, her bare arms.

"I took her by the shoulder, asking her why she stole from the coffers of the holy Pentacle. 'Hunger,' she said. 'Have you no husband to keep you?' I asked. 'No,' said she, 'I have no husband, for I can neither weave nor spin.' I searched her face and found in it no trace either of fear or desire, loathing or longing. So, while the law entitled her hand to be placed on the block in payment for the silver, I took that hand in troth instead and placed on it my own ring of gold.

"After the marriage, I showed my bride the bachelor's apartments that were to be her married home. All that was mine was hers, I told her, except for the locked room under the eaves, to which I alone kept a key. She nodded and asked whether a carpenter might be hired to install an airing cupboard.

"My wife was true to her word, and neither wove nor spun, contenting herself with tending the herbs and teaching herself to fashion the blown-glass vessels I used in my work. I waited for her to disobey me, as I thought she must, by taking the key and opening the locked room. This she did not do, rapt instead on the installation of her cupboard.

"This tore at me in a way you cannot imagine. Having so rashly married her, I was frantic to discover something undeserving in her. But a wife with a more even temper no man ever had. She seemed content to spend her days working glass in the fire, afterward giving me my bath before taking her own. She catered to my appetite in everything; I never went off to bed unsatisfied. Surely, no better wife!"

Caitlin shuddered. Through the drug her mind worked the name over and over, turning it inside out: *Tybitha.*

The Necromancer leaned over her, studying Caitlin's features, as if he saw something of his wife there.

"One day, I discovered my stock of poisons was depleted. Not a large amount, but some hand other than my own had tampered with the drug jars. I challenged my wife; she admitted taking it and claimed it was to kill rats. I let the matter drop. What was she, after all, but a lovely thief? If she had guessed the secret of my longevity, she ate the poison herself only out of vanity, to stay time's march upon her beauty.

"It was nothing so womanly as that. How slowly the realization dawned!

"She was my enemy, come out of the wilderness to finish what she had begun. She had taken a new guise, arming herself with youth and beauty, to steal from me my inheritance, a precious touchstone of past and future. She had come, so bold as to take the name *Tybitha,* taunting me with the simplicity of it. And I too drunk with her to see the meaning of it, a wasp trapped in honey.

"How witless I was, not to see it sooner! I had set the locked room as a test for her, and while I waited for the trap to spring she had turned the airing closet into an alchemist's chamber fit to rival my own. While I slept, drugged with love and trust of her, she turned my house inside-out, searching out my secrets, forcing herself to eat the poison as I ate it. In her airing cupboard she gazed into a crystal of her own making, for she had told me one untruth. Where her mother had spun silk, the daughter spun glass.

"At last one day I discovered her in my most secret hiding-place, about to set her hand upon the stone. I could not kill her—not only had love made me incapable, the poison had brought her a little of my own immortality. So I took her name from her, her youth and beauty, and her reason, and sent her off into the wood."

"*Abagtha.*"

"Yes. The word for an old woman's winding sheet. Two things should have taught me she was of Myrrha's blood: She was named after Tybio, and she had those same eyes, the owl's eyes, as her nine-times-great-grandmother. Did you never guess? *Think:* Kiss—lip. Grey—hare."

Harelip, thought Caitlin. "Myrrhlock."

"None other. Not long after Abagtha's banishment my touchstone told me an assassin had been dispatched to waylay me. This despite the precautions I had taken." Caitlin thought of the book in Milo's library, with the pages torn out. Myrrhlock continued.

"I awaited him with pleasure; here at last was a test of my immortality. When the assassin arrived, I was surprised to see a girl of no more than thirteen, unarmed, remarkable for the fact that she had one blue eye and one green. This was before the nature of the threat had made itself clear, and I was careful she did not suffer too greatly. But each year thereafter there came a child, until one day as I was at my books I read in an ancient text how a prophet should come out of the wilderness and be undone by a child with one green eye and one blue. The runes were remarkable: *forest* for green, *sky* for blue.

"I saw now what I was up against and acted quickly, but those who had already gathered against the Pentacle saw to it some of the children were spared. So I have waited, for a hundred years and again another hundred, knowing every year will bring its circle of seasons, and perhaps a child, one eye on the forest, the other on the sky. But my patience, my poison, is running out. I need more and more of it, so that there can never be enough. Without my killing food I will die. But you offer me another way." Myrrhlock picked up one of the silver knives.

"I had long ago read of a creature that has aspects both of the male and female and is capable of recreating itself endlessly. Here, I thought, was the way to escape my poisonous addiction.

"But this, too, presented a problem. In each new infancy, I would lose memory and leave myself vulnerable to my enemies. I needed to create a perfect vessel into which I could transfer my thought, my soul, my self." Behind the mask the Necromancer's eyes gleamed, and one of his gauntleted hands reached out to caress Caitlin's cheek. "And where was there ever made a more lovely urn?"

The drug had nearly worn off, but Caitlin could hardly tell, she was so paralyzed with fear. The Necromancer's voice washed over her like ether.

"But first, a few adjustments. Your heart, for instance, must be filled with a mixture of sweet resin and lead, and your blood replaced with quicksilver. Then I will go in your body to Chameol and destroy my enemies once and for all. They will crown me queen, and the very straits will run red with blood." The knife skimmed over Caitlin's trunk, making a light cut, and Caitlin's gasp was like the sound of the flesh parting, the blood beading in the gap.

"*No!*"

The Badger started for Caitlin, as if to stop the welling of all that blood. He was flung across the room by a powerful blow, although Myrrhlock had not touched him. Dazed, the Badger took in the retorts and crucibles, the animals pacing in their cages. Wiping a little blood from his mouth, he turned to the Necromancer.

"What unnatural thing—"

"Unnatural?" Myrrhlock laughed. "Shall I tell you what is unnatural? Shall I tell you of your own birth? It is well known to me. A curious economy of forefathers, in that your grandfather served as your father as well. The word, I think, is incest? Unfortunate that the girl should have hung herself, especially since she waited until the child had reached maturity to do it. You have proved a nuisance to me."

Caitlin was slipping under the edge of a darkening mist. *Don't listen to him. Badger, my eyes. Look at me.*

The Badger stood in the middle of the room, mute. Then he lunged at the Necromancer, only to be flung the length of the room again. There was the sickening crack of a bone, and the Badger cried out.

"Do not try to save her. Save yourself. Turn now and leave while it is still charity that I extend to you." The Badger clutched his arm and said nothing. Myrrhlock grew angry; the darkness upon the mask shifted like a thundercloud. The Necromancer set the silver knife beside the amulet on the table where Caitlin lay.

"Do you really believe the life you intend for her would be *saving* her? Yes, I can see it: You will make a wife of her, a brood animal for the getting of your mooncalves. For such they would surely be. You yourself have seen it, the blight passed on through the blood. They carry the brood to the river in the dark of night and drown them."

The Badger saw in Caitlin's eyes that human armor of fear, which is love also. He could not stand the sight and looked away. It's not true, he thought, but he could not summon his voice to say it. And feared it was true. The pain in his arm was not to be borne; he clenched his teeth and closed his hand on the stone that was in his pocket, the stone he had taken from the dragon's throat.

As his fingers clenched it—so hard it cut his palm—the Badger felt strength beginning to return to him, the pain itself charging through him like the anticipation of disaster, or desire.

Caitlin's own hand closed around the catstone. No sooner had her fingers tightened around the amulet than she felt the Badger's strength flowing into her, her own will passing into him. For the dragon's heart and the catstone were pieces of a single stone.

Damn it all, he cried, *you're the strong one!*
This time it's your turn to be strong.
And if I fail? We're done for.
No. We have not come this far to end this way.

Myrrhlock perceived none of this, intent on the white-hot mixture in his crucible. "When I am done with her, I will tend to you. In the meantime, think well on this: If you choose not to cooperate, I will pluck from you all memory and thought except the vision and sensation of her eternal agony. If you are reasonable, and I hope you will be, a place will be made for you in the temple. Did you not once wish to be apprenticed to an apothecary?"

"Yes. You sent me off with a death-warrant."

204 🐦   THE SPELLKEY

"That was the abbot's doing. He paid for his miscalculation with his life."

I can't get near him, the Badger thought frantically. Caitlin's own answer slid into his brain, pushing aside the pain.

The stone! Armed!

With a single movement of his arm the Badger hurled the stone into the center of the mask. Myrrhlock gave an inhuman cry as the mask shattered into a thousand fragments. The Badger caught a glimpse of a face he knew—the abbot's harelipped secretary: ". . . the magician's lips where his sister had kissed him split, and his hair went white." Then the Necromancer gave a terrible shudder, his figure distorted into something out of nightmare, an apparition of wings and sightless eyes and a maw of purple flame. The horrific thing wavered in the chamber, as if in a death spasm, and vanished.

Neither of them could recall later how they left the collapsing chamber with their lives. They woke in the snow, to the ache of healing, to see little Winna bending over them, the saving tears standing in her seer's eyes.

18
the spellkey turns

o far had the thorn pierced there was no retrieving it. The abbess sank into a fever and could not be roused. The nuns circled around her bed in confusion.

"Look!" said the youngest, who was standing at the window.

A woman was riding boldly through the gates of the convent upon a piebald horse. She was dressed like a soldier, and her copper hair shone in the winter sun like a shield. The dogs and children of the village danced around her as she came, and strange figures in rags, shoeless— inmates from the asylum. They could even pick out the old abbess. All wore garlands of flowers, though where they had come from in the heart of winter there was no telling.

The nuns watched her approach, not knowing what to do. They had been warned against her coming: Beware of witches, they were told, and with hair like that surely she must be a witch, as surely as if she had one blue eye and one green. Every four hours through the night they were accustomed to being wakened, assembling in the choir stalls to pray for protection against the legion of unbelievers.

But the abbess lay in a fever, and they knew not what to do. Witch or not, the woman on the horse had an air of command. Though their hearts leaned over the windowsill toward the banner of copper hair, the nuns hesitated.

Then the youngest remembered the old rhyme her grandmother had used to say to her when she was very small:

> Dogs and madmen dance around
> Coppercrown is come to town.
> She'll ride a pie-horse in the gates
> To carry away the child that waits
> Hie me up so I can see
> When Copper-Copper-Coppercrown
> Comes riding through the town.

The bowl of compresses broke on the floor. With impatient hands the young nun wrested the wimple from her head and let it fall on the stairs. Out into the snow she ran, heedless. This was the thing that had been foretold. The young girl knelt at Iiliana's feet, raising a flushed and ardent face to her queen.

The eldest nun had followed. Iiliana helped her loosen her wimple and cast it off, the hairpins sinking into the drift and vanishing, the grey hair tumbling around the old woman's head insubstantial as smoke.

"I thought I would not live to see this day," said the old nun weeping. "After so many years it seemed as if they must only be legends after all."

"Iiliana!"

Elric came up with Winna in his arms. He caught Iiliana in an embrace, Winna and all.

"Enough," Iiliana protested. "You'll crush the child."

He handed Winna over. "What's wrong? Can't I be glad to see my sister?"

"Is she all right?"

It was understood that she meant Caitlin.

"You had better have a look at them both."

"I will examine her—as for him, I think you and Asaph had best tend to that."

"Have a little pity!"

The Badger sat across from Asaph and Elric at a table in the abbess's chambers. At the Badger's outburst the others traded a glance.

"Everyone has been treating me like a child who's too young to know what's going on. I'm not a *fool;* I know I'm no part of your plans for Caitlin. But I do think, before you turn me out with a fresh horse and a new suit of clothes, that you could tell me what it was all *for.*"

There was a silence before Asaph finally answered. "There is an ancient brotherhood, the knights of Chameol. I am one such knight, as is Elric. You have met others, though you did not know it: Fowk the lockpick, and Leier. We are knights without armor, no arms but our wits, and in swearing fealty to Chameol we forfeit our bloodline, our names, our right to marry, to own more than we can carry in our pockets. So you see it was not so much a lie, my playing a monk. The vows are the same.

"We are sworn to Iiliana, pledged to defeat Myrrhlock and destroy the very Pentacle itself. The verse on the missal and the runes in the Devil's Sieve tell of a great seer, an otherworld daughter, who will come with a knight-without-a-sword to destroy the Pentacle and restore the age of knowledge and light."

The Badger stared into this face he knew so well, and not at all. This was an Asaph he had never seen, sober in fact and humor. His wounds ached, and when the Badger spoke it was in pain.

"That all sounds noble, but it explains nothing. *Why?* Why the gilt on the missal? Why pretend to go mad, and let me believe you were dead? Why kill the deer in the forest and leave me to rot in prison?"

"We are sworn to serve the Spellkey. Often we must serve in ways that seem cruel. But we are sworn to—"

"—let suffer and die."

"No—"

"Yes!" The Badger rose from his seat, trembling. "I tell you, yes!" He pointed at Elric. "I saw him turn over the body of the relic-seller. You are sworn to murder, and worse, all of you. And you, Asaph, who pretended to be like a father to me—" The Badger's own words choked him.

Elric had risen, too. "I'll go."

"Are you telling me what the riddlespinner showed me was a lie?" the Badger asked when the door had closed behind Elric.

"No—when Elric found him Dice was already dead, by Myrrhlock's hand, or the abbot's."

"And the poison on the reins?"

"Myrrhlock. We had no hand in that."

"And if Caitlin had not found a remedy? I suppose my death would have been unfortunate, but necessary."

"You don't understand. Some deception was necessary, but it was not all a lie. How can I say where my vows left off and love began? You could either be a son to me, Badger, or a prophecy fulfilled. Who was I to claim you? We are all of us merely clay, mold for the Spellkey."

"So this has all been for Caitlin's amulet?"

"No—it is a stone of power, but your sacrifices were not made for it. The Spellkey is the journey from Thirdmoon to Ninthstile. As the runes tell it, the road is the shaft of the key, and each stopping place along the way a ward for unfastening the lock. The Spellkey is the test for telling the true seer and her knight. You might have succumbed anywhere along the way, swayed by love or wealth or the call of the Pentacle itself.

"It was Elric's task to see that you were thwarted at every step and, too, to watch over you; it was he who saved you from the apothecary. Had you become an apprentice there you would not have lived out the week. Elric was to tease out the weakness in you, to trip you up. If you were not the ones, we had to know before you reached Ninthstile. We could tell you nothing, not reveal ourselves, because you had to act out of what was in you, and in you alone." Asaph laughed.

"You almost ruined it, you know. Elric couldn't penetrate the court of Fifthmoon, because you would recognize him. So he played his wild card, sent in a mercenary, a hired-sword who'd never held a lance in his life. Shooting his last marble into the circle, he called it."

The knight rose. "Now it would be best if you slept. A room has been prepared for you."

The Badger paused at the door. "I was rash—I'm sorry for what I said."

"No, be glad we are both still here, to be quarreling!" The face changed briefly into the one Asaph had worn in his cups, then it was again this new face, the one the Badger did not know.

But he would grow to know it.

In the hall outside his room he met Elric. The two men stood and faced each other, and again Elric felt that this was no longer a stableboy in front of him. There was something in the way the Badger winced and arranged his arm in its sling—the gesture of an old man. Looking at him, Elric felt a curious twinge.

"Does Caitlin know you belled her?"

Elric was too startled to answer.

In the dim light the Badger's eyes gleamed. "Yes," he said softly. "The riddlespinner showed me that, too."

"Does Caitlin know?"

"She may have guessed. I've said nothing to her."

Elric nodded, matter of factly, a man being told he was going to the gallows: *Da: just so.* "Myrrhlock would have killed her if he had found her; it was before he knew her value to him living. So I had to protect her, hide her where they would never think to look. And I had to keep the village idiots from drowning her in a ducking chair. So I hid her in plain view. Dressed as a village witch and madwoman, Myrrhlock would dismiss her as a charlatan who was no threat to him. And with the bells, the villagers would feel safe and let her alone."

"Let her alone? Did you never think about what they did to her? Did you think it stopped with the *bells?* No—don't answer. There was nothing you could do to stop it, I know; it was perhaps even necessary and, besides, it is all in the past, all for the best—"

Elric's gaze was grey and level and betrayed nothing of what was in his heart. "I might have done something to prevent it, if I had known. But I did not, and whatever happened to her—yes, even that—was better than death at Myrrhlock's hands. And if I need forgiving, isn't that for her to say?"

They fell silent, each thinking of Caitlin, newly belled, falling asleep in the barrow that first night, waking hour by hour to the sound of her own bells. Elric broke the silence.

"We were raised on the hope, Iiliana and I, that in our lifetime the two would come, the otherworld daughter and her knight."

"A tanner's daughter's bastard."

"No, a knight. The rune can also mean simply a servant or companion, even a child, so we never knew what we were looking for. Whenever there was word of a child born with seer's eyes, a knight would be dispatched. I was twelve when I was sent off to the Weirdwood."

"It's finished then. You've found her."

"You still don't see. Not her, the both of you. The otherworld daughter *and* her knight. You have not only found the Spellkey, but unlocked it."

Iiliana had put the catstone on a ribbon and tied it once more around Caitlin's neck. Caitlin put up a hand to touch it.

Her heart was full of contrary emotions, wine and oil that would not mix. She had not expected to leave Myrrhlock's chamber with her life and was marveling yet at her escape. In all her experience Caitlin had found that others always rescued you with an end in mind. Abagtha had taken her in and raised her to be a nameless slave. Even the Badger had unfastened the bells only to place a collar of another kind around her neck.

It looked as if she had been saved again, and Caitlin looked up, wondering what would be asked of her now. Iiliana's face was frank and kind. Caitlin worried. She was wary of honesty and kindness: They were a rune tongue she had never mastered, though she was fluent in the sister tongues, ruse and ruthlessness.

"This stone—how often I tried to part with it, so the dreams would stop! But it was as if it owned me, not the other way around. How could it kill Abagtha and not me?"

Iiliana touched the stone she wore around her own neck.

"The old stories say that when Myrrha fell dead, her spinning hand struck a stone. The old woman saw this and came looking for it, and with a simple spell gave it the power of a dreamstone. You know that some stones seek out water; this stone seeks out dreams. It cannot spin a dream, only magnify the dream within the dreamer. After Tybitha became Abagtha she was full of hollowness, and when she put on the amulet the hollowness consumed her. When you put it on, you began to understand your dreams and to remember them. Myrrhlock knew the dreams would lead you to him, but he also knew the stone could give you the power to destroy him. So long ago he sought out the stone and shattered it. This was his undoing: The pieces fell down wells, were ploughed into fields, carved into necklaces—even fed to dragons. Each piece has the power of the whole and, once shattered, Myrrhlock could never gather them together again."

"And is he destroyed?"

"For the present he has retreated. Our battles against him have just begun in earnest, I fear. But they need not be your battles."

"What do you mean?"

"You have a choice. You may come to Chameol and be honored as our seer. All our secret arts will be open to you, and the ancient runebooks. You will be prepared to take your place as a high oracle. Or, if it is really what you want, your otherworld sight can be taken from you, and you may go back into the world as an ordinary woman. But if you choose Chameol, you must come alone."

Caitlin nodded. "Would I be blind, then, if I chose to remain in the world?"

"No, you would see and dream as other women do, but you would not be able to move between the dream world and the waking one as you do now." Iiliana paused. "You would lose all memory of what has happened, of me and Chameol, and of the tanner's son. That will seem unduly cruel to you, but if you were allowed to remember even a little it would jeopardize our fight against Myrrhlock. The Badger is a part of what you must forget if you do not choose to join us."

"Then it is no choice at all."

"Have you not often wished your dreams away?"

"Often, sometimes daily. What good have they been to me, after all? Certainly they never spared me any pain or warned me of danger. When they offered me a glimpse of the future it was contradictory. In one dream I would see myself laughing, happy—the next I would see my own death."

"The dreams mirrored your own confusion. On Chameol, you can be taught to master them, to make them come at your bidding, and to tell the actual from the possible."

"When must I decide?"

"I sail for Chameol in a week's time. If you come at all, you must come then."

Morning arrived and found the Badger seated at table. He had not been to bed, although he might have put his head on his arms for an hour in the darkest part of the night.

He cut a very different figure than he had when he set out for Moorsedge on a late summer day months before, his thoughts on the new life he would make as the rising young apothecary. It would be too easy to say he looked older, though he did. He was leaner, and his face bore the traces of travel through unfriendly climates: briar scratches, winter sunburn, and a glaze to the eyes as if he could no longer sleep through the night—it is a trait found in soldiers even when they have returned from battle.

This morning the Badger's jaw glittered with a gold stubble; there were lines around his eyes, and a certain way his hands lay on the tabletop. He had not merely become a man, he had become mortal.

In his hand he held two marbles, one blue and one green. His thoughts were on the fortune-teller in Moorsedge. What had she said? He would make a perilous journey and lose what he valued most.

Caitlin had come into the room, and stood looking at the marbles in the Badger's palm. With a cry she ran up and seized them, as if to throw them into the fire. The Badger caught her hands and stopped her, and they struggled silently for a moment. Each soon saw neither was about to gain the upper hand, and the fistfight degenerated into a kiss. The marbles rolled forgotten into a knothole in the tabletop and nested together, cockeyed.

Suddenly the Badger broke away, and the look on his face was so appalled Caitlin turned from him.

"Don't—don't look at me that way."

"Not you, me! How can you stand to touch me? When I think of what he said, it makes my flesh creep."

Caitlin remembered Myrrhlock's version of the Badger's birth.

"You don't believe him?"

"In my heart I think I have always known and never wanted to believe it. And I can never know it's not true. Everyone who ever knew the truth is dead."

"What does it matter to you and to me? It is a terrible thing, if it's true, but a thing of the past. Anything can be forgotten." She turned his face to hers. "Look at me. I, of all people, know this!"

"Don't you see? A mooncalf, that's what I am. Now do you see? The blood is bad, bad blood will tell. Monsters breed only monsters."

Caitlin said nothing. She was thinking how that morning a drop of wax had curdled in the water of her basin.

The Badger had set a wider space between them, looking at her soberly, as if to paint her every feature on his brain. "I had come to think that it was only a matter of winning you over, of making you care. I never thought it would mean giving you up."

Her heart was beating fast. "And are you? Giving me up?"

"It won't come to that. You're going to Chameol."

"Yes." To Chameol, to the moon, from waking to dreams. It is a terrible thing, sometimes, to watch someone you love asleep, Caitlin thought. It was as if you watched yourself as you slept, afraid your soul would not be able to get back into your body. Terrible, to be ever after alone, separate even from yourself, your own thoughts a stranger's.

"What will you do?" was all she said.

"I don't know. I won't say it doesn't matter; it does. But I'm not sure I can care about it today."

Caitlin went to see the shutters and door were latched. When she turned, he saw her hand unlacing her shirt.

"Is that a wise idea?"

"No, but I want to be foolish with you a last time." She came to him with her blouse slipping from her fine shoulders where her heavy hair should have lain. He put a hand to her warm skin and she covered it with one of her own.

"For the next hour," she said, kissing his ear, "you are forbidden to say anything that isn't an endearment."

"Yes," he murmured into her neck.

She shook him by the shoulders. "Yes, what?"

"Yes, my beloved angel."

They were laughing, and then suddenly holding each other, wracked with sorrow. You must tell him, she thought. The wax, falling from the taper, spinning in the basin, forming the rune for *acorn*, and then the rune for *kindle*. But there was no way to tell him, and all language had left them but kisses.

Outside, Elric put his hand to the latch. He had a proposal for the Badger and had not seen Caitlin go in. Iiliana had; she appeared beside him and gave a little shake of her head.

"Here, I wanted you, anyway." She snapped a pair of shears in her hand, sharp and handy jaws.

"Your hair wants cutting. No arguments."

In a few days they had reached Big Rim. A ship was found, one even the rats had abandoned. Iiliana was well pleased, and bought it for a niggling sum. In the morning the ship was nothing but an unseaworthy bulk; by afternoon, whether by skill or charm, the ship shone, straining at its moorings as if eager for the journey Iiliana mapped out for it. The sails billowed even though there was a calm, and all along the waterfront people stopped to stare at the ship and its odd crew. Every hand was a woman, her hair lately shorn from convent or asylum. The ship's rigging was alive with them, as if the ship had been overrun with flying squirrels.

Up on the dock, Caitlin stood in the cape Iiliana had given her, velvet blackness sweeping around her like the hair she had given up. Elric, outfitted for hard riding, stood before her and handed her a box.

"A repayment," was all he would say.

In the box lay his copper hair, nested in the braided black coil of her own.

"When your hair is grown to the length it was, we'll meet again." He wanted to tell her of the bells that often haunted his sleep, but Elric knew there was no saying it. Some vows he must keep.

Iiliana put a hand on Caitlin's shoulder. "Farewells all said? The tide's not at my bidding, and this one is on the way out."

The Badger stood holding Motley's bridle. His eyes met Caitlin's. "There have been enough farewells, I think."

"Yes," Caitlin agreed, thinking there was something in his eyes she had not seen before. It made him look like Elric.

She did not know that Elric had cheated her, holding back part of the measure of her hair. A braided circlet of it cinched the Badger's wrist, hard and black as ebony, hidden by his sleeve.

The Badger was impatient to make a start, but Elric watched until the ship was out of sight. He squinted a little, looking into the sun as he had to.

At last he swung into the saddle and they headed out of the town.

When they had reached the edge Elric reined in Maud, turning to the Badger.

"Still want to go on?"

"Tell me again, about the vows."

The Badger was thinking it was little enough to give up: His name, Matthew Tannerson, was easy enough. It was not as if he ever used it. And never having had a home or money he would hardly miss them. The third requirement was the reason he had accepted Elric's offer in the first place.

"It's not monkhood, mind," Elric said. "It's just that you can never marry."

The Badger nodded. He doubted he would want to, between nightmares of mooncalf children, dreams of—

"I'm ready."

Looking, Elric thought for the first time that the odd name suited him. At last the Badger had the look of a badger: a quick animal way of glancing around him, poised, keen, hungry. Yes, Elric thought, you are ready. "Do you see those woods?"

"Yes."

"When we pass into their shadow, you will be a knight of Chameol."

The Badger nodded.

"There will be no turning back," Elric warned.

"There rarely is."

So the stableboy of Thirdmoon See died that day, and a knight of Chameol was born. In the days that followed the Badger learned to ride so that his horse's hoofprints hid those of Elric's horse, and the path showed nothing of their passing. As Motley picked his way through the light snow, his rider hoped he would learn in time to make his heart like the path: unmarred, betraying nothing of trespassers there.

The *Double Dolphin* made good time to Chameol. Iiliana and Caitlin stood together on deck as the shroud of mist fell away to show the island before them. Winna came up, yawning, and Caitlin took her in her arms, wrapping the cape around her. She was surprised when Iiliana spoke.

"You are trying not to think of him. That's bad. You must think of him often, even speak of him. Hearts are more fragile even than glass, for glass resists acid. Hearts do not."

"I wasn't even thinking of him, to tell the truth." To tell the truth? The wax, then, a single drop, falling in the basin, spinning a thread. Caitlin hugged Winna closer.

The dolphins came up to the side of the ship to greet them, leaping from the waves in the mist, calling their greeting. The crew pressed to the rail.

"See, Winna?" said Iiliana. "Your new home."

Winna's lip trembled, and she raised a troubled face to Caitlin. "Will I see them again, my mother and father?"

Suddenly Caitlin had a clear vision of herself sitting in an arbor in autumn. There was a cradle at her feet, and Abagtha's old book of spells lay open in her lap. Before her the leaves of the arbor shook, giving up a figure dressed like a thief and wearing the face she loved best in the world.

"Yes," she said to Winna. "You will see them again. I'm sure of it."